As they passed under a lamppost, Logan looked down at her.

Being this close, his heart raced like he'd set off a trip wire. His grandmother's words echoed in his head. *Take a chance.* Before he realized it, he and Serena had reached her door.

"Thanks for walking me home. It was very gentlemanly of you."

"My pleasure, but I have to admit, I have an ulterior motive."

Her brow wrinkled. "You do?"

He moved into the space between them. Surprise lit her eyes, then a slow smile curved her lips. He inhaled her lavender scent. Placed his hands on her hips. Leaned down and whispered, "Too bad there are no fireflies to make some magic."

"That's okay. I think we can make our own magic."

She slipped her arms around him and stood on tiptoe. He lowered his mouth to hers, brushing her lips with his, once, twice, before settling in for a long kiss.

Dear Reader,

How do you trust someone? Especially when you have secrets you've been hiding your entire life? Serena Stanhope has secrets and she's unwilling to reveal them, until Logan Masterson shows up in her life. It's bad enough that she finds him extremely attractive and he manages to get under her skin. But reveal her past? That's a tall order.

Welcome back to Golden and the Meet Me at the Altar series. The Matthews brothers are still hunting down leads on their widowed mother's boyfriend. And Serena might just have the answers they need. But as we all know, nothing in life is a given. Even when we try to hide the truth, it has a way of being exposed, especially when love is involved.

I hope you enjoy Serena and Logan's story. They gave me a run for the money, but I enjoyed every moment I spent as these two walked down the rocky road to love. And their path was more rocky than others.

Happy reading!

Tara

HEARTWARMING

Trusting Her Heart

———

USA TODAY Bestselling Author

Tara Randel

Recycling programs
for this product may
not exist in your area.

ISBN-13: 978-1-335-51080-8

Trusting Her Heart

HARLEQUIN®
www.Harlequin.com

Printed in U.S.A.

Tara Randel is an award-winning *USA TODAY* bestselling author. Family values, a bit of mystery, and, of course, love and romance are her favorite themes, because she believes love is the greatest gift of all. Tara lives on the west coast of Florida, where gorgeous sunsets and beautiful weather inspire the creation of heartwarming stories. This is her ninth book for Harlequin Heartwarming. Visit Tara at tararandel.com. Like her on Facebook at Tara Randel Books.

To Karen Rock, my wonderful critique partner
and, best of all, my good friend.

CHAPTER ONE

"My dear, if I didn't know better, I'd think you were trying to elude my grandson."

Serena Stanhope was most definitely trying to stay off Logan Masterson's radar. So far so good, even though his grandmother came up with every reason under the sun to make Serena's hiding impossible.

"He only gets to town once in a while. I was really hoping you two could get to know each other."

In the two years she'd lived in Golden, Georgia, Serena had learned that Mrs. Masterson was a notorious matchmaker. It was well-known she was bound and determined to see her two grandsons stand at the altar. Problem was, neither was engaged, dating or playing the field. Serena was afraid the woman had ulterior motives by showing up here today, but couldn't deny she enjoyed Mrs. Masterson's company.

"I've been really busy." Serena's excuse danced off the tip of her tongue as she tidied a stack of sales slips and placed them in a plastic bin beside the register. "The summer flew by, and with all the new art projects I've started, I simply keep missing him."

Mrs. Masterson, petite, with an expertly coiffed head of white hair and dressed in a pastel blue suit, turned to view Serena's store, Blue Ridge Cottage. "I will admit, your newest creations are lovely. But so is having a life, and you, my dear, do not have one."

If this comment had come from anyone else, Serena might have been offended. Even if it might be a teensy bit true. But this was Gayle Ann Masterson, matriarch of the venerable Masterson family, who were very important in Golden.

All the more reason to steer clear of them.

Serena walked from behind the counter, her flat sandals clapping against the tile floor. She'd dressed in a blue-and-white patterned dress today—her store colors—and hoped it emphasized her point. "My life is the store."

Mrs. Masterson huffed, then checked her watch.

Personal conversation averted, Serena thought. "Is there anything I can help you with today, Mrs. Masterson?"

"I told you, 'Mrs. M.' will do. And can't I drop in to visit one of my favorite tenants?"

Business was slow today, and her assistant didn't come in until later this afternoon, so Serena was happy for the company. "Certainly, you can. I thought maybe you were shopping for something specific."

"You know I adore your store."

Serena grinned as she gazed at her colorful merchandise. "So do I."

Blue Ridge Cottage was Serena's dream come true. Her refuge, as well as the business in which she poured all her creative energy. She tucked a strand of long hair behind her ear, then picked up a box of stationery, running her finger over the clear top, still amazed that she'd been fortunate enough to meet and surpass her goal.

One entire wall of the store featured original hand-drawn greeting cards and postcards. She came up with every design herself, inspired mostly by the beautiful north Georgia mountains. Nature had always appealed to her as a subject and thankfully she'd found a way to capitalize on a theme she loved.

Tables were scattered around the showroom floor and offered original stationery, fancy pens, bookmarks and a host of other related paper supplies. Some days she had to pinch herself at the reality of all this being hers. She'd scrimped, saved and worked hard to land here. There was no going back.

She crossed the room to a rustic hutch, bought at a garage sale and repurposed, the shelves now containing colorful boxes of stationery. Serena picked up a box tied with a jaunty sage-colored ribbon and inhaled the scent of crisp paper. "What do you think of this new print?"

Mrs. M. took it, tilted her head. "Let me guess. The view from Bailey's Point?"

"Yes. I hiked up there and took tons of pictures. Came up not only with the writing paper, but a series of greeting cards. So worth the trip."

During college, Serena's roommate, Carrie, had dragged her to the mountains for a minivacation. Serena had been instantly enchanted. The small towns, untouched woods and waterfalls, winding roads and brick houses among tall trees, made easy subjects for her artwork. She could spend hours in one place, perched on a rock or at the edge of a scenic mountain overlook, sketching the local sights her customers had come to expect from her. Golden had captured her fancy immediately, enough that when the time came, she'd made the decision to settle here and open her first store.

The quaint downtown, with six blocks of multicolored buildings that housed all kinds of tourist shops, restaurants and small businesses, had beckoned her as she drove down Main Street. Once she roamed the sidewalks, she fell in love with the homey touches, from the cast-iron lampposts supporting hanging planters overflowing with flowers, to the inviting aromas from the local coffee shop and bakery. She was hooked. Right then and there she'd decided to make Golden her home.

"Are you sure?" her BFF, Carrie, had asked. "You've always talked about settling in a big city."

Breathing in the fresh mountain air laced with pine and wildflowers, being serenaded by cheery chirping birds, she couldn't have been any more sure. While Carrie, who'd created the website for Serena's business, had declined her invitation to move with her, Serena counted her blessings every time she unlocked the doors to her very own store and viewed the town she called home from the wide window.

Mrs. M. replaced the box, drawing Serena from thoughts of her good fortune. "Hmm. Explains why Logan keeps missing you."

Yes, fortunately it did. She had no intention of being matched with anyone. "I have to keep my designs fresh and new."

Her landlady did not look convinced.

Serena bit back a chuckle. She really admired the older woman. Sweet, with a backbone of steel, she had given Serena her first real chance in a brick-and-mortar retail store. Located in the middle of a block on Main Street, it was a prime location in this up-and-coming vacation town. The business that had started online had grown into the building where she was standing today and was everything she'd ever hoped for.

No way would she let anyone take this away from her.

"I still love your original work," Mrs. M. said. "Your aunt Mary was a wonderful influence."

Aunt Mary. Right. The legend behind the business. Silently cringing, Serena went about straightening merchandise.

"It's a shame she passed. I would have loved to meet her."

"She would have loved you, too," Serena said over her shoulder as she replaced the box.

"I don't like the idea of you all alone."

"We've had this conversation many times," Serena said, her movements brisk as she fussed around the shop. "I'm very happy the way I am."

Mrs. M. arched an eyebrow. "Single?"

Serena suppressed a grin, then said, "There are many single women who live rich and productive lives."

"You don't even have a pet."

"Maybe someday."

She'd always wanted a cat, but she and her dad had jumped from town to town growing up. There was no way they could look after an animal, or at times, afford one. Her upbringing had been unconventional at best, but she'd loved her father and went along with his schemes.

"Since you're here, I have something I'd like to run by you," Serena said, pressing a hand to her stomach. She hadn't planned on broaching the subject today, but since Mrs. M. had stopped by, there was no time like the present.

Interest gleamed in Mrs. Masterson's blue eyes. "Anything."

"You remember how I told you I started my business right out of college."

"Something about a business model in a financial class?"

Serena smiled at the memory. "Correct. We had to conceive and build a business—on paper, that is—and since I loved to doodle, I came up with greeting cards. After creating the business plan, figuring out how to launch the idea and acquiring funding, I was hooked."

"Didn't you work for a greeting-card company right out of school?"

"For two years, to get experience, but I was actively drawing, building up inventory. Once I had enough product, I launched my website."

Shaking her head, Mrs. Masterson frowned. "I don't understand doing business over the computer." She held up a hand to stop Serena from explaining the advantages. "I've heard it all, mostly from you, my dear. But I've also been in business a long time, and let me say, there is nothing like face-to-face transactions."

Said the outgoing extrovert who dealt in local real estate.

"That's the main reason I opened the store, once my online presence grew," Serena continued. "But at least I had an established product and a bottom line, which made the timing perfect to branch out." Breathing in the soothing scent of lavender—she'd hung dried sprigs of her favorite flower around the shop—she got back on track. "Having said all that, I'd like to expand. I was wondering if you might be interested in investing in my company, BRC, Co."

"An investment opportunity? Hmm." The older woman tapped her chin with a finger. Her shrewd eyes narrowed.

Trying not to let her nerves get the better of her, Serena wandered to the counter. The business wasn't in dire straits yet, but paying back personal debts had kept her from reinvesting in the store like she'd hoped. Just to look at the store, Mrs. Masterson might wonder why she needed an influx of cash, and she'd be right. The debt was private, coming from her own savings dipping lower and lower every month.

"Why now?" Mrs. Masterson finally asked.

"To be honest, I didn't project my costs accurately enough for the Summer Gold Celebration. We had more foot traffic in town this summer than the prior year. My printing invoices have risen, and I'd like to offer more classes, which means ordering more supplies." Serena paused, licked her dry lips. "I have a copy of the proposal in my office if you're interested."

"So you're looking for more than our current landlord-slash-tenant dealings?"

"Yes. If you feel comfortable investing,"

Serena said quickly. Asking for money was tricky, no matter how much practice a person had. "If not, I'm happy with our current arrangement."

When Serena had arrived in town, she'd known at first glance that she wanted her store located in the whitewashed two-story building. After contacting the rental agency and learning the amount of the monthly rent, she thought it might be too much for her budget. Until she found out the rent included both the shop downstairs and a roomy apartment upstairs. It was tight, but she had enough capital to get started. That was two years ago. Her reputation was growing, as evidenced by steadily rising online sales. But her heart was here in the store, talking to customers and encouraging people to recapture the lost art of writing letters and cards, of all kinds, and all the things that went with that personalized effort.

She'd immediately painted the front door to the shop a bright sapphire blue. She placed an antique table she'd found at a thrift store right in front of the large store window, arranging the best of her inventory in an appealing display to catch the eye of shoppers passing by. Blue Ridge Cottage, stenciled in bold white letters, took center place on the main window along with an Open/Closed flip sign in the corner. The hours were posted on the door. Her assistant had come up with a sandwich board to put on the sidewalk directly in front of the store to advertise specials of the week and class schedules featuring painting and calligraphy, to name a few.

Along with her rent, Serena also received weekly visits from Mrs. M. She liked to think that beyond the professional aspect, she and Mrs. Masterson were friends of sorts. Perhaps the widow's visits were more about getting out of the house and being with people than about business. Either way, Serena enjoyed their chats.

"As you know, I never make a decision on the spot."

Serena did know that. The Mastersons owned a huge bulk of real estate in Golden, corporately and privately. Mrs. Masterson had her own business dealings as well as property she leased. Serena had heard her call her monthly income "mad money."

"Why don't you give me your proposal. I'll look it over and run it by my financial adviser if I'm interested."

"That would be great. I'll be right back." Excitement rushing through her, Serena quickly went to the small work space she called an office to collect the proposal. She'd spent nearly a month going over projections, assembling all the information an investor required—profit-and-loss statements, balance sheets, projections—and placed them all together in a professional presentation. When she returned, Mrs. Masterson had moved to the window. She checked her watch again, the third time since she'd come into the store, Serena noted.

"Here you go," Serena said. "If you need to get to an appointment, we can sit and talk another time."

Mrs. M. waved her off. "No hurry."

"Are you sure? You've been looking at the time ever since you came in."

"Oh, that? It's nothing."

Mrs. Masterson didn't do anything without a reason. By her cagey expression, Serena suspected she was up to something matchmaking related.

After slipping the folder into her large handbag, Mrs. Masterson crossed her arms. "I'm afraid I will need to get moving along fairly soon. My son scheduled a meeting at our office."

"Like I said, I'll be happy with whatever decision you come up with." Securing the money would be the best scenario, but Serena knew better than to pressure potential investors.

The store phone rang. "Excuse me." She hurried to the counter, reaching over to pick up the handset. "Blue Ridge Cottage."

For the next ten minutes, Serena took a special order for a baby announcement, also part of her business model. She'd become the local go-to for unique wedding invitations, special birthday and anniversary party invitations, and baby announcements. When she hung up, she was surprised to see her visitor still in the store.

She asked Mrs. Masterson if she would like some coffee, when a wide smile curved the older woman's lips and her eyes lit up.

Wondering what had brought her such pleasure, Serena joined her at the window and felt her own smile slip when Mrs. M.'s grandson Logan Masterson strode into view. He stopped to read the sandwich board situated on the sidewalk, giving Serena a moment to drink him in. Not that she needed to—she'd memorized his good looks the first, brief, time they met.

The man was tall and broad-shouldered, with a military bearing. His wavy dark brown hair caught the sunlight perfectly. Sunglasses were perched on an aristocratic nose. A five-o'clock shadow dusted his cheeks, even though it was just after noon. Dressed in a striped button-down shirt with the cuffs undone, indigo jeans and shiny boots, he glanced in the window and saw his grandmother, and a devastating smile brightened his handsome face.

Swallowing hard, Serena wanted to escape, really, she did, but her feet wouldn't move—mutinous body parts. The door opened and the sound of a car horn and laughter floated in with him. He removed his sunglasses to reveal intense coffee-colored eyes. It was then, Serena decided, that she was a goner.

LOGAN MASTERSON WALKED over to his grandmother and placed a kiss on her soft cheek, then sized up the owner of Blue Ridge Cottage. The woman had been impossible to nail down. Every time he'd come to Golden, he'd tried to speak with her, but always ended up talking to her employee, who told him that her boss was conveniently out of town or on a business trip. It was almost like she knew he'd been hired to uncover her background. He'd worry about that fact if he wasn't sure he was the best PI around.

"Grandmother, how are you this fine day?"

The woman he adored lightly tapped his shoulder. "Fine, if not worried about you."

Yes, he'd been running late due to a problem he'd been dealing with at his Atlanta agency. There were a dozen investigations requiring his managerial skills, but he wouldn't trade the satisfaction of owning his own business against a few time constraints.

After eight years in military intelligence, he'd opted out. An army buddy had opened a PI agency in Dallas, and offered him a good job. He'd worked there for a year and discovered that he genuinely liked helping people seek justice and uncover secrets. Maybe because of the truth that his own family had kept from him.

But eventually, he missed the foothills of the southern Appalachians and decided to head back to Atlanta. He had every intention of working for another agency, but his friend's farewell advice came in the form of encouraging Logan to open his own office. He liked the idea of being the boss, so he returned to his home state, went about obtaining all the pertinent licensing and insurance, then started taking cases. Word spread, clients increased and, four years later, he employed half a dozen other investigators. Logan was thankful his employees were pretty self-sufficient, but every once in a while, though, he had to insert himself in a case. Today had been one of those instances.

"You always tell me to work hard instead of hardly working. I was following your advice."

Grandmother rolled her eyes. "Don't go throwing my words back at me. I know how you are."

She really didn't, thank goodness. But that was a concern for another day.

Shrugging his shoulders to relieve the tension after the ride in his SUV from the city to this mountain town, he glanced around the store, then met Miss Stanhope's gaze.

"Well, I finally get to talk to the elusive store owner."

Her shoulders tensed. "We've talked before."

"For about two minutes. Not much time to get to know someone."

"I have a business to look after," she said, smoothing the skirt on her sleeveless dress. She moved her gaze from his, but not before he caught a glimpse of her unusual blueberry-colored eyes. He'd forgotten how startling they were, especially in contrast to her rosy complexion and midnight black hair.

He wanted a chance to look at them again, because, yeah, she intrigued him.

The phone rang, breaking his moment of reflection. Tossing her long straight hair over one shoulder, Serena turned and made her way to the counter.

His grandmother elbowed him as he watched her go.

He yelped, "Hey, what was that for?"

"You're messing up my plan," she said in a loud whisper.

He knew what her sneaky plan entailed and didn't want any part of it. He lowered his voice. "I told you, Grandmother, I can find a woman on my own."

"You're taking much too long. I want to see you happy before I die."

Calling his grandmother dramatic was an understatement.

"Look, I'm in town for the meeting," he said, leaving out the fact that he was doing a little reconnaissance work while he was at it. "Not to look for a wife."

"Can't you multitask?"

He coughed out a laugh.

Grandmother sighed. "Turns out I need your expertise while you're here. Let's go get coffee before the family meeting."

At the mention of family, Logan's stomach

clenched. As much as he'd tried to untangle himself from the family business, his grand-mother bound him up in emotional ties he couldn't escape. That meant quarterly meet-ings. He'd much rather have major surgery than sit in his father's boardroom.

Digging into the front pocket of his jeans, he extracted a few bills and handed them to his grandmother. "Why don't you head over to Sit a Spell and order our drinks. I'll be there in a few."

Grandmother's eyes narrowed. "What are you going to do?"

"Chat up your friend like you want me to."

With a slight harrumph, his grandmother waved at Serena and left the store. He was now alone with the woman who had caused more useless legwork to and around his hometown than he cared to admit. Putting on his PI game face, he strolled up to the reg-ister as she hung up the phone.

"Aren't you leaving with your grand-mother?" Serena asked.

"I will, but first I wanted to talk to you."

"About what?"

"Grandmother playing matchmaker."

Serena's gaze flickered away for a flash and returned.

"Is that why you disappear every time I arrive in town?"

"I don't…" She tried to mask the annoyance on her face, but failed. Crossing her arms over her chest, she glared at him. "Your grandmother's actions aside, I have had legitimate reasons for being away, not that it's any of your concern."

"Fair enough. Matchmaking or not, I care about my grandmother, and she thinks highly of you. I wouldn't want to see her disappointed, say, if her good opinion were to change."

Her eyes grew wide, the unusual color more pronounced. "For heaven's sake, why would I disappoint her? She's been more than wonderful to me. And a friend."

He shrugged to give off an air of nonchalance.

She looked at him accusingly. "Do you grill all her tenants?"

"I'm a bit overprotective that way."

"Well, you have no reason to think I'd do anything to hurt her. Or go along with her tactics."

"Good." He sent her the reassuring smile he'd patented to ease subjects into believing they had nothing to worry about. "Just wanted to make sure we're on the same page."

Serena rubbed her right wrist. "Anything else?"

"No." He turned, stopped and caught her gaze again. "I like your store, by the way."

Confusion swept over her features. "Thanks?"

Chuckling, he strode outside. He'd learned a long time ago the best way to pick up information was to keep your subject off guard. Serena wouldn't know what to make of him now and that would work to his advantage.

Crossing the street, he met his grandmother, already seated at an outdoor table at the busy coffee shop. A warm rich scent wafted from the store, making Logan's stomach grumble. He'd missed lunch in his haste to get here and now realized how hungry he was. Holding up one finger at his grandmother, he ducked into Frieda's Bakery to buy pastry. Not even close to the healthy food he normally consumed, but Frieda made an apple fritter he couldn't resist. Stepping back out to the sidewalk, he unwrapped a treat and took a bite of sweet apple chunks rolled into tasty dough and offered the other one to his grandmother.

Mouth full, he met his grandmother's stony glare.

"You didn't do the 'I worry about my grandmother and I have my eyes on you' routine, did you?"

Logan swallowed, took a seat and stretched out his legs. "When have I ever made my intentions known to your tenants?" Reaching out, he took the drink his grandmother had ordered and leaned back in the chair.

"Young man, I needed your help years ago. I can handle myself fine now."

"I don't doubt it for a minute." He took a sip—Delroy and Myrna Hopkins still had the best coffee he'd tasted anywhere—and lifted one shoulder. "I enjoy making people squirm."

"You don't trust anyone, do you, Logan?"

"Only you." He straightened, set down the fritter on a napkin and leaned across the table to cover her soft, wrinkled hand with his. "No one will ever take advantage of you again."

Grandmother patted his hand in return. "I thank you for your grizzly-bear efforts, but I must ask you to stop scaring my tenants."

Blowing out a put-upon sigh, he picked up the fritter. "When did you lose your sense of fun?" he asked, then finished off the doughnut only to start the second one.

"Since you began this mission to protect me." She withdrew her hand. "Besides, I like

Serena. She's all alone and I feel rather motherly toward her."

Another reason she was pushing this match. She had a big heart. As much as he would have liked to tell her he wasn't interested in romance, he couldn't reveal the truth to his grandmother. His good friend Deke Matthews had called in a favor and Logan meant to do well by his buddy. Yes, Serena had been hard to catch up with over the summer, but she was telling the truth—she had been working on designs for her greeting-card business. He hadn't been able to find out much else about her, and for a guy who sniffed out lies for a living, she was turning into a major project.

"Tell me what you wanted to discuss," he said, changing the subject.

"It happens to be about Serena."

He raised an eyebrow.

Grandmother pulled a folder from her purse. "She's offered me a business proposal. I haven't had time to read it yet, but since you do all the background checks on tenants and businesspeople I work with, I thought you should look into this."

Huh. What were the odds his grandmother would give him an avenue to investigate this woman? And why did his Spidey-sense go haywire at the request? *Because two different people have asked you to check up on the same woman.* Circumstances like this didn't happen easily, or often, so he decided to look at this newest development as a gift. One thing he'd learned in PI work, and life in general, was that people lied. And some lies were more devastating than others.

He understood Deke's concern. His friend was trying to find information about a man his widowed mother was dating. Since Logan was superprotective of his grandmother, he got why Deke and his brothers were concerned. The man in question seemed too good to be true, with reason. One of Deke's brothers had discovered this man had lied about his employment and their mother refused to listen to the warnings.

Even though Deke's mother and the subject lived in Florida, they'd found a link, phone calls between the man and Serena's store number. That was when Logan had been called in. So far he hadn't uncovered much. Serena's personal history was spotty—there was a huge gap between her childhood and when she started her business. Any PI worth his salt knew that was a major red flag.

And now Serena wanted to do a business deal with his grandmother? Heck, no. Not until he learned more about who she was, what she was up to and if there were legal reasons why he couldn't find a complete history on her.

"So will you look into this for me?" his grandmother asked.

"Like I always do. Please tell me you haven't told Serena what I do for a living."

Ever since his grandmother had been scammed by some former tenants who'd skipped out on paying a few years ago, he'd been keeping an eagle eye on her. She'd suffered a health scare at the time—the doctors thought she had cancer. Thankfully it turned out to be a minor problem that was cured, but she'd been weak and off her game.

Afterward, she and Logan had come up with a deal. Grandmother would give him the name of anyone interested in renting from her or working with her and he would do a full background check, besides checking out references, to make sure they were on the up-and-up. It had turned out well for both of them. She hadn't been duped again.

"I imagine keeping her in the dark about our conversation will make it easier to do your job. And no, I haven't said a word, so she won't find out from me. I wanted you to win her over on your own merit, not from my glowing recommendation.

"I know you have your reasons why your life in Atlanta is private from your life here, even though I would love to brag on you. I really wish you'd open up more, but that's your choice, so mum's the word.

"But, Logan, go easy with respect to Serena. She's a lovely, smart young lady and you could do worse than find a woman like her."

The jury was still out on that call.

"I have to ask, are you working this hard to get Reid married off?" Logan's brother had been trying to avoid their grandmother's machinations as strenuously as he had. The difference was, Reid lived in Golden, in close proximity to their grandmother's interference, while Logan thankfully lived an hour south.

His grandmother shook her head. "I haven't found the right woman for your brother." She pointed at Logan. "But don't you worry— there's a woman out there for him, and one for you."

"And on that note," Logan said, rising and scooping up the now empty cups to throw in the trash, "I say we get to that meeting. Father hates it when we're late."

"Yet you're tardy at least ten to fifteen minutes every time."

Logan offered a forced smile. "What can I say? I love to create tension."

Grandmother sighed as she collected the folder to return to her purse. "Well, you're very good at it."

"Hey, we all have our thing."

Once she rose, he hooked her hand through his arm and escorted her the three blocks to the family office. They walked slowly. It was a muggy afternoon, the last dog days of summer. September was half-over and he couldn't wait for the temperatures to drop and the leaves to change color. Autumn had always been his favorite season growing up, until...

As they arrived at the two-story office building, his grandmother squeezed his arm. "I'd tell you to behave, but I know you won't listen."

Grinding his back molars, he remained quiet. These meetings were important to both his brother and grandmother, and that was the only reason he still attended. He really didn't care what his father thought about him. Nothing would make him respect the old man again, so he didn't even try. But he did love the woman who connected him to his family and would do anything for her, including sit in the same room as his father.

It all boiled down to family love and honor, he supposed. He'd never be the Masterson team player his father wanted him to be, but he was honest enough with himself to know that was okay. He didn't want any ties to the empire. Nor would he ever be a carbon copy of his father. The older man's lies had dictated that Logan would be his own man.

So for now, he'd go along with everyone, but then ferret out Serena Stanhope's secret.

As the office's glass door closed behind him, he focused his gaze back down Main Street. The owner of Blue Ridge Cottage was hiding something, and it was going to be his great pleasure to expose the truth.

CHAPTER TWO

WRAPPING HIS HAND around the doorknob to escape the boardroom after the long meeting, Logan cringed when he heard a deep voice. "Son, a moment, please."

Almost made it.

He closed his eyes for a brief second, loosened his grip on the knob and turned. Waited.

"You didn't say much during the meeting." His father spoke in an authoritative voice. "I wanted your opinion on the bid for that parcel of land in Atlanta."

There was a reason Logan didn't contribute. He wasn't involved in the day-to-day running of Masterson Enterprises, nor did he care to be. His PI business was gaining momentum, so his energy went toward that future, not one with ties to the past.

"Whatever you think is fine."

His father, tall, like himself, with thick, dark hair streaked with gray, struck a commanding pose. His success came from the fact that he didn't back down, which essentially meant making people cower until he got his way. Not a business model Logan would ever choose to adopt, but it worked for Arthur Masterson.

There had been more than one argument while he was growing up, when Logan refused to give in to his father's demands. Tensions had come to a head when Logan found out his parents had lied to him about the circumstances surrounding his birth. After his father made excuses for brushing aside the truth, Logan joined the military. The two hadn't agreed on any one thing since.

"When are you going to get your head into the game, Logan?"

Reining in his temper, Logan kept his tone even. "We've had this conversation a dozen times. I'm here for Grandmother, not to be part of the behind-the-scenes operations. You have Reid for that. I don't know how much clearer I can make it that I'm not interested."

"There will come a day when you'll need to give up that hobby of yours and come home to help Reid with the company."

Hobby? Logan was good at what he did. Had started his agency from the ground up. Nothing had been handed to him, not even the seed money his grandmother had loaned him. He'd paid it back, with interest. "You're not helping your case, Dad."

"And this stubborn act of rebellion is getting old. Things were mishandled. Mistakes were made. You joined the military to get back at me. But it's been years and we need you to step up here in Golden."

"Wow. Did you really say 'mistakes were made'?"

"Leave the past where it belongs, son."

Anger, hot and heavy, crept over Logan's skin.

"We have many plans going forward in the upcoming year. Your mother and I would like you to be present."

"I've explained this to you more than once. I'm here for Grandmother."

Hoping his point would hit home—doubtful—he reached for the knob again when the woman he called mother moved into his peripheral vision. He was about to be double-teamed.

Her cloying perfume choked him. "Logan. I was hoping we'd visit before you left us again."

"I have some things to attend to."

"Really?" She arched her artistically shaped eyebrows. "In town?"

"Yes."

"Then you don't have an excuse not to come to the house for dinner tonight. Seven?"

He must be off his game today. First, Grandmother trying to embroil him in her matchmaking ploys, then his father talking over him and now his mother asking him to dinner. He'd rather not eat than share a meal with the two of them.

"Let me see how my time is," Logan answered. "I'll let you know." His investigating had better come up with something worthy for him to endure such family togetherness.

His mother's eyes went dewy and she laid a graceful hand on his arm. Bonnie Masterson had sacrificed a lot for him, loved him when she didn't have to. His darned heart went and got soft on him as he met her searching green gaze, her heart-shaped face framed by pale blond hair. He never could say no to the woman, even though they would never be close.

"I'll see you at seven."

Bonnie's smile spread. "Wonderful. I'll have Alveda make a plate of your favorite fried green tomatoes."

With a nod to his parents, he said, "I'll see you later."

He jogged down the stairs, burst out the front door to the street and stopped to breathe in fresh air. How did they do it? Even when he steeled his heart against them, they won. Shaking off his strange mood, he strode over to the mountain vacation business of Put Your Feet Up. His meeting with Deke Matthews should have started ten minutes ago.

He entered and caught Deke and one of the business's owners, Grace Harper, in a serious lip-lock.

"Kids, I thought we went over the legal ramifications of inappropriate PDA in the workplace."

The couple jerked apart. Grace's pretty face flushed, while a smirk curved Deke's lips.

"We got tired of waiting for you."

Logan apologized. "The meeting went long."

Deke gave him a searching look, then nodded.

"Tell you what," Grace said. "Why don't you guys head over to Smitty's? You'll have some time to talk before the Oktoberfest committee descends on the place."

"Sure you don't want to join us?" Deke asked, his hand resting on Grace's shoulder with casual ease. They'd fallen for each other when Deke came to town to follow a lead on his mother's mystery man—a lead that led directly to Serena Stanhope.

"I promised my sister I'd finish up a few calls before going back to my law office." Grace turned to Logan. "She had to take the kids to the doctor."

"Things are going well here?"

Deke nodded as Grace said, "My sibs are all in, which means I actually get to practice law, so yeah—" she glanced at Deke "—things are good."

Logan had known Grace, along with most of the population here in Golden, all his life. She'd always been focused and serious, so he wasn't surprised she'd gone into law. Deke was also on more of the quiet, reflective side. He assumed that was what made them a good pair.

He'd first met Deke when an investigation by his agency overlapped with an active police case of his. A woman had come to the agency, concerned that her husband was involved with some shady people. After tailing the guy for weeks, Logan soon discovered the husband was involved in several robberies. The cops were called in, Logan and Deke compared notes and, in the end, discovered the connecting link that led to Deke making an arrest. They'd gone out for a few beers after closing the case and had been good buddies ever since.

"Let's hit it," Logan said. Ready to get down to business, he stepped out onto the sidewalk while Deke said goodbye.

A few minutes later they were walking north to Smitty's, a neighborhood hangout off the beaten tourist path. While most of the businesses in town catered to visitors, Smitty's was the one place where locals could escape and let off steam in the rustic pub after a busy day, or just hang out with friends.

"You know," Logan said, "you don't have to rub your sappy relationship in my face every time we meet."

"And you could have more information about my mother's boyfriend, but you don't."

Logan cringed. "Sorry about that. This case wasn't the slam dunk I'd hoped it would be."

After pulling open the heavy oak door of the log-cabin-style pub, Logan motioned in Deke and then followed. The dark interior was soothing coming on the heels of the intense late afternoon sun. He blinked, waiting for his eyes to adjust. Their boots echoed over scuffed wood floors as they took a corner table. Classic country boomed from the wall-mounted speakers scattered around the room. Once seated, Deke didn't waste any time.

"Anything new?"

Logan rested his elbows on the table. "Nothing since the last time we talked. Serena's past is murky, to say the least."

"She and her father are good."

"Your mother still standing by her man?"

"Tightly."

Logan scowled.

Deke had called, asking him to check the connection between Serena Stanhope and James Tate, the man his mother had started dating. Since Deke and his brothers were all involved in law enforcement, they decided to get a PI involved instead of risking their positions by doing a background check for personal reasons. A PI in Florida had found calls on Tate's phone made to Golden and discovered that number belonged to Blue Ridge Cottage. Since the lead had shifted from Florida to Georgia, Logan had then taken over this end of the investigation.

"My brothers and I laid off," Deke said. "I've done my best to stay out of Serena's eyeline, hoping my mom would lose interest in the guy, but that hasn't happened. Mom is stubborn. The only way to get her to see reason is to present her with credible facts showing her why we're concerned." He grimaced. "Even then she won't be easy to convince."

Logan took his phone from his pocket and pulled up a document. "I did a background search on both names Tate and Stanhope. The information overlaps between a deceased Tate and a confusing past on Stanhope. I'd say he stole the Tate identity he's using now. Stanhope, however, is legally still alive, even if there hasn't been any activity in his credit, health care or any other traceable matters over the past ten years."

"So he is a con man."

That had been the consensus between the brothers and investigators working the case after the initial information on the subject was revealed. Logan didn't see that fact changing anytime soon.

"The next step is producing evidence to prove our theory. Serena is the key. It's no coincidence they have the same last name." Logan met Deke's steady gaze head-on. He'd learned a long time ago that when dealing with clients, it was best to be straightforward, even if you didn't have concrete answers. "Right now, all I can confirm is that Stanhope is using another man's identity. Weird thing is, he's not doing it for financial gain.

There's been no record of Tate's social security number used to open bogus accounts or credit cards. He strictly took the name because it matched up closely with his own date of birth and physical resemblance."

"Which he could argue is a coincidence. How many other people in the US have the name James Tate?"

"Right. As far as I can tell, he's not stealing a dime."

"Then why not use Stanhope, his real name?" Deke mused.

"Maybe he used it in a prior con job and can't afford to be associated with it."

Deke nodded, then asked, "Serena?"

"So far, no link. The calls from Tate stopped about the time you found out what we suspect is his real name."

"Think he warned her?"

Logan shrugged. "That would be my guess."

Heavy footsteps approached the table. "You guys ordering?"

Deke glanced up. "Nice customer service, Jamey."

A smile appeared under a heavy beard. "Like you expect niceties."

"We get them when Sarah is working."

"Her day off, so you get me in all my customer-relation glory."

"Ginger ale," Logan said, then looked at Deke.

"Same."

"My tab," Logan told the pub owner as he walked away.

Deke rested his elbows on the scarred table-top and leaned forward. "So what's next?"

"I keep tabs on the pretty store owner. I'm hoping she's the avenue that leads me to the information we need."

"Why does that smile of yours tell me you're going to enjoy that?"

"I don't know." Logan shook his head. "It's like I've met my match with her and can't wait to start sparring."

"And you wonder why the ladies don't think you're romantic."

Logan threw up his hands. "Hey, I'm not looking for romance. I want to wrap up this case and stay out of Golden for as long as I can."

"Not if your family has anything to say about it."

Logan scoffed. "I'm not asking for their opinion."

After yelling something through the kitchen

door, Jamey returned with their drinks. "You guys staying for the Oktoberfest meeting?"

"I am," Deke answered. "Grace is joining me here."

"You're really getting involved in that festival mess?" Logan asked as he picked up his glass.

"I am."

He shot Deke a pitying look. "Count me out."

"Really? What if I were to tell you Serena will be attending."

Logan took a swallow of the sparkling beverage, then carefully placed the glass on the table. "Then I'd say Oktoberfest just became my favorite holiday of the year."

"I CAN'T BELIEVE I got roped into the festival committee," Serena muttered as she and her store manager, Heidi, made their way down the sidewalk to Smitty's.

"Aren't you the one always telling me you adore Golden? So you act like a good citizen and get involved."

Serena would love to, if she wasn't afraid of getting too close to people, especially Deke, the son of her father's girlfriend.

Deke had come by the store a few times after first arriving in town with friendly questions she knew not to answer. Once she learned who he was, her fallback position was to be wary. Eventually Deke had backed off. They were polite whenever their paths crossed, but he had a look about him that kept Serena's antenna up.

Since landing in Golden, Heidi Welch had become a good friend in the short time they'd known each other, and lately she'd interacted with Grace Harper. Since both Heidi and Grace had lived in Golden longer than Serena, they seemed to know everyone, along with the best places to have fun. While Serena loved being included, being accepted as part of a group, it also made her nervous. Every day she prayed her past wouldn't be revealed.

"Even if I was right in the middle of a new card design?"

Heidi shot her a sideways glance. "You can't use that excuse because you're always working on one design or another."

True. Serena used drawing as a way to escape the world around her. Hours flew by as her colored pencils, charcoal or watercolors filled her sketchbook with shading, tone and contrast. Engrossed in her work, she didn't worry about the past catching up with her.

The new series, inspired by the beautiful

mountain vistas and dense woods surrounding Golden, had been more time-consuming than she'd envisioned. Good, because the quality of her work would bring sales; bad, because she was behind on her deadline. She'd hoped to have her proofs to the printer before presenting her business proposal to any potential investors. Would Mrs. Masterson be intrigued by the merit of the proposal, or know someone else who might find Serena's business interesting enough to invest in?

"You're being secretive about this business proposal," Heidi said as she led the way. "Any reason why?"

"No. It's just…the more I create new ideas, the longer it seems to be taking me. I had so many flashes of creativity in college, which launched this whole company. But as more of my designs get out there, I want them to be different. Which means more time spent making sure every line, every splash of color, is fresh and innovative."

"Glad to hear the artist is back."

Serena stopped short, her sandals catching the sidewalk seam, causing the pedestrians behind them to swerve in order to miss running into her. "What do you mean? I've always been an artist."

Heidi grinned, her light brown hair highlighted with a bright red streak in the front and pulled back in a high ponytail. Her amber-colored eyes sparkled. "Not when you're caught up in the business aspect of the store. I don't know why you didn't let me put the proposal together. I'm way better at numbers than you."

Yes, Heidi had a mathematician's brain. She was also very shrewd, which meant Serena kept the company's information, mainly the truth of its origins, a secret. Only one other person in the entire world knew about Aunt Mary and how she figured into the company lore. Serena planned on keeping it that way.

"Aren't you busy enough with inventory, marketing, online sales—"

Heidi held up her hand. "I get it. I have work to do."

"It's not like I didn't ask you for advice."

"You did, which makes me happy. I know you're busy with your designs and I just wanted to help."

Serena threw an arm over her friend's shoulder to tug her close. "I appreciate it."

"Doesn't mean you have to get all gooey on me."

Releasing her, Serena laughed. "We wouldn't want that."

"No, we wouldn't," Heidi muttered in her patented "keep your distance" tone.

"Someday you're going to return one of my hugs."

Heidi resumed walking. "Don't count on it."

Swallowing a chuckle, Serena was about to tease her friend when a voice called out, "Hey, ladies. Wait up."

Serena smiled as Grace Harper strode toward them. Brisk and to-the-point, the blonde woman dating Deke had initially made Serena uncomfortable until she got to know her better.

"Headed to the meeting?" Grace asked as the three strolled down the sidewalk together.

"Do we have a choice?" Serena replied.

Both Heidi and Grace sent her identical frowns.

"We've discussed this," Heidi said. "If we want more tourists, we need these festivals."

"The Summer Gold Celebration was a start," Grace said, "but I don't think we pulled in the numbers the festival committee was looking for."

Puzzled, Serena said, "The foot traffic was pretty good."

Heidi nodded. "It was better than summers past and our sales were up, but I'm sure you've noticed the lag this month. After Labor Day we see less tourists. Kids go back to school and our bottom line drops. Oktoberfest draws an older crowd, hopefully with money to burn."

"We've already seen vacation packages slow down a tick at Put Your Feet Up. Tourists eager to view the fall foliage won't be here until October."

Serena turned to Grace. "But aren't you spending long hours getting your practice started?"

"I am. Though I still put in time at the family office." Grace shrugged but looked anything but repentant. "What can I say? I'm all about control."

Heidi looked around Serena, sending Grace an amused glance. "Really? Seems to me a certain tall, dark and handsome tour guide has tempered that streak."

Grace's eyes grew dreamy. "Yeah, Deke is pretty awesome."

Serena and Heidi exchanged eye rolls.

"Look, you two, once you each find the right guy, you'll become as sappy as me."

"Count me out," Heidi said, picking up the pace to beat the others to Smitty's.

"What about you, Serena?" Grace asked,

her smile bright. "You don't have a boy-friend. Are you looking?"

An image of Logan Masterson, his winning smile and sharp gaze, filled her head. While he was very attractive, he also sent out a vibe that made Serena nervous. "Right now my focus is on the store."

"But one day?"

Serena laughed. "People in love are annoying. You think everyone should join your club."

"It's not exclusive." Grace held open the heavy door after Heidi disappeared inside the dimly lit pub. "Maybe I can set you up with someone. There are some nice single guys in town. Any of the Wright brothers are a catch."

Serena's eyes went wide at the suggestion. "Good grief, no."

"Afraid you might actually meet a guy and fall in love?"

Yes. That would be a disaster.

"How about you concentrate on Deke," Serena told her friend, "and leave us single ladies alone."

"Fine," Grace huffed. "For now."

Serena followed Grace inside, hoping her friend would spend more time dwelling on her own relationship with Deke and forget about setting her up with any of the bachelors currently residing in Golden.

A crowd had already gathered, and the assembled group was upbeat and merry. Once her eyes grew accustomed to the low lighting, Serena sought out a table near the back of the room, where she could observe the meeting without getting involved. She was all for drawing tourists to Golden to make the town profitable, her store included, but old habits had her keeping to herself. Working on committees meant people getting to know you, and until she paid back her debt, she couldn't risk being found out.

She'd just slipped onto a hard wooden chair and hooked her purse over the back, when the chair next to her scraped across the floor and a tall male dropped down.

"Fancy meeting you here," Logan said, placing his glass on the table.

Great. She really didn't want to field questions about why she'd been out of town or if she was going to take advantage of his grandmother. "Don't you have any other store owners to badger?"

"Nah. Only here to sit in on the meeting."

"You don't even live here."

"Doesn't mean I'm not interested."

He looked up and waved. To her dismay,

Grace and Deke joined them. Now she had two men giving her more attention than she wanted.

"This should be a good meeting," Deke said, sinking into a chair after making sure Grace was seated.

"The Tremaines are at the helm, so it'll be intense," Grace added.

Carter and Lissy Ann Tremaine were the town's "it" couple. Carter's family, like the Mastersons, had helped found Golden. While the Tremaines were about branding and being in the public eye, the Mastersons were about real estate and making money. But from what she'd understood, Logan had some kind of business in Atlanta and didn't participate in the day-to-day running of the Masterson business, which made Serena wonder about his sudden interest in the town's activities. Could his grandmother have upped her matchmaking game? Squirming in her seat, she crossed her fingers, hoping her conclusion that Mrs. M. had lured him here was correct.

"Uncomfortable?" Logan asked, leaning close enough to Serena that his spicy citrus scent surrounded her. His intense gaze made her want to shift away, but she forced herself to be still.

"Busy. I had to close the store to come to this meeting."

"No help?"

"Heidi, and she's here, too."

Logan scanned the pub. "Everyone is getting in on the town spirit."

"That's one of the things I like about Golden."

He turned to look at her, his eyes capturing hers, and she fought back an unwanted shiver. "Town spirit?"

"Yes. It's nice to see everyone coming together."

"Something you aren't used to?" he asked.

She wasn't touching that question, so she asked instead, "Why are you here tonight? You weren't part of the town's summer festivities."

His eyes shuttered. "I live and work in Atlanta."

"Doing what?"

"Information retrieval."

She sent him a puzzled look.

"I find things for people."

"What kinds of things?"

Before he could answer, a server stopped by the table for their drink order.

"So why the interest in Golden now?" Serena asked as the server hurried on.

"My grandmother. Also, Deke's a friend, so we've been catching up."

"Your grandmother mentioned you still have ties to the family business."

"I do. It's a small part, but gets me to Golden once a quarter." He took a drink from his glass. "You? Family, I mean?"

"Not locally."

"But you have family?"

"Sure. Doesn't everyone?"

His amused gaze met hers. "Vague."

She stared ahead, trying to ignore him.

Before Logan could say anything else, the Tremaines called the meeting to order, which suited her fine.

They began with a recap of the summer celebration, statistics and a discussion about what generated the most interest. And could this be translated into even more tourist traffic in a few weeks' time. Suggestions were made to play up the quaintness of the town, drawing on its history as part of a gold-rush craze in the 1800s, to appeal to vacationers. The town had been established when people from far and wide arrived to pan for nuggets after a gold vein was discovered in the mountains on the outskirts of Golden. Tourists could try their luck to this day in some of the panning locations found around town.

But as much as there was to offer in Golden and the surrounding areas already, twenty different people had twenty different suggestions. Carter finally reined in the discussion and read off all his own ideas.

"Carter always did like to listen to himself talk," Logan muttered under his breath for only Serena to hear.

She grinned. Logan had the preppy-looking man pegged. "I take it he's not a favorite of yours?"

Logan sat close enough that his shrug brushed against her arm. "Competitors. Mostly from his point of view."

"In high school?" she asked.

"Yep. Gotta love memories from good ol' Golden High."

Curious about the handsome man beside her, Serena made a mental note to research Golden High School. She figured both men were in their early thirties, so she could narrow down the years they attended.

"Well, he seems invested in placing Golden on the map."

Logan leaned closer and a trickle of pleasure danced over her skin. "How about you? Part of Team Golden?"

She shifted, widening the space between

them. Put starch in her tone. "As long as I have a store here, yes."

His gaze met hers again. The way he gauged her, as if trying to uncover all her secrets, took her breath away. *Danger, Serena Stanhope, danger.*

Panic rose and she sucked in air too quickly, almost choking. Logan reached over to slap her on the back as Deke and Grace sent curious glances their way.

"You all right?" he asked in between her coughing.

No, she wasn't.

Logan's knowing gaze unnerved her in more ways than one.

CHAPTER THREE

THE COMMITTEE MEETING wound down after the particulars of Oktoberfest were discussed and job descriptions handed out. To Serena's dismay, Heidi volunteered them both to serve food during the three-week event. She couldn't get out of it without questions being hurled in her direction, so she smiled and graciously went along with the idea. Once the meeting had been adjourned, Serena jumped up and headed straight to the ladies' room.

Logan couldn't know, could he? She stared in the mirror, searching her soul. She'd been careful. Had kept her nose to the grindstone. Hadn't created any red flags. Aunt Mary's story was carefully crafted and cemented. So what did he think he knew?

All during the meeting he'd peppered her with questions that hit too close to home to be considered random curiosity about a store owner in a town where he didn't even live. And the way he kept leaning into her space? Like he was trying to trip her up? It had worked, all right, if her startling response to his proximity was any indication.

Or could he actually be going along with his grandmother's matchmaking attempt?

She hadn't had many serious relationships with men throughout the years, but she did recognize the early stages of attraction. She couldn't ignore Logan's tantalizing spicy scent or keep from meeting his gaze when those dark brown eyes caught hers. When he'd brushed his shoulder against hers, she'd tried to control the rush of anticipation without success. His appeal was like a beam, pulling her toward him when she should be running in the opposite direction.

What was it about this attraction that scared her so much? How Logan had swooped in and claimed her attention? How she'd reacted to his presence? Or was it more about him finding out who she really was?

Throwing cold water on her face, she took several deep breaths and calmed her nerves. She could handle this. She'd kept her past hidden up until now, hadn't she? She'd continue doing so, no matter that a handsome man with broad shoulders and a gorgeous grin weakened her confidence. Smoothing her dress, she walked back into the main room.

Conversation about Oktoberfest flew around

her, and she heard something about how working together made everyone family, but she focused on scanning the pub, looking for a certain good-looking dark-haired man, instead of engaging in the discussion.

"You'll love it," a voice said near her ear as the group milled about and folks visited before heading home. Still distracted, Serena jumped when Heidi elbowed her. "Did you hear me?"

"Huh?" Serena turned her attention to her employee. "Sorry, I wasn't listening."

Heidi followed her gaze across the room to Logan, who stood talking to the pub owner.

"Ah, so that's how it is."

Serena felt her face flame. "Not at all. There's nothing going on."

"Really? Then why are you so jumpy?"

"Because I have a class that starts in—" she glanced at her watch "—thirty minutes and I want to get back to the store to set up."

"You did that before we left," Heidi reminded her.

"Well, I need to get back."

Heidi looked at her as if Serena had forgotten her own name. "If you say so."

"I do. Are you coming with me?"

"If you don't mind, I'm going to grab a burger. I'll be there in time for the class."

"Okay, see you in thirty."

Serena scooped up her purse and fled the pub, leaving the raucous music and loud voices behind her. Heart beating, she pulled her cell phone from her bag and hit speed dial. Even though she'd told Heidi she was going to the shop, she took a detour into Gold Dust Park, crossing under the stone arch at the entrance. She sat down at the first vacant picnic bench she encountered.

When the ringing finally stopped, her father's voice came across the line.

"Serena. What a surprise."

"Hi, Daddy. I know we were going to limit our calls, but, well, I think I have a situation here."

"Deke, right?"

She had told her father about Deke's curiosity last spring, when he'd come into the shop to introduce himself and the probing conversation had turned to family. When she found out later who Deke was, her father hadn't thought dating his mother a problem at the time. They'd both successfully kept their past a secret, hadn't they? Deke had backed off, as her father had predicted he would when she voiced her concerns, and everything had returned to normal, making Serena feel a bit foolish. After her bout of nerves, her father suggested they only talk when necessary, and up until now, there'd been no problems.

"There's this guy, Logan Masterson. I don't know him very well, but he seems interested in why I'm in town, do I have family, all the questions I've been trying to avoid."

"Serena, no one knows who you are in that town. Your past is safe."

Safe, but for how long? There had to be a list of people interested in her past, but her father had conveniently stuck his head in the sand while she righted wrongs.

"It's probably me being overly cautious, but I'm wondering why after two years anyone is asking about my family."

"Well, um, I'm sure it's your imagination. You suspected Deke was interested in you, but nothing ever happened, so you were wrong about that."

Was she? Just because Deke had backed off didn't mean he hadn't called in reinforcements. Logan definitely looked like a reinforcements kind of guy. How else to explain his attempts to meet up with her all summer?

"You've always been too nervous for your own good," her father scolded, but Serena caught a note of worry in his tone.

Suddenly she was sure she wasn't overreacting.

"Daddy? What's going on?" She paused as a terrible thought rushed into her head. "You haven't started any new scams, have you?"

"Of course not. I promised you years ago that I was going straight and I've kept my word."

Relief washed over her, but she still suspected he wasn't on the up-and-up. "Then why do I feel like you're up to something?"

"No scams."

His quick answer didn't reassure her. "What aren't you telling me?"

The silence on the other end seemed to drag on forever. Finally, her father spoke, his voice light and happy. "Jasmine and I are getting serious."

Serena blinked. Not what she'd expected. "Explain *serious*."

"I think I'm in love."

Definitely not what she'd expected. Ever since her mother had died when Serena was eight, her father had never seemed interested in other women.

Lifting her right hand, Serena gazed at the angel wings tattooed on her inner wrist. The ink had been a tribute to the mother she'd known briefly, yet who had made a big impact on Serena's life. All that remained were fuzzy recollections of her mother encouraging her innate artistic abilities. Memories of a woman who'd smelled like flowers and had squeezed Serena in loving embraces. Their little family had been happy until a brief illness had taken her away, leaving Serena with a father who couldn't deal with life.

It wasn't until years later, when her father had made her a part of his scams, that she'd learned her mother had been the driving force behind keeping him legit. With his moral compass gone, he'd reverted to shady tricks, dragging his unsuspecting daughter with him until she was in so deep there didn't seem to be any way out. Serena was still trying to outrun the shame.

"And she knows all about me," her father said, breaking the silence.

Serena froze, then stuttered, "You—you told her?"

"No details. Just that I was a bit of a con man in my day."

"A bit?" Serena choked out.

"I didn't want to run her off."

Serena spoke her deepest fear aloud. "Is there any way Jasmine could have sent Deke to spy on me?"

"Why would she? I told you, her sons are law enforcement. If they knew something about me, they would've confronted me by now."

Or maybe they'd use reinforcements?

"So far I've played it cool and haven't run into any problems, Serena. It's more that they've got a problem with the idea of their mother dating. But their father is gone. It's time to move on. She's told them she's happy, and it seems to have worked." He chuckled. "Quite a woman, my Jasmine is. You'll love her."

"I don't understand why you ever told her about me."

"How could I not brag about my successful daughter?"

His words made her chest constrict. She loved her father, no matter his faults. "You're sure no one is snooping?"

"I can't see any way a person would know the truth. At least not through me or my beloved."

Her father in love? As much as she was happy for him, she couldn't shake the feeling that this was behind the sudden interest in her life.

"I'm sure you're overreacting, like you did with Deke," her father continued. "Take a few deep breaths. Be nice to the new guy and evade like I taught you to. You'll be fine."

Said the man who lived hundreds of miles away. Yes, he was sticking his head in the sand, appropriate, since he lived in Florida, and Serena would now have to keep her guard up all the time.

Did he have to fall for a woman with sons in law enforcement? Just when she thought maybe, just maybe, she could lead a life without looking over her shoulder, her father might have jeopardized her future.

But he'd never see it that way. Her father was a romantic at heart, one who could sell you swamp land in Florida. She'd have to handle this alone.

"You're probably right, Daddy. Thanks for listening."

"Anytime, my sweet girl. Now, I have to run. Love you."

"Love you, too," she replied, already moving the phone away from her mouth.

A group of people walked by, reminding Serena where she was. She hurried to the store, unlocked the front door, flipped the sign to Open and dropped off her purse in the office. After starting the coffee maker, she collected the class supplies she'd stacked on the counter and carried them to the empty table on the showroom floor, where she laid out the paper and pens for the 7:00 p.m. calligraphy class. With only minutes to spare, she forced herself to corral her runaway emotions.

Her father in love. This spelled disaster.

Serena shoved away the conversation with her dad and concentrated on the students, who had started to arrive.

"Coffee will be ready in a jiff," she told the women. "Or let me know if you'd like sparkling water instead."

Members of a local Purple Hat Society were signed up for tonight's calligraphy lessons. Serena had been thrilled, since working with customers connected her to the community. The ladies, age seventy and up, were a hoot. They spoke their minds and always seemed to enjoy the class, especially the refreshments Serena offered as part of the experience.

As the women got settled, she picked up a pen, recalling how she'd discovered her love of everything writing related in college. She'd taken all kinds of art classes on campus, but had loved calligraphy from the very beginning. All her dorm mates had asked her to sign their names to greeting cards in the fancy script, and now she shared that talent in the classes she offered here in the store.

"Now, ladies," she said to the group of six

sitting around the table, "this is a beginner class, so we'll be using ballpoint pens instead of the finer pen nibs. If you keep at it, you can advance to dipping in ink later." She walked around the table, handing out alphabet templates. "Tonight you'll trace the letter patterns to get a feel for the decorative writing."

The door opened and Heidi hurried inside, waving as she crossed the room to the counter.

"If you ladies will excuse me, I need to talk to Heidi for a moment. Go ahead and get started."

She met her employee at the counter and pulled out a day planner from the shelf. "If you wouldn't mind entering my schedule into the database and printing it out, I'd appreciate it."

"Sure. Anything else?"

"Call Mrs. Keene and let her know the baby announcements are in. Otherwise it's slow tonight."

"Mind if I take off after doing this? I have a huge spreadsheet I'm working on."

Heidi took bookkeeping jobs as well as working for Serena.

"Sure. I'll lock up and see you tomorrow."

"Thanks."

Serena started to walk away when Heidi stopped her. "You were the topic of conversation tonight."

Turning on her heel, Serena composed her features. "Really? Someone was interested in me?"

"Yep. Logan." Heidi grinned. "And you said there's nothing going on."

"I barely know the man."

"Well, you must have made an impression. Looks like one of us might be joining the dating club."

Better to let Heidi think Logan might be romantically interested in her than in the probable truth—that despite her father's assurances, Logan was only interested in her family's shady past.

As LOGAN EXPECTED, dinner was superb. Not his normal choice, since he stuck to a healthy diet, but he wouldn't say no to honey-baked ham, coleslaw and corn bread, although he skipped the vegetables drowned in butter.

The formal dining room of Masterson House was a bit staid for his taste. Fresh flowers placed in a crystal vase on the sideboard overpowered the savory aroma of dinner. His loft in Atlanta was more his style—big windows washing the space in plenty of natural light, exposed brick walls and dark wood floors, industrial kitchen and contemporary furnishings. As far away from traditional as you could get.

"Logan, how are things in Atlanta?" his brother asked as he cut into a slice of ham.

"Busy. Took on two new cases this week."

"Interesting?"

"A divorce and a large chain store wanting to beef up security." He'd been thrilled to expand into security work and hoped this was just the beginning. "That job will be time-consuming but worth it in the long run."

"Divorce?" Their mother wrinkled her nose. "Rather unseemly, don't you think?"

Yes. It was. But it was also life and, unfortunately, a staple in his business.

"Talking about marriage," his grandmother said, "I'm still waiting for my grandsons to tie the knot."

Logan shook his head. "Smooth, Grandmother, considering we were talking about the opposite of marriage."

She shrugged. "I take my cues where I get them."

Logan swallowed a chuckle.

"I bought my tickets today for the Golden Ladies' Guild fall fund-raiser."

Logan shot Reid a look and received the same panicked reaction in return.

"It's for a good cause. I would love my grandsons to accompany me."

"I'd have to check my calendar," Logan said around a forkful of slaw.

"Me, too," Reid echoed. "I have some out-of-town meetings scheduled."

His grandmother smoothed the cloth napkin on her lap. "Do you two think you can really outmaneuver me?"

"No," Logan admitted. "But we can try."

She laughed. "I'll text you the date and you *will* pencil me into your schedules."

"Yes, ma'am," the brothers said in unison.

"I've also been thinking about wedding dates." The older woman's light blue eyes took on a faraway glaze. "Spring is beautiful, with the promise of new beginnings. Late summer is lovely as well. Or the fiery autumn colors make a beautiful backdrop to the ceremony."

"Grandmother, don't you think you're getting ahead of yourself?" A flicker of skepticism laced Reid's comment. "Logan and I don't even have girlfriends."

"Which is easy to remedy if you'd listen to me."

"Gayle Ann, I want to see my sons married as much as you," their mother said, "but don't you think this in-your-face method is a bit…high-handed?"

"How else can I get them on board? They don't take my hints." She scowled at Logan. "And there are some perfectly wonderful women right here in Golden."

"What if I told you I'd found the love of my life in Atlanta?" Logan teased.

"I'd say bring her for a visit so I can determine if she's right for you."

Logan laughed. "If I didn't know better, I'd think you didn't trust me."

"With your love life, no." She leveled a stare at Reid. "And you're not out of the clear, either, young man."

Alveda, the family cook, whose graying hair was pulled into a severe bun, swept into the dining room to check on the ham platter. "Is everything okay?"

"Perfection, as usual," his father complimented, rare praise coming from the normally indifferent man.

As she passed by Logan, her bony hand rested on his shoulder as she leaned down and said, "I've got pecan pie for dessert."

Logan groaned. "You're killing me." He glanced at the thin woman who'd been cooking for the family since he was a child. "But make sure to bring me a big piece."

"With vanilla ice cream?"

He closed his eyes and groaned again. "Yes, please."

The older woman chuckled as she returned to the kitchen.

"Grandmother, about this fund-raiser." Reid visibly cringed as he said the words. "What does it entail?"

"Tea. Finger sandwiches. Speeches. Lots of women."

"Aren't you forgetting Oktoberfest?" Logan reminded her.

"That's for tourists. Only locals attend the ladies' guild activities."

Logan reached for his glass of sweet tea. "If it's at Smitty's, count me in."

Their mother gasped. "You can't be serious."

"He's not," Grandmother confirmed, "but I rather like the idea. Since I'm on the committee, I'll make the recommendation for next time. This year's party already has a venue."

"Tell us when and where," Logan said.

"Excellent. I'll have my picks for your future brides there with bells on."

A smart remark about not needing any women, nor any bells, was on the tip of Logan's tongue, but his grandmother's happy expression kept him silent. Later, he and Reid would have to strategize on how to hold on to their single status.

A fleeting image of Serena flashed through his head. Her long black hair. The unusual blue eyes that snagged his attention. When he'd leaned close to her at Smitty's, he'd picked up the scent of lavender. She'd tried to move away, leaving him to wonder how he affected her. Was she as interested as he was? He'd love to find out. If his grandmother invited her, the fund-raiser might not be so bad after all.

Of course, the question was, would Serena attend? She was pretty jumpy around him. Guess he didn't blame her. Grandmother had probably mentioned she was trying to marry him off. That would easily explain why she was uncomfortable. Who wanted to be pressured into a relationship?

But despite her obvious misgivings, he liked her. Was impressed by her business, which he knew firsthand was not easy to start. She had an online presence as well as the store, and after checking out her website, he had to admit she was pretty savvy. Now, if he could unravel her past...

"The boys will find appropriate women to

marry, Mother," his father said as he pushed away his empty plate.

"Boys?" Logan arched an eyebrow as he recognized the grimace on his brother's face. "In case you haven't noticed, Reid and I are grown men."

His father waved a hand to brush aside Logan's point. "Men take care of their responsibilities, which you have not."

"Not this again," Logan muttered under his breath.

"Yes, this again. Until you take your rightful place in Masterson Enterprises, we will continue to have this conversation."

Logan glanced at his brother. "Why don't you say anything?"

Reid rolled his neck. "I'm doing what I can," he growled.

Their father frowned. "What's that supposed to mean?"

Reid turned to their father. "I work hard for the company, Dad. I wish you'd give me a little more credit."

"I only meant it would be nice for your older brother to work with us."

Reid rose and tossed his napkin on the table. "Which he clearly has no interest in. And if you weren't so obsessed with Logan coming back, you'd see that I've made many important advances for the company. Brought in a lot of business since I've worked there full-time."

The door from the kitchen swung open as a heavy tension blanketed the room. Alveda returned with pie slices loaded down with ice cream for Logan and Reid.

"I'm not hungry," Reid said as he stalked out of the room.

"Oh, dear," Grandmother said under her breath.

"Why do you do this?" Logan asked his father, who sat at the head of the table like he was a king. "Reid is everything you need for the company, yet you treat him like his contributions don't matter."

His father's eyebrows rose. "I do no such thing. Reid is integral to the success of the company."

"Do you ever bother to tell him?"

His father crossed his arms over his chest. "Why should I praise Reid for work he knows he does well?"

"Because it's nice to be acknowledged every once in a while. But then you wouldn't know how to do that, would you?"

Okay, maybe that was harsh, but his father couldn't seem to get off the "come back to the company" bandwagon. For Pete's sake, he'd never been part of the company to begin with. While Reid had gone to Clemson for business, Logan had disappointed by joining the army. Still, hope sprang eternal in his father's mind. Which was aggravating because Reid was a good fit for the company.

"I won't have you talking to me like this," his father said in his pompous tone.

Logan rose. Slowly folded his napkin and placed it on the table beside his untouched pie. "Works for me," he said and strode from the room.

Fifteen minutes later he found his brother on the wooden platform overlooking a small lake on the property. The last orange streaks of light colored the dusky sky as the sun sank into the horizon. Logan dropped down into a chair beside Reid, enjoying the serenity of the view, and inhaled the sweet scent of freshly mowed grass. "Another stellar dinner."

Reid stared over the placid water. "You know he only gets riled up when you're in town."

Anger, and a flare of guilt he ignored, washed over Logan. "He doesn't like that he can't control me."

"And you think I'm a coward for not standing up to him?"

"No, I never said... Okay, I can see how it might come across that way."

"Logan, you walked away."

He had. After his senior year of high school, he'd walked away from family, a scholarship to the University of Georgia and the treachery of his father's actions.

When he opened his mouth to argue, Reid held up a hand.

"And I get why. But it was a long time ago and you've made a good life for yourself in spite of what Dad did. Can't you forgive?"

It wasn't like he hadn't considered sitting down with his folks before. But every time he contemplated bringing up the past, his stomach rebelled and he couldn't do it.

"Look, Reid, I'm sorry to pull you into the middle of this."

His brother shrugged as if he was used to it. Which brought all the old emotions crashing over Logan again.

He didn't want to talk about his father any longer. This conversation never got them anywhere, so he asked the question that had been bugging Logan since he first talked to his grandmother this afternoon. "Does Grandmother seem okay to you? She's really pushing this 'marriageable women' thing and I want to know why."

Logan couldn't help but worry about his grandmother. Her illness had been scary and he hated the idea of her getting sick again.

"I haven't heard anything, but then I moved out."

Surprise lifted Logan's eyebrows. "Really. What brought that on?"

"In a few years I'll be thirty. I've let Dad guilt me into staying in the big house for far too long."

Big was an apt description of the Masterson home.

Built in the early 1900s after his great-grandfather settled in Golden, the house and grounds held the genteel air of another time. Pierce Masterson had arrived in Golden to pan for gold. Once the vein was depleted and people moved on to places like California, Pierce stayed in Golden. With the money he had managed to save from the gold he'd mined, he bought property. Then more and more until he was buying and selling land from here to Atlanta. When he married his true love, Lila, they'd built the house the current Mastersons resided in today. It was tradition—generations living under one roof. And Logan had broken that tradition when he'd moved out as a teenager and never come back.

The Greek Revival–style two-story house was white brick, with two sitting rooms as well as a formal living room, large kitchen and five bedrooms. Southern elegance abounded in every room. A large front porch featured rocking chairs and a swing. He and Reid had had a blast growing up here, discovering treasure in the attic, running around on the ten-acre grounds and fishing in the lake, until he'd accidentally found the incriminating evidence that created a schism between him and his family. There were lots of good memories here, if he'd let that one—huge—bad moment go and try to make things like they were a long time ago.

"Where'd you move to?" Logan asked.

"I bought a place a few blocks off Main. It's small, but I've been working on it. Just finished remodeling the kitchen and I'm starting on the living room next. Maybe I'll flip it once I'm finished."

"Good for you."

Reid slanted him a sideways glance. "Don't patronize me. Just because you chose a different path doesn't mean I have to feel bad for sticking with the family."

"Ouch. Guess I deserved that."

"Maybe you want to quit starting arguments when you come to visit. It upsets Grandmother and my mother is always out of sorts afterward."

Logan gripped the arm of the chair, his knuckles turning white.

Reid pushed forward in his chair, his face contrite. "Logan… I'm sorry. I didn't mean—"

Logan rose to leave. Couldn't get out of there fast enough. "It's okay. You don't have to apologize. Trust me, I know full well she's not my mother."

CHAPTER FOUR

SERENA RAN ALONG the winding back roads of Golden. Long tree limbs stretched overhead to catch the sunlight filtering through the leaves. A recording of Keith Urban's sultry voice streamed from her earbuds. Wisps of hair had escaped her ponytail, sticking to her neck, the long length sweeping over her back in a rhythmic motion. A light sheen covered her skin as she moved quickly in the early morning dawn.

She loved this time of the day. Folks were still fast asleep while she viewed the woodland landscape as she ran her usual five miles in solitude. This was her personal time, when she could think through problems, come up with creative ideas or focus on the business before her busy day started.

She'd mentally gone over her list for the day—get proofs to printer, advertise an upcoming class, review finances again. The last item had her cringing, but it was necessary, especially if she wanted to be one step ahead of a possible investor. Mrs. M. might be her friend, but the wily woman would do her due diligence before parting with her money. Serena didn't blame her.

Breathing in the crisp air that signaled a welcome change in the weather, she couldn't ignore the nagging concern over the past few days. Her last conversation with her father weighed heavily on her. She needed to figure out how to keep her carefully constructed life intact. Hadn't she done everything she could to rectify her part in her father's…jobs? Wasn't she working to make things right even though shame still defined her after all this time? Granted, she'd been a kid when the scams took place, but deep down she'd known that what her father was doing was wrong. She'd been too scared he'd leave her, loved her only parent way too much to not go along with his schemes. Now she hoped with every fiber of her being that her steps to make amends would count for something in the end.

She'd convinced herself she needed investors to accomplish that.

She rounded a bend in the damp, leaf-strewn road and crested the top of a steep hill. She stopped and jogged in place, taking in the scene below her, heaving steady breaths as she regulated her heart rate.

Golden. The leaves showed a slight change in color, signaling the upcoming showcase of autumn foliage that would bring tourists to the area in droves. How she loved this sleepy town. From the lively characters who lived here to the friendships she'd made in a short time. Sure, Carrie, her best friend from college, still surfaced in her life, but beyond that, she'd never had anyone to confide in.

Well, maybe *confide* was too intimate a word. Carrie knew enough, but she didn't know everything. At least Serena had Heidi and Grace to pal around with now. They'd gotten her excited about Oktoberfest when in the past she'd have shied away from working too closely with others. But this was Golden. People here were quick to pull you into their universe once they accepted you. Even though she'd been standoffish at first, a natural position she'd honed over time, they'd broken down barriers and she could truly say she was one of them.

Unless the truth exposes you.

Stomach swirling now, she shook off the foreboding and picked up her pace. Controlling her downhill run, she hugged the side of the road as she drew closer to town. She'd taken this same route for over a year now, knew the pitfalls of the terrain. As she made it to the bottom of the hill, a pickup truck suddenly zoomed behind her. With her earbuds in place, she didn't hear the loud engine until the truck was upon her. Jumping out of the way, she misjudged her stride and turned her ankle. She lurched to a halt, then tumbled into the soft grass.

"Watch where you're going," she yelled, but the truck careened around another corner and disappeared from view. Once the object of her anger vanished, her ankle began throbbing with a vengeance.

Yanking the buds from her ears, she muttered "Shoot" under her breath. After she brushed the grass and dirt from her black capri running tights, she viewed her ankle with concern. With her palms, she pushed herself upward to gingerly test if she could put weight on her right leg. She cringed as pain shot along her foot and up her calf. So much for continuing her run back to the apartment.

Resigned to hobbling, she reached the north end of Main Street, her momentum increasing as she limped down the street's gradual incline. Few people and fewer cars were out and about at this hour, as only early risers were stopping at Sit a Spell for a morning shot of caffeine. Even from here the rich aromatic coffee scented the air.

She tried not to put much weight on her swelling ankle, but barely succeeded. By the time she reached Blue Ridge Cottage, she'd pulled out her key, ready to make her way through the narrow alley and up the wooden steps leading to her residence. She almost tumbled when a voice broke the morning silence.

"Are you okay?"

Looking out, she held back a groan. Logan crossed the street, concern etched on his handsome face, a steaming coffee cup in hand. This morning he wore a gray-and-white-striped dress shirt, charcoal slacks and black loafers.

"Depends on your definition of *okay*," she answered as she leaned against the building.

His eyebrows formed a V when he frowned. "Really, what happened?"

"Truck. Me jumping out of the way." She pointed down. "Turned ankle."

He knelt down before her, his hand lightly grazing her skin as he examined the injured joint. An unwanted but undeniable shiver rushed over her. Good grief, he was only being a concerned citizen.

"I'm fine," she told him, trying to shift away as his warm fingers palpated the bone.

"You should probably have it checked out," he said, rising when he got the hint she didn't want him in her personal space.

"It's not bad. I've injured it before, so I can tell. A little bit of ice, ibuprofen and keeping my foot up should do the trick."

He didn't look convinced. "You're sure?"

"Positive." She'd been taking care of herself for a very long time. This minor setback was no different. "What're you doing here so early?"

"Grandmother needed a report from me. Thought I'd beat the city traffic and drive up here early."

Was that his only reason? His unwavering attention had her guard up big-time, which was a shame. If she was going to blow her life up over a guy, Logan would make it really easy.

"Why don't I help you get home."

She waved him off. "It's right here."

He looked up. "So, you're living over the store?"

"Yes. The apartment was empty and your grandmother was kind enough to let me move in."

"That's Grandmother. Always looking

out for others." His gaze caught hers, full of meaning. "That's why I look out for her."

Warning received. "Then we can both agree, your grandmother is special."

His intense expression softened and a smile played around his mouth. It lit up his entire face and almost put her at ease. Almost. It was his body language that had Serena deciding to call this conversation quits.

"So, I'm going to go upstairs to get ready for work." She inched from her position. "Thanks for checking on me."

One dark eyebrow rose. "No way I'm going to leave you alone. I'll follow to make sure you're okay."

Her inner defenses reared. "Really, go do your thing."

He stood his ground.

"Stubborn man," she muttered under her breath as she resumed her wobbly journey to her apartment.

"Did you say something?"

"How thoughtful of you," she said over her shoulder.

Her reply earned her a burst of laughter.

She straightened her shoulders and gripped the railing. After only two steps, Logan swooped in beside her, his strong arm wrapped around her waist. She shot him a cool stare despite the riot going on in her stomach. He smelled way too good and was way too close for her peace of mind.

"What do you think you're doing?"

"I can't watch you struggle. It's too painful."

Her voice rose as she said, "I'm the one who twisted my ankle."

"And I'm the person who is going to make sure you don't fall down the stairs."

She held back an eye roll. "I'm capable."

"No one said you weren't." His voice caressed her skin as his breath wafted over her cheek.

Torture. Beautiful torture. Why did she respond to this man the way she did?

He'd made her nervous enough when they'd sat side by side at the meeting at Smitty's. But this? Was he intentionally encroaching on her space? Sure felt like it.

Instead of arguing, she picked up the pace to reach the landing so he'd leave her alone. She had to remember this was the man whose sweet charming grandmother had decided to pair them together. Yes, he was handsome and seemed to be a gentleman, but that was no reason to let down her defenses. After this episode, she'd keep her distance. Yes, that would do the trick. Distance.

They finally reached the door. Logan removed his arm and watched her fumble with the key. Could she look any clumsier?

Once she had the door open, she half turned. "Thanks again."

"My pleasure." He indicated the apartment with the hand holding the coffee cup. "If you need any help, I'll be here all day."

"I think you did more than enough. I'll, ah, see you around?"

"Count on it."

Then he was moving down the steps and around the side of the building.

"Why?" she quizzed the universe as she went inside, closing the door behind her. Leaning against the solid barrier, she let out a breath. Could she take much more of Logan hanging around Golden?

After taking a few steps, she tossed the key on the kitchen table. The apartment was a good size for her and, best of all, it was her own. It had taken six months to furnish and decorate to her liking, but as she viewed the homey space now, she realized it was worth it.

The kitchen was along the back wall. The dark wood counters, white cabinets and island had been refurbished before she moved in, creating a rustic charm she loved. The wood floors had been sanded and refinished and suited the open-concept style. Her cozy navy couch commanded the living area, and was scattered with pillows in various patterns and bright colors. An oversize armchair with a comfy blanket draped over the back matched the other details. Two wide windows framed by sheer panels overlooked Main Street. There were two bedrooms separated by a bathroom, which she now hobbled to. Glancing at a big clock on the wall, she hustled as fast as her weak ankle would allow. She needed to be downstairs to open the store in an hour.

Even after a brisk shower, Serena's ankle continued to throb. She swallowed a pain reliever, slipped into flats, discovered her ankle was too swollen and switched to slippers that matched her pale blue sleeveless A-line dress. Not that slippers made a great fashion statement, but at least she'd be comfortable. She finished with her makeup and, after taking one last look in the mirror, deemed herself ready to take on the day.

Once downstairs, she flipped on the lights, scooped coffee into a filter and unlocked the front door to Blue Ridge Cottage. Open for business.

This morning she would be working by

herself, which was fine. Friday mornings were usually busy when the tourist traffic picked up, but she'd be able to take care of housekeeping logistics and still wait on customers. By late morning she'd contacted the printer, sent off her designs and taken a special order. This was why she loved her store, why it was all hers and, if everything went according to plan, she'd be doing this for a long time to come.

Just before lunch the door opened. Mrs. Masterson strolled in, dressed in her signature two-piece suit, today in a rose shade. Not one hair was out of place and her lovely smile graced the room.

"Good," Mrs. Masterson said, getting right to the point. "I was hoping to speak to you alone."

"Should I be worried?"

"On the contrary. I've been going over your proposal and would like to invite you to dinner tonight. I have some questions and have asked my financial adviser to sit in. How does that work for you?"

Serena certainly wasn't going to refuse. If Mrs. M. was interested, she'd go to the moon and back. "It would be my honor to come to dinner."

"Excellent. I know you close at six, so I've

asked Cook to have dinner ready by half past. That should give you time to drive to the house."

She'd heard all about the large house and the beautiful grounds surrounding the mansion. Whenever Heidi went out there to visit Alveda, the Masterson's cook, she gushed over the stately architecture and the history of the place. If it had been for any other reason than securing money, Serena would probably decline. It was one thing to visit with Mrs. M. when she stopped by the store, another to step foot on her family's property. Serena's embarrassment about her shameful past was never far from her mind.

Nerves started to quake in her stomach, but Serena pasted a confident smile on her face. "I'll head over as soon as I lock up."

Mrs. M. patted her hand. "And don't let my son's reputation scare you. I'll keep him in check."

Her son's reputation? Serena swallowed hard. She hadn't been scared until now. Nervous, yes, but not scared.

"See you this evening," Mrs. M. said in a singsong voice as she swung open the door and then left.

A few minutes later, Heidi walked in.

"Thanks for letting me come in late this morning. I had a huge job to finish."

"Sure. Anytime," Serena answered, her mind on the upcoming meeting. She ran numbers through her head. Considered bringing samples of her work to show she had a handle on future products. Maybe a chart or two…?

"Earth to Serena."

She blinked at her employee. "Sorry. I have good news."

Heidi tilted her head.

"Mrs. M. is interested in talking about the proposal."

"That's huge."

"I agree. It was a long shot asking her, but now it's paid off."

"When is the meeting?"

"Tonight. At Masterson House."

Heidi's smile slipped.

Serena's nerves went haywire again. "What?"

"Nothing. She doesn't ask just anyone to the house."

"Oh, no. This is too much pressure."

"Calm down."

Serena moved from behind the sales counter and Heidi noticed her limp.

"What happened?"

"Near miss with a truck. No biggie. Now tell me about the Mastersons."

"I'm sorry. I didn't mean to freak you out. They're kind of…set in their ways. Give them the answers they want to hear and you'll be fine."

Serena frowned. "What if my answers aren't what they want to hear?"

"You're a saleswoman. Sell it, sister, and you'll get that investment."

The door opened and a group of women walked in. Heidi went over to assist them, leaving Serena to wonder what she'd gotten herself into.

LOGAN STEPPED INTO the foyer of the grand house, brushing his shoes on the mat before setting foot on the highly finished wood floors. Spending time in Golden meant family dinners, which he'd been able to avoid for quite a few years now. He hoped to learn more about Serena and soon, so this didn't become a habit.

He poked his head into the formal living room to spy his grandmother seated on the sofa, reading from a navy folder. Serena's proposal.

"Still going over the numbers?"

She glanced up, sending a smile his way. "Weighing my options." She closed the folder and patted the cushion next to her. "I know we met for breakfast to go over your take on Serena's business, but I feel like this is a very important decision." She shook her head. "Maybe I'm making too big a deal of all this."

Logan bent down to brush a kiss on his grandmother's cheek then settled beside her. "Nothing wrong with rereading it until you feel it's right. What does your gut say?"

"That Serena needs me. That she'd do well with the new funds she'd have."

"There you go. You're not wrong very often."

"Perhaps." She stared out the wide picture window, taking in the full view of the picturesque grounds. The grass was a deep green; the trees were full of foliage that showed just a hint of the fall colors to come. It was cooler today. The windows were open and a refreshing breeze flowed through the house.

Blinking, she turned back to him. "And what have you been up to today?"

"Stopped by Reid's house."

Her brow wrinkled. "I do worry about him."

"He's a big boy, Grandmother. Moving out on his own was a good thing. It'll give him the time and space he needs to sort out his future."

"Your father isn't happy."

"Because he isn't getting his way."

When his grandmother opened her mouth, probably to defend her son, Logan stopped her. "He and I might never see eye to eye, but he should realize that allowing Reid some distance will be good for everyone in the long run."

"I suppose." She sighed. "I never thought my grandsons would end up being so difficult."

Logan placed a hand on his chest. "Why, Grandmother, I'm hurt."

She batted his arm. "Hardly. You have so much armor protecting you, I doubt anything penetrates."

Maybe, but it worked in his favor. Nothing and no one could dare hurt him if he kept his heart behind sturdy iron bars.

"I also had a meeting with a client."

"Here in Golden?"

"Yes."

"Word of your PI agency must be spreading."

"I can only hope." He leaned back to rest an arm along the back of the sofa. "Since you'd asked me to dinner, I worked at Smitty's after my appointment instead of going to Atlanta and back."

"Isn't it noisy in that place?"

"I block it out."

"That is one thing about you—you are focused."

Footsteps approached from the hall. Logan glanced over to see his father enter the room. As always happened, he stiffened, but took soothing breaths to keep the man from breaking his composure.

"Logan. Good to see you."

"Dad."

His father glanced around. "Where's Reid?"

Logan exchanged a glance with his grandmother. "Since this is a business dinner," she explained, "I thought he could miss tonight."

His father looked at his watch. "It's six fifteen."

Grandmother rose and walked over to pat her son's arm. "Patience," she said just as the doorbell rang. She set off to answer it.

Alone with his father, Logan stood. His father shoved his hands in his pants pockets. The uneasiness in the room swelled. Female voices carried from the foyer, and when his grandmother entered the room, the sight of Serena by her side caught him off guard. Serena was the business dinner?

"Arthur, this is Serena Stanhope. Serena, my son, Arthur."

Serena held out her hand. "Pleased to meet you."

His grandmother's smile was cagey. "Logan, you've met Serena."

He nodded in her direction, not missing the way her eyes widened with surprise. Apparently, his grandmother had neglected to inform her who would be at this meeting.

"Alveda is ready to serve dinner, so if you all don't mind, let's head to the dining room."

Serena sent Logan another anxious glance, but his father engaged her in conversation as he led her to the other room. He noticed the slight limp, which probably explained the flat shoes and told him how she was doing after the morning's mishap.

"Coming?" his grandmother asked, clearly amused.

Impressed by her duplicitous skills, he joined her. "Grandmother, you never fail to surprise."

"It's my prerogative as matriarch to keep my family on their toes. Besides, I've already told you you're taking far too long to find a wife."

He expelled a long-suffering sigh. "I don't suppose there's anything I can say to get you off the marriage bandwagon?"

"How long have you known me?"

He chuckled in response.

Logan took a seat across the table from Serena. She nervously folded her fingers and rested her hands by the place setting. She was lovely, the contrast of the pale blue shade of her dress making her blueberry-colored eyes more striking, which further stoked his interest. That didn't mean she was the woman for him, despite his grandmother's hopes.

He met her gaze and asked, "How's the ankle?"

"Much better, thank you."

His father raised an eyebrow but Logan didn't add any details.

The kitchen door flew open, and his mother, wearing a peach-colored dress, her cheeks red and hair slightly mussed, hurried to take her place at the table.

"I'm so sorry. Time got away from me."

Logan slanted a glance in his father's direction to catch a look of disapproval.

As she shook out her cloth napkin to place on her lap, she said, "I hope I didn't keep you waiting. When Gayle Ann informed me that the dinner hour had been changed, I lost track of time." She looked across the table at her husband. "Guild business."

Gayle Ann waved a hand. "Don't worry.

Bonnie, I'd like you to meet Serena Stanhope."

His mother's eyes sparkled. "The owner of Blue Ridge Cottage?"

"Yes."

"I love that little store. You have such treasures."

"Thank you."

Bonnie went on to talk about the meeting, but Logan kept his attention on Serena. Her shoulders were stiff, her smile forced. Clearly she was uncomfortable in this setting. It made him wonder if she was nervous because she was sitting in the Masterson dining room or if it was more.

"So tell me, Serena. How do you like living in Golden?" his father asked after the cook had served the chicken and vegetables and they'd all dug in.

"I love it here. Everyone is so gracious and the tourists are wonderful."

"Blue Ridge Cottage is your first store?"

"Yes."

"She started her business online," Grandmother informed them.

"What made you decide to open a store?" his father continued.

"The company is growing. And I love to meet my customers in person."

"Where did the name come from?" his mother asked.

Serena put down her fork and patted her lips with her napkin. "A special cottage."

"Aunt Mary's?" Grandmother asked, and Serena nodded. "Her aunt is the inspiration behind the business," she added, as if possessing insider knowledge.

"In what way?" Logan asked.

"She encouraged my art," Serena said before bringing a forkful of vegetables to her mouth.

Logan drank from his water glass. Eyed Serena over the rim. What was with all the abbreviated answers? Most of the business owners he knew loved to talk about their stores, but Serena grew increasingly uneasy. Not the best way to interest an investor.

"Is this cottage local?" his father asked.

"Outside of town. It's a small place, set back in the woods."

"Serena is quite the artist," Grandmother told them. "She draws all the sketches for her products, right, dear?"

"Yes. This area is an artist's dream."

"I so wish I'd taken art lessons," Logan's mother said. She glanced at him and smiled. "Didn't have much time while raising two active boys."

Logan nodded her way. His mother wasn't one to get nostalgic. Maybe because Reid was so noticeably missing?

"And your family?" his mother asked Serena.

"No one local." She reached for her glass. "This meal is absolutely delicious. Makes me feel guilty that I don't have more time to cook."

When the conversation moved on to cooking shows, Logan didn't miss the relief that crossed Serena's face at the change of topic. There was definitely more to the woman than met the eye.

After Alveda had removed the plates, his grandmother pushed back her chair. "Why don't we have dessert in the living room? Serena? Logan?"

Everyone rose. He followed the ladies, again checking Serena's gait to make sure she was okay. She took the first chair she came to, stretching her foot out before her with a grimace, which told him it must still ache.

Grandmother picked up the Blue Ridge Cottage folder. "I've reviewed your proposal. Spoken to my advisers."

Serena gripped the arms of the chair.

"I'm inclined to invest, but I still have a

few questions. There are areas I'd like cleared up, for my peace of mind."

Serena glanced from his grandmother to him. Swallowed. "And those would be?"

Grandmother flipped a few pages. "While all your expenses are clearly documented, there is one thing missing."

Concern crossed Serena's face. "Missing? I'm sure I included everything you need to make a decision."

"The finances are as I expected."

Serena bit her lower lip. "Then what is unclear?"

"The proposal is all very cut-and-dried. Why expansion? Why now? What's missing is your passion."

Before Serena could say a word, his father strolled into the room. He stood along the back wall to listen.

"I didn't realize I needed to explain my passion for Blue Ridge Cottage."

Grandmother lowered the folder to her lap. "Serena, I have invested in many different businesses. Anyone with a good accounting program can work the numbers." She leaned forward. "When I visit you at the store, you're so animated when it comes to your products." She held up the folder. "I don't get that feeling when I read this."

A red flush spread across Serena's cheeks. "Since this is my first foray into looking for investors, I didn't think…" Serena swallowed. "I'm afraid I have to take full responsibility for not making my passion more clear."

Logan had to admit, he was impressed with the way she handled herself. Grandmother could be a tough critic.

"It would be in everyone's best interest if you reworked the proposal. Show me what really matters to you and your company." His grandmother's face was stern, her gaze never leaving Serena's. He knew that look, the one that said, "I know you have it in you to do better." The look that had pushed him to succeed more times than he could count. "You don't want to give this proposal to other would-be investors knowing they will have the same impression."

Serena squirmed in her seat. Alveda chose that moment to enter, carrying a tray of dessert plates.

Logan had dealt with his family his entire life. These types of conversations were commonplace and he could handle the grilling. He might be investigating her, but the panic on her face proved she was in over her head. For reasons he didn't want to examine, he found himself sticking up for her. "I think we can give Serena the benefit of the doubt."

"Indeed." Grandmother ratcheted down the tension by smiling. She took a bite of cake and then said, "Why don't you fix this and a few other pertinent details I've flagged and resubmit it to me."

"I will." Serena glanced at everyone in the room. Her plate rested on her lap, the food untouched. "I appreciate you giving me a second chance."

They all rose, setting the dessert plates on the coffee table. Grandmother carried the folder to Serena. "My pleasure, dear."

Logan observed his father silently leaving the room. Then his grandmother snagged his attention. "Logan, would you mind walking Serena to her car?"

"Of course, Grandmother."

"And I'll be by the store next week. That beginner's drawing class you advertised has caught my fancy."

"Thanks again, Mrs. M."

His grandmother gently touched Serena's cheek. "Always, my dear."

Clutching the file to her chest, Serena began an unsteady path to the front door. He opened it for her, following her onto the wide veranda. The temperature had dropped, the mid-September air just a touch cooler as they ventured outside. The wind picked up, carrying a discernible hint of autumn. Crickets hummed their nightly serenade as darkness fell quickly around them.

"I'm so embarrassed," Serena said in a voice so low he barely heard her. "I thought I'd done a complete job."

He had to admit, he had reservations about her sketchy past, but the misery on her face tugged at his heart. It looked like she truly regretted her mistake. She'd come across as a very capable businesswoman, so her error had to sting.

"Hey, no one is perfect. At least Grandmother didn't outright dismiss your proposal."

"I guess." She looked up at him. "Thanks. You didn't have to defend me."

"You were already having a rough day. Bruised ankle and all."

"More like bruised ego." She shook her head, her hair brushing her shoulders.

"It's your business. It's personal and, let's face it, most owners want to control all aspects."

She averted her eyes.

"Chalk this up to a rookie mistake. Thankfully it was my grandmother who read it first. You can make adjustments and go from there."

"I don't know..."

He gently took her by the shoulders to face him. "My grandmother likes you. She's in your corner, otherwise she would have outright dismissed your proposal instead of pointing out the problems."

"I suppose."

"Get Heidi to help you this time."

She nodded. Moved away. "I should be going."

He took her elbow to help her down the wide steps. Their footsteps, Serena's unsteady, crunched over the tiny pebbles of the circular driveway. Once at her vehicle, he opened the door for her.

"Here's an idea," he said after she tossed the folder onto the passenger seat. "Be honest about your love for the store and you won't have a thing to worry about."

She met his gaze. His chest tightened at the sadness reflected in the blue depths of her eyes. The rising moon highlighted her creamy skin, her delicate cheekbones. Her gracefully curved lips. If she wasn't a case he was working on, he'd be seriously tempted to ask her out.

"Good night," she said, slipping behind the wheel.

As she drove away, he was conscious of the prickly awareness he'd tried to dismiss ever since he'd met her. There was something about her he couldn't ignore. An energy that drew him to her despite his good intentions to keep it purely professional between them. His instincts, however, told him she was going to be nothing but trouble.

CHAPTER FIVE

"You look like someone stole your dog," Heidi remarked. It was Monday and Heidi had turned up to find Serena behind the counter on a tall stool, hands cupping her face as she stared at her laptop. Colored pencils were scattered around, but the open sketch pad in front of her was nearly empty. Moments before she'd been doodling until her thoughts became too overwhelming to create anything worthwhile.

Quickly tapping the computer pad to remove the image on the screen, she said, "I messed up."

Heidi's eyebrows rose. "I doubt that."

Serena pushed back from the countertop. Today she'd put on a cheery yellow dress, but it did nothing to lift her spirits. Her ankle still ached, keeping her from the morning run that always calmed her nerves. "Really. I should have had you look at the finished proposal. I've never put one together before and Mrs. M. picked up on it. Said my passion was missing."

"In a business proposal?" Heidi held out a hand. "Let me see."

She hesitated, but then reached under the counter and handed the papers over to Heidi. After reading the proposal, Heidi glanced at her. "It is rather dry, and that's coming from an accountant. Although…"

"What?"

"You didn't use the suspense category like I told you to."

"I thought it sounded fake, so I left it out."

"No, it's real."

"It's okay to record money in that account if I needed it for emergencies?"

"Sure. It's better if you're more specific, but it still works."

Heidi flipped through the pages again. "Would you designate the category for business or personal reasons?" She pointed to a different numbered account.

"If it's for personal reasons, place it here."

Serena nodded, glad Heidi hadn't waited for a reply. She wasn't entirely sure how to answer that question.

So there were other ways of documenting money that went directly to her, especially since she was the owner of the company, but the dollar amounts were above normal operating expenses. How did she explain it? *Oh, did I forget to mention that when I was a teenager I helped my father swindle decent hardworking families out of their money, so now I'm anonymously paying them back?* Yeah, that would go over well.

Keeping her mouth shut, she picked up a dark blue pencil and shaded in a section of the waterfall she'd been sketching. Honestly, she wished she was there right now, in the depths of the forest, away from what might ruin her life if the truth was revealed.

What her father had done was horrible, but at the time, Serena was still grieving her mother and she'd gone along with him. Initially, he told her that she was simply helping him with his job. Every daughter would want to help out her dad.

She was just thankful to see her father reengage in life after suffering through the depression that had paralyzed him after her mother died. But as she got older, she realized the company he represented didn't exist. That he had set up a scam and every dime went straight into the Stanhope family coffers.

At first she'd wondered why they changed their last name so often. As she got older, she kept detailed records in a notebook of the money they received and where it had come from, not asking the whys and wherefores. In retrospect, she should have been curious, asked more questions, but she'd been young and so happy to have her father back to his old self, none of it sank in right away. By the time she figured out the reality, she was his accomplice.

Heidi flipped through the proposal. "From a quick glance, it looks like everything is in order. Want me to go over this with a fine-tooth comb before you resubmit?"

"Would you mind?"

"It's what I do."

While Heidi went to the small office, Serena dropped the pencil and tapped the laptop again. Senior pictures from Golden High School filled the screen. After some of the comments Logan had made at the Oktoberfest meeting, she'd searched online to find the old yearbook. He'd been on multiple sports teams, captain of the baseball team senior year, involved in student government, crowned prom king. He was smart. Involved. Going places. The exact kind of guy who would never understand her shadowy past.

She shook her head and let out a glum sigh.

Her father's fake business had lasted about five years, until Serena entered high school. Shortly after, her father had an angina attack, and the money they'd made went to medical bills. Even though the condition was more of a scare, it was serious enough for him to take stock of his life. They settled down, and he got a job selling insurance and, much to her surprise, held on to it.

Eventually, she went to college, working her way through school by securing grants and loans while holding down multiple jobs. By then her dad had moved to Florida and they never spoke of that period of their life again.

But she never forgot. Even while her father battled his heart issues, she'd promised herself she would find a way to repay the people they'd swindled. She pledged to do it, but never told her father, worried about how her decision might affect his health. Then her father turned over a new leaf and she was just grateful he'd walked away from his schemes.

A few years later, when she was going through their storage unit, she came across the book she'd used to keep track of the names of all their marks and how much these people had sent to the fake companies. She'd sunk to the concrete floor, her heart racing and tears slipping from her eyes. Right there, she'd renewed her promise to pay them back. She was still working at it today, putting away a certain amount each month to go toward the refund program. So far she'd anonymously reimbursed ten people out of the twenty-five they'd scammed. Paying them back might increase the odds of looking guilty if law enforcement ever found out, but she couldn't live with herself unless she tried.

Tonight she planned to check another person off her list. She'd started with the ones they owed the most money to and had worked her way down. So far she hadn't been caught, but she had no idea how long her luck would hold out.

"Here you go," Heidi said as she walked back into the store proper holding out the papers with sticky notes on them. "Log in to the program and fix the places I highlighted. Add your personal story and I think Mrs. M. will be happy."

Serena tapped the computer to get rid of the image. "Thanks. I'm sorry I didn't have you take a look first."

"I get it, but next time know that I'm on your team. I would never do anything behind your back and would point out any issues."

"I know." Serena quickly looked over the notes. "That's it? Just the one area of concern?"

Heidi shifted her weight.

"What?"

"Are you investing money elsewhere?"

Oh, no. "Why would you ask?"

"There are large amounts that come out of your savings every once in a while."

"That goes to family members who need money." They weren't *her* family, but Heidi didn't need to know that.

"Huh. You never talk about family."

Knowing the only surefire way to get Heidi off her trail, Serena said, "I could say the same about you."

With a *humph*, Heidi spun on her heel and returned to the office. Serena held back a smile. Heidi was nearly as tight-lipped about her family as Serena.

"It's none of my business," Heidi called over her shoulder as she walked back to the office.

Serena's head jerked up. She hurried after Heidi. "What is none of your business?"

Heidi's fingers flew over the calculator. "What you do with your money."

"It's nothing nefarious," Serena assured her friend. Not now, anyway.

Heidi twisted around in the office chair. "And I get how important the store is to you. When something belongs to you, it's hard to let others in."

"Yes. That very idea was pointed out to me the other night." How had she allowed the conversation to move into this area? With a hard shake of her head, she returned to the sales counter.

Heidi followed and asked, "By Mrs. M.?"

Serena gathered up her pencils and closed the sketch pad. Her advanced calligraphy class would start soon. "No, um, Logan." As she moved, she tripped over the stool leg and bumped the laptop. The dark screen came to life, showing the last image she'd called up, Logan's senior picture. She let out a quick squeak but her friend had already seen the screen.

Heidi sent her a knowing grin. "Oh, yeah. And when did this conversation take place?"

"After dinner at the Mastersons' house."

"Interesting tidbit you left out."

She shrugged, even though her heartbeat was racing. "It's no big deal."

"Really. Then why do you get all flustered when his name comes up?"

"I don't know. He...confuses me."

"In a good way or a bad way?"

"Both?"

Heidi laughed. "Explains why you're looking him up. He was definitely in the 'it' crowd in high school."

"What can you tell me about him?"

"I haven't seen him much since he left town a long time ago. I used to be close to the Mastersons, but honestly, we lost touch through the years.

"Listen, I'm going to run by the printer then grab some coffee," Heidi said. "Need anything while I'm out?"

"No."

"See you in an hour." Heidi strolled to the door, then stopped and turned, amusement sparkling in her merry eyes. "Speak of the devil."

Serena glanced out the large store window to see Logan and his brother walking on the other side of Main Street. Logan was dressed in another button-down shirt and jeans. Headed to Smitty's? And why should it matter?

When she didn't respond, Heidi laughed and headed out into the sunny Golden afternoon. Once she was gone, Serena went to peer out the window to catch another glimpse of Logan.

What was it about him that had her at wit's

end? Sure, he was handsome. He loved his grandmother, which spoke volumes about his character. Gave her the chills when he caught her gaze or leaned a little too close. Good grief, could she be experiencing real feelings for the man? Were Mrs. M.'s matchmaking efforts working?

That wouldn't do. Not now. Not with any man until she repaid her debt. Besides, Logan suspected her of something. That was the real reason a relationship with him would be risky. She was right to be wary. So why did that disappoint her so much?

Brushing aside her regret, she made the changes to the proposal and printed out a clean copy to drop off to Mrs. M. She was crossing the sales floor to get the calligraphy supplies when the front door opened and she heard a familiar voice… "Surprise!"

She turned and her jaw dropped. Her best friend from college stood just inside the door, two large rolling suitcases at her side.

"Carrie? What are you doing here?"

"Hoping you don't mind putting me up while I take an impromptu vacation."

Warning bells clanged in her head. "That doesn't sound like you. You love your job."

Her smile dimmed the tiniest bit. "Things change."

Noticing her friend's unease, Serena pulled her into a hug. After they squeezed each other tight, Serena stepped back. "I'm sensing there's a story here."

Carrie's gaze slid away.

"Why don't you take your things upstairs and we'll catch up a little later."

"You don't mind?" Carrie asked in an uncharacteristically subdued tone.

"Are you kidding? I've missed my partner in crime."

The old nickname brought a small smile to Carrie's lips.

"Thanks."

"What are friends for?"

"Remember that," Carrie said, then quickly gripped the luggage handles and escaped to the apartment.

"So how did dinner go the other night?"

Smitty's at lunchtime was loud and busy, and the day's special feature of meat loaf smelled great. Logan settled into the hard pub chair before answering Reid's question. His brother's hair was messy and he wore a T-shirt and jeans, a far cry from the usual suit and tie he sported at the office. If anything, Logan was determined to find out what was going on with his less-than-communicative brother.

"Grandmother is worried about you."

"You covered for me, right?"

"I told her that everyone should give you space." Logan pinned his brother with a curious gaze. "That's what you want, isn't it?"

A muscle jumped in Reid's jaw. "For now."

Tired of sidestepping, Logan asked, "Are you going to tell me what's up?"

Before Reid could reply, the pub owner ambled over. Shot Logan a wry glance. "This is the most I've seen you in town in years."

"What can I say, Jamey? I'm in demand."

Reid laughed. "He thinks he is."

"Hey, it's the truth. I've got a lot of irons in the fire."

Reid raised an eyebrow. Jamey chuckled.

"I'm not feeling the respect here, guys."

Jamey slapped him on the shoulder. "As long as you use Smitty's as your base of operations while you're in Golden, I'll respect you every day of the week."

Logan glanced up at the gregarious pub owner. "And if I take my business elsewhere?"

"All bets are off."

"Figures." Logan shook his head, but couldn't deny how much fun he'd had hanging out with old friends since the case had brought him back to Golden. "I'll have today's special."

"Me, too," Reid said, and the owner set off to the kitchen.

The brothers sat in silence for a long, drawn-out moment before Logan spoke. "So what's going on with you?"

Reid ran a hand through his thick hair. "I'm thinking of leaving Masterson Enterprises."

Shock whipped through Logan. "No way."

A busy server delivered two glasses of iced tea before attending to another table. Reid grabbed the glass and took a long drink. Logan knew his brother well enough to recognize the procrastination tactic.

"What's really going on, Reid?"

Depositing his glass back to the scarred tabletop, Reid folded his arms and leaned forward. "Before I say anything, please know this has nothing to do with your decisions."

This couldn't be good.

"You took off right out of high school, Logan. I get why. The point is, I did the good-son thing. I went to college. Aced school. Came home to be part of the family business. And all I ever hear from Dad is how he wants you on board."

Logan understood why Reid was upset. He

hated that his father overlooked the son who actually wanted to be involved in Masterson Enterprises.

Reid met his gaze, eyes weary with emotional fatigue. "Bottom line? I'm not really sure what I want to do. That's why I bought the house off Main. If I step down from ME, at least I have a place to stay while I figure out my next steps."

"You always did your best thinking when you were working on a project," Logan remarked. "You think Dad is going to fight your decision?"

Reid shrugged, but Logan could feel the weight of his gesture.

"I'm sure he will, but he can't make me do anything. I'm not a kid any longer. Time he saw me as a man."

Logan heard the unspoken "like you." Again, he hated that his brother had to come to this crossroads. As Logan had discovered, the initial pain of a life-changing event was enough to bring you to your knees, but ultimately made you stronger. Or more stubborn in his case? His own epiphany might have come earlier in life, but he was still proud of his younger brother for taking a stand now.

Logan lifted his glass to swallow the cool

iced tea, then asked, "You're going to tell Grandmother?"

"Yeah. To be honest, it wasn't until I bought the house that things fell into place. I needed time to wrap my head around my decision. I can tell Gran now."

Logan nodded. His brother was in for a battle. "Look, you know I have your back, right?"

Reid's gaze, clear now, met his straight-on. "Always."

"Then let me help you out."

"In what way?"

An idea had been forming in Logan's mind ever since the night he and his brother had talked out by the lake. He'd learned a long time ago to go with his hunches. He only hoped his brother was open to his suggestion.

Jamey returned, setting two heaping plates of meat and potatoes before them. The savory aroma had Logan's stomach growling. Once the plate was half-empty, he returned to their conversation.

"Here's my proposal. Let me move in with you for a while."

Reid lowered his fork. "Move in with me?"

"Yeah, unless you're afraid I might ruin your romantic mojo."

Coughing, Reid made a fist and thumped on his chest. "No worries there."

"Good. If I'm close by we can strategize."

"Strategize what? I'm not entirely sure what I want to do with my future."

"Sure you are. You just haven't worked it out in your head yet." Logan scooped another forkful of meat loaf, the tangy seasoning reminding him that his culinary skills in the kitchen were sorely lacking.

"You'd give up living in Atlanta? Away from Dad?"

"For a while. The PI office is running smoothly, so my people can handle things until I get back. I'm working on a case that has me coming up to Golden pretty frequently, anyway. If I'm here, I can focus without the distraction of driving back and forth. Plus, you have the honor of using me as your sounding board."

Reid let out a sharp laugh.

"Okay, a brotherly shoulder to lean on?"

Reid pushed away his plate. "I don't want you to blow into my life, pressing me to make decisions. You'll be another version of Dad."

Logan placed a hand over his heart and reared back. "You wound me."

"I'm not kidding, Logan." His brother's

tone was infused with steel. "I can figure out my life on my own."

Logan viewed the conviction on his brother's face. Felt it to his toes. "I hear you. I'm not here to meddle. I only want the best for you."

"And I need to figure that out, just like you did."

"Fair enough." As much as Logan wanted to help his brother, make his decision easier, he knew Reid had to go about this his own way, on his own timetable.

The server removed their plates. "Honestly," Logan said when he'd left, "you'll be doing me a favor by letting me stay with you. I need to get to the bottom of this case."

"And this case has to do with Serena Stanhope?"

Logan shot him an irritated glance. "You're way too observant for your own good."

"Dude, it's not rocket science. Anytime you two are in the same room, there's this tension that hovers between you. And I'm not sure it's just to do with business."

Was there? Despite listening to his gut, he couldn't ignore the attraction. Was that part of the reason he was hot on this case?

"I'll admit I'm interested."

Reid snorted.

"But it's still a job. And if you don't mind,

I'd appreciate you keeping your opinions to yourself. At least until I close the case to the satisfaction of my client."

"You got it. And yes, you can stay with me for a while." Reid sat back in the chair and grinned. "My big brother, bitten by the bug."

"I haven't been bitten."

Reid observed Logan in a way that made him antsy. "It had to happen sometime."

"What had to happen?"

"Falling in love."

His chest tightened at his brother's words. "I think you've overstated. I barely know her."

"But you're making strides to remedy that?"

He was, in order to close the books on Deke's case. At least that was what he told himself.

"I'll admit she is a very fetching subject, but that's as far as I'll go."

"Right," Reid scoffed before finishing his drink.

They paid for lunch and headed outside. The strong afternoon sun warmed Logan's shoulders, but he welcomed the slight crispness in the air, which meant fall was officially on the way.

They'd started walking back to Reid's place when both their phones pinged. Logan pulled his from his pocket and read the caller ID. "Grandmother."

Frowning, Reid looked up from his phone. "Me, too."

They both tapped the text icon and looked at each other with identical expressions.

"The tea party," Reid groaned.

"Saturday." Logan replaced his phone in his pocket. "She wasn't kidding about getting us to attend."

"And we gave her our word."

They took a few steps.

"You know what this means," Reid said.

"That she's got an unsuspecting female picked out for each of us." Logan placed a hand over his stomach. "Are you feeling what I'm feeling? Like our lunch was bad and we'll be laid up for a few days?"

Reid chuckled. "That won't work. Gran will drive you to the hospital to have your stomach pumped before she'd let you skip this event."

Logan dropped his hand. "It was worth a try."

"Face it, bro, she's got us good."

Logan's gaze wandered to Blue Ridge Cottage of its own volition. He wondered if Serena was involved with the guild. Would she be at the tea party? If so, he could use the opportunity to question her some more.

Or simply enjoy her company.

Yeah, there was that.

Erin was involved more in the guild, so if she
knew anything important, Faith could find out
once she got to question her sister more.

"Anything else, Mrs. Hamilton?"

"No, dear. Thank you."

CHAPTER SIX

THE GOLDEN LADIES' GUILD held its annual tea
luncheon at the historic Sever House, which
was set on the far side of Gold Dust Park. It
had been built in the early 1900s by Ronald
Sever for his bride, and the ladies' guild had
taken over care of the structure decades ago.
A three-story Victorian, white with black
shutters and a wide wraparound porch, the
house was, in Serena's estimation, a dream
come true. She and her father had only lived
in tiny apartments, so the idea of raising a
family in a gorgeous house like this was a
staple of her daydreams.

Reality was quite another issue.

The lower level was divided by a wide stair-
case, which was located in the center of the
house. The two main living areas were large
open spaces, with high ceilings and broad
windows that allowed plenty of natural light
to brighten the space. The house was available to rent for weddings, parties or meetings, such as today's. Both rooms had been

transformed into fashionable afternoon-tea rooms; complete with round tables and dainty chairs, pink-and-white linens and tiered serving plates. Along one wall sat a long table with pots of tea and platters of cookies.

"Good grief. There's enough pink in here to give me a toothache," Heidi griped as they made their way into the gathering. "It's practically autumn and not a harvest color in sight."

"Be nice," Serena whispered. She smoothed her palms over her sheath dress, designed with an explosion of colorful flowers over a white background. "It was sweet of Mrs. M. to include us today."

"I like it," Carrie said as she viewed the brightly decorated surroundings.

"That's because you look like a guild lady," Heidi pointed out.

"And what's wrong with that?" Carrie countered, looking down at her flattering peach dress. "It reminds me of the times my grandmother took me to tea."

"When you were a little girl?" Serena asked.

"No. Last month," she answered sheepishly.

Heidi choked over Carrie's reply.

"Hey, my grandmother rocks."

Serena had to hand it to Carrie and Heidi—
so far the two women had worked together
without a fuss. Carrie still hadn't revealed to
Serena why she was here, but she was helping Serena in the store as a way of making
up for crashing at her place without notice.
And Heidi, although she would never admit
it, didn't mind spending less time at the store
because her accounting clients were increasing and she could work a few more hours at
home.

"Ladies." Mrs. Masterson clasped her hands
in front of her chest and hurried toward them
as other women from town began to arrive.
Her pantsuit was as pink as the afternoon-tea
decor. "Thank you for coming."

"Like we had a choice," Heidi said under
her breath, tugging at the blue lace skirt of
her dress.

"You did," Serena said through her smile.
"I told you that you could stay at the store."

"And then remind me that I'd let Mrs. M.
down? No way."

Serena stepped forward to greet the older
woman. "We're so happy to be here."

"Ah, and you brought your friend."

On one of Mrs. M.'s visits to the store,
she'd met Carrie and the two had quickly
bonded like long-lost friends. Heidi already

had an ongoing relationship with Mrs. M., since she'd been in town the longest, and if Serena didn't miss her guess, the older woman had a soft spot for the usually prickly Heidi.

Carrie grinned. "I like your style, Mrs. M."

The older woman preened. "I can't take all the credit. The committee had a clear vision and created this beautiful English tearoom." Mrs. M. took Serena's arm and pulled her from her friends. "But I have a problem, my dear."

"Is everything okay?"

"Yes. I must leave before the festivities start and I have a favor to ask."

Relieved and eager to help, Serena said, "You name it."

"I invited some additional guests. They might feel a bit out of place and I was wondering if you wouldn't mind sitting with them."

Serena knew and hated the feeling of being out of place. Sure, she usually ended up in that position intentionally—self-preservation and all—but it still didn't feel good. "It would be my pleasure."

"You're such a special girl." Mrs. M. glanced at her watch. "I must run. They'll be here shortly. And thank you again."

Mrs. M. turned to walk away with Serena hot on her heels. "Wait. Who are your guests?"

"You'll recognize them when they walk in." Mrs. M. wiggled her fingers at Carrie and Heidi and disappeared into the kitchen.

"What's up?" Carrie asked as she wandered over, a cookie in hand.

Still puzzled over the woman's abrupt departure, Serena lifted a shoulder. "Mrs. M. had to leave. She asked me to look out for some guests she invited."

Carrie glanced around the room. "This place is starting to fill up. Heidi snagged us a table, so we should sit."

Serena bit her lower lip. "I should probably wait by the door."

Carrie shrugged. "I'll be at the table."

Women entered the house in groups, all dressed in lovely summer dresses, some even sporting wide-brimmed hats or fascinators made trendy by royal weddings, but no one Serena recognized. Mrs. M. had said she would know who her guests were, but as the minutes passed, she was stumped. She was just about to give up and head to the table, when the door opened and two tall men, dressed in tailored suits and ties, walked in.

Her mouth fell open. "Logan?"

"In the flesh." He closed the door behind him. "This is my brother, Reid."

Serena shook Reid's outstretched hand, shocked to her toes to find Logan standing here. "I don't understand."

"Grandmother."

A smile tickled her lips. "You're her guests?"

He nodded, clearly unhappy.

Serena placed a hand over her mouth as a laugh escaped her.

"Go ahead. Laugh away."

"Sorry." She frowned, still baffled. "But your grandmother knew this was a tea luncheon. When she said she had guests arriving, I assumed she meant other women."

"Gran is cagey," Reid said, and Logan added, "And invited us, anyway."

Humor and respect for Logan mingled in her heart. "And you still came? How sweet." Logan scanned the room, his eyes narrowing. "Where is Grandmother, by the way?"

"Oh, she had to leave."

"What?" the brothers cried in unison.

"Something came up, but she asked me and my friends to keep you company."

Logan glanced at his brother. "She really did it."

"Like there was any doubt?" was Reid's strangled reply.

"Did what?" Serena asked, missing the meaning of the brothers' exchange.

Logan shoved his hands in his pants pockets. "You do remember that our grandmother is a matchmaker."

"Yes, but she wouldn't…"

Logan caught and held her gaze. "Oh, but she would."

Serena looked away as she felt her cheeks heat.

"I need something to drink," Reid muttered, running a hand through his neatly styled hair.

"You'll have to wait for a proper drink until we go to Smitty's later," Logan informed him.

Reid brushed by them, headed across the room to the tea table.

Serena looked back at Logan. "I can't believe your grandmother would invite you guys. You're the only men here."

"I'm sure it's part of her grand plan to lure Reid and me to a room full of women and see what happens."

"You make her sound calculating," Serena said, defending her friend.

"Grandmother to a T. And she has her sights set on you and me together."

Even though she suspected as much, the

idea flustered Serena. "C'mon. Let's take a seat."

With his hand at the small of her back, they wove through the tables. Was it overly warm in here? The temperature had been pleasant until Logan arrived. She slipped a finger under her collar and flapped it back and forth to whip up a breeze. Goodness, Logan had an effect on her. When she reached the table, Carrie's eyebrows arched and Heidi let out a delighted chuckle.

"She did it again, Logan?" Heidi asked.

Logan pulled out a chair for Serena, then sat beside her.

"She's getting desperate." He tugged at the knot of his tie. "The pressure's heating up."

Reid walked up with a dainty china teacup and saucer in his large hand. "You gotta be kidding me," he said as he examined the delicate china.

Heidi let out another laugh. "Classic."

Shaking his head, Reid took the vacant chair between Heidi and Carrie.

Serena introduced the brothers to Carrie, who said with a smile, "You guys must really love your grandmother. Either that or she's holding something very damaging over your heads."

"That would be preferable," Logan said,

taking his napkin from the table to place on his lap. "She's afraid she'll die before seeing us get married."

Carrie's smile grew bigger. "I knew I liked that woman."

Guild members moved about the room, chatting with one another before lunch was served. Bonnie Masterson stopped by the table, her hair artfully styled, her makeup applied to highlight her beautiful face. Her hand flew to her chest. "She actually got you here? I can't believe it."

Logan and Reid both rose. "Mother."

She put her hands on her hips. "I'm sure if I'd asked you boys to attend you would have said no."

Reid kissed her cheek. "You didn't have to. I'm sure Gran told you her plan."

Bonnie didn't even bother looking guilty. "Of course she did," she said as she gave Logan a hug. "Now behave and I'll talk to you both before you leave."

"Great," Logan muttered under his breath as he took his seat, and Serena heard him.

"You know," she said quietly, leaning in his direction, "you've made two women in your life very happy."

A corner of his mouth kicked up. "Only two?"

She blinked. She didn't know what to say, so she took her cloth napkin with trembling fingers and shook it out before placing it on her lap.

Before long the high-pitched chatter echoed off the ceiling. The brothers were good company, keeping conversation at the table lively. Serena couldn't deny the cascade of shivers every time Logan's arm brushed hers. Like the night at Smitty's, he sat close enough that she couldn't miss his citrus cologne. Or the way his coffee-colored eyes grew darker when she caught him looking at her. Thankfully the sandwiches were tiny, because she'd suddenly lost her appetite.

When she pushed away her plate, he tilted his head toward her.

"Nervous?" His whisper brushed over her ear, setting off a cavalcade of sensations.

Serena jerked. "I've, um, never been to an event like this before."

Lame, lame, lame.

Logan shrugged. "It's not a big deal. The guild women are always getting together for some event or fund-raiser to support Golden."

"And I'm sure they do great things in the community. It's different than how I grew up," she admitted.

His expression turned curious. "Your mother wasn't involved in any civic groups?"

Serena rubbed the inside of her wrist. "She died when I was young."

His glance moved to her wrist and back. "I'm sorry."

She sent him a wobbly grin. "Thanks. She was awesome."

"I'll bet."

His tender smile took her breath away.

Afraid her heart was slipping into the "falling for the guy" zone, she straightened her shoulders. Focused on the conversation around the table.

"We're definitely hitting Smitty's after this," Reid said as he pulled apart two slices of bread to figure out the filling inside.

"Tell you what," Heidi said. "For being good sports, we'll buy you guys a beer."

"Deal," Reid said quickly before anyone could renege.

Serena took the china teapot from the center of the table to pour herself more tea, then held it out to Logan to see if he wanted a refill. He nodded and tried to fit his finger in the small handle of his cup. He gave up and wrapped his strong hand around the entire thing.

"So does your grandmother do this often?"

Carrie asked, the amusement twinkling in her eyes indicating that she was in Mrs. Masterson's camp.

"More so lately," Reid told her. "Logan lives in Atlanta and misses most of her prying, but I've learned to dodge her invites."

"You know Mrs. M. adores you both," Heidi said as she nibbled on a cookie.

"She does," Reid affirmed, "but you do remember all those times we hid out at the lake until her guests left." Reid turned from Heidi to speak to the table. "Gran always managed to invite a daughter around my age to her parties."

Serena brushed her fingers across the napkin on her lap. "You two grew up together?"

"Kind of," Heidi said, shooting Reid a look.

"That tells me nothing," Serena said.

"When I was in high school, my mom and I had some problems. Alveda opened her home to me and I moved in." She shrugged like it was no big deal. "I used to go to the main house and hang out in the kitchen with Alveda."

"Who knows how to make an actual sandwich," Logan grumbled as he held another small square in his fingers.

Serena figured this lunch was nowhere

near close to filling him up. He'd need an entire platter to satisfy his hunger.

"Who's watching the store?" he asked.

"Lisa, one of the girls who takes an art class. She fills in for me every once in a while."

"Still, this is a Saturday afternoon. I'm surprised they dragged you out of there."

She chuckled at the vision of Carrie on one side, Heidi on the other, gripping Serena's arms as they yanked her out of Blue Ridge Cottage. "I was there all morning and I'll check back in after the tea."

One of his dark eyebrows arched. "You won't be joining us at Smitty's?"

She couldn't resist asking. "Do you want me to?"

His commanding gaze held hers, sending a shiver over her skin. "I do."

The intensity in his eyes mesmerized her. Never before had a man focused his attention on her as if she was the most important woman in the room. Yes, she normally shied away from getting close, but with Logan it was different. It was like he sensed her reservations but found her special, anyway. Letting go of her qualms, she said, "Then I'll make sure to be there."

His intimate smile warmed her to her bones.

Once lunch was finished, there were a few speeches and then everyone mingled before heading home. Logan stayed by her side, which secretly thrilled Serena, until his mother called him away. She joined Heidi, who was checking her phone, and her gaze returned to Logan's broad shoulders as he crossed the room. Her smile dimmed when his mother pulled him into a conversation with a beautiful woman she didn't recognize.

"Heather Baine," Heidi reported.

Serena tried to act disinterested. "Really? I don't know her."

"The Baines are old money. Like the Mastersons."

Serena's stomach sank. His family would expect Logan to be involved with someone with a pedigree, not a scam artist's daughter.

"Don't worry, though. I heard her college boyfriend was going to propose."

Serena infused a little attitude in her voice. "I wasn't worried."

"Tell that to your face."

Serena gaped at Heidi then rearranged her expression to appear unconcerned.

"What's got her upset?" Carrie asked as she walked into their circle.

"Green-eyed monster," Heidi quipped.

Serena sputtered over a denial that didn't quite reach her tongue.

Carrie peered at the guests, not having to be told the topic of the conversation was Logan. "He's not interested in her."

Despite herself, Serena asked, "How can you tell?"

"Because I sat across the table from you two, and trust me, Logan only had eyes for you."

Her stomach did a funny flip, a mix between joy and nerves. She wrapped her arm around her best friend. "You always know what to say."

Reid joined the group. "Are you ladies ready to get out of here?"

"So ready," Heidi said, jumping at the chance to escape.

"I'll meet you out front," Serena told them. She went to their table to retrieve her purse, checking her phone to see if Lisa had texted.

Relieved to find no messages, she started when Logan stopped beside her. "Checking on the store?"

"Yes. No problems, but I need to go back and close up."

He escorted her to the door. "You know,

with the right people in place, your business can run successfully even if you aren't there."

"I've put so much of my heart and soul into Blue Ridge Cottage, I guess I worry."

"You have a sound business, Serena."

Her shoulders rose as she inhaled. "I'm getting better at letting go."

They stepped onto the wide covered porch.

"Everyone needs some fun time, you know."

She pulled her sunglasses from her bag and slipped them on. "Are you trying to tell me something?"

"Maybe you should let your hair down."

Her hand flew to her hair, which she'd pulled back in a tight bun. Not sure how guild women presented themselves at fund-raisers, she'd gone for what she hoped was tasteful. Logan took her hand in his and grinned. "I meant metaphorically."

"I know." When he didn't let go, she squeezed his hand. "Thanks."

"Just be who you are," he suggested, which sent her stomach fluttering into a frenzy. Could having fun get her in big trouble? Guess she'd have to find out.

"Hey, you two, get over here," Carrie called. Serena hesitantly released his hand, missing the touch immediately. Oh, dear, she had it bad. "We're all going home to change then meet up at Smitty's for dinner."

"A real dinner," Reid added.

Logan glanced at her. "You'll be there, right?"

Going for lighthearted instead of lovesick, she said, "Where else would I be?"

"Great. Otherwise I'll have to come get you myself and make sure you have a good time."

Her heart tumbled. "You're promising to entertain me?"

His killer grin said it all.

AT HALF PAST six the group sat around a table in Smitty's, engaged in lively conversation. As agreed, they'd all changed into more comfortable clothing. Logan sported a pullover and jeans. And while he enjoyed seeing everyone in a jovial, relaxed mood, one person was conspicuously missing. Serena.

He leaned over to Heidi. "I thought we were all showing up tonight."

"What can I say? Customers came in right at closing. True to form, Serena told us to head over here and said she'd join us."

He appreciated Serena's work ethic, but whether she knew anything about his case or not, someone had to show this woman how to relax and enjoy her free time. He rose. "Be back soon."

"Where are you off to?" Reid asked.

"To find the absentee member of our group."

He didn't miss the glance between Heidi and Carrie. Or his brother's grin. He'd just stepped away when Jamey arrived with their drinks.

"Taking off so soon?"

"I'll be back."

His lips twitched. "Ah, I see how it is."

"How what is?"

Jamey merely shrugged his broad shoulders, but waggled his eyebrows at the group. For which he received laughs. The innuendos were getting old. Especially since the only thing he'd done so far was spend a little time with Serena.

"Hey, that's my friend you're talking about," Carrie yelled at the pub owner.

"How do you know? I never mentioned a name," Jamey countered.

"Like that was a mystery," Heidi joked.

Shaking his head at their banter, Logan strode from the pub.

He was met by a purple sky with a slash of orange as the sun hovered over the horizon. Traffic still moved slowly down Main and the voices of tourists carried along the sidewalks.

He ignored the tantalizing scents tempting him as he passed the bakery, keeping a steady pace to Blue Ridge Cottage. According to the hours posted on the front door, the store closed at six. He wasn't surprised when he pushed open the door to find Serena at the sales counter checking out a customer.

She glanced up when he came in, surprise in her eyes. "I'll be right with you."

He nodded, roaming the store while she finished the transaction. His grandmother had gushed over Serena's artwork, but he'd never taken the time to study it. He was surprised by the skill shown in each scene of forest animals in their natural habitat, or brightly blooming flowers, all captured in a range of dazzling colors.

After seeing out the customer, she locked the door. "What are you doing here?"

"You said you'd join us at Smitty's."

"I will. I have…" She stopped and glanced at her watch. "Oops. Time got away from me."

He picked up a decorative box and glanced at the woodsy scene sketched on the note cards. It was so real, so inviting, he could imagine himself in the forest, hiking a well-worn path. Inhaling the pine boughs as he passed by. "Your artwork is beautiful."

"Thank you." She walked back to the counter and pressed a few keys on the cash register. "I find this part of Georgia so inspiring."

"You do it justice, that's for sure. No wonder Grandmother is a fan."

He strolled over and leaned against the counter. The scent of lavender surrounded him. Under the fluorescent light, Serena's memorable blueberry-colored eyes shone. She still wore the same dress from the tea party, one that flattered her. With the two of them alone, the outside world shut out, he could imagine that this was the beginning of a date. A time to discover each other and see where things went. Problem was, she was a job. He couldn't forget that.

Pushing away the reality, he said, "From what I've read about you, you've kept true to your initial concept and made it a success."

"I've always loved to draw. Being able to make a living from my gift is more than I could ever have imagined."

"Why is that?"

"I guess I wondered if I'd be fortunate enough to go after my dream." She rubbed the inside of her wrist the way he'd noticed before. Silence blanketed the room, not in an awkward fashion, more a comfortable stretch in time. "It was tough for us after my mom died."

He reached over the counter and gently took her right hand in his. Felt the soft shudder when he turned her hand to reveal angel wings tattooed on her inner wrist. "For your mom?"

She nodded. Swallowed. "When she left... it felt like our entire world had fallen apart."

He knew the feeling. Had experienced it in his own way.

She pulled her hand from his and rested her palms on the counter. "We had a few rough years. Things got better when I went to high school."

"Then I'm happy to see your hard work has paid off."

She glanced around the store. Smiled so brightly it made his chest ache. "It has."

"You did promise to have a little fun."

"I can't help it. Even if it's closing time I let people stay and browse."

"It's Saturday night, Serena. Don't you ever stop being a store owner?"

"Is that even possible?"

"Yes. So why don't you get changed and we'll join the others, who are way ahead of us in the partying department."

She sent him a sheepish grin. "I get it. Time to join the party."

Within minutes she had the cash register

emptied and the lights off, and they closed the back door.

"I need to run upstairs to change."

"Take your time." He followed her up. "How's the ankle, by the way?"

"Better. I kept off it all week to be sure, but this morning I went out for a long-overdue run."

"I suppose I don't have to tell you to be more aware of your surroundings?"

"Left the earbuds home today."

She unlocked the door to her apartment and led him inside. It was cozy and homey, like he imagined Serena's place would be.

Really? You've been imagining her place?

He swallowed a groan. Yeah, he had. And not in a professional, PI kind of way. What was wrong with him?

"Be right back." She went to one of the bedrooms and closed the door. While she was changing, he'd have a few minutes to check out the place.

As much as this wasn't his intention when he'd come to collect Serena, he took advantage of the situation. Quickly, he went through her kitchen drawers. Nothing useful. Rifled through a basket on the counter filled with receipts. Opened her personal phone book. Nothing under "Stanhope." Flipped through to find any family names. Found a number for "Dad." One of many, he discovered. The five previous numbers had been crossed out. He made a mental note and continued his search.

Her reading choices were eclectic. Her living room neat as a pin. No way could he safely check out her bedroom, so he'd have to be happy with the one thing he did find. Taking a seat on the couch, he pulled out his cell and added the number he'd memorized to his notes. A door opened and Serena joined him.

"Thanks for waiting."

"It was well worth it," he said as he rose, his gaze sweeping over her. She'd changed into a swirly patterned blouse and jeans, and touched up her makeup. But best of all, she had released her hair from that restrictive bun and let it flow freely around her shoulders. He walked over. Lifted a section. Was overcome with the scent of lavender again. "I see you took my words seriously."

A becoming red stained her cheeks. "Don't think for one minute that I did this for you. I like my hair down."

He leaned close to her ear. "So do I."

With a small laugh, she pushed him away. "Let's go. We wouldn't want to keep the gang waiting."

As they walked through town, it was all

Logan could do not to take her hand in his. This wasn't a date, he had to keep reminding himself. He suspected she had information about the man he'd been hired to investigate. He needed to keep his wits about him. Yes, Serena was beautiful, but she clearly had secrets he needed to ferret out.

As they passed the park, fireflies flitted about in the entrance. Serena laughed, clearly enchanted.

"Oh, my goodness." She pulled her phone from her back pocket. "I have always wanted to do a series of cards featuring fireflies." After snapping a few pictures, she scrolled through the gallery. "I can't think of anything more beautiful than twinkling lights coming from these tiny creatures."

Logan stood back, watching the joy on her face. "I have to admit, I don't give them much thought."

"Then you're missing out." She turned to him. "Did you know there are over fifty species of fireflies in Georgia, each with their own distinctive flash?"

"I do now."

"The male puts on a light show to attract a mate."

"Really? Now, that is interesting."

"You probably don't think about them

much since you live in the city. All the bright lights hide their magic. To be honest, I never really noticed them until I moved here." She smiled at the tiny lights dancing in the air. "I don't know. They have a way of making me happy. Especially after a long day at the store."

"So you come here to visit with your flashy friends?"

"Don't laugh. They're easier to talk to than people sometimes. No judgment. No back talk. They listen, blink their lights and go on their merry way."

"And it bothers you that people judge?"

She lifted a shoulder, as if her admission was no big deal. "Sure. Doesn't it bother you?"

"Only if I let it."

She blew out a sigh. "Then you're tougher than I am."

They stood in the deepening shadows, enjoying the light show. The smoky scent of cooking meat wafted their way from Smitty's. After a few moments he turned. Glanced at Serena. Wondered why she looked so sad. Or what she was hiding.

She noticed his attention and laughed. "You probably think I'm silly."

"Far from it." He ran his fingers over her

hair. Placed a finger under her chin and tipped her head back. She blinked at him. Interest shone in her blue eyes. Taking a chance, he lowered his head and brushed his lips over hers. Lightly, just like the fireflies darting about in the air. When she returned his kiss he moved closer, placing his other hand on her waist. The air was cool, the night special, and he was falling for a woman he should be investigating.

She pulled back. Gazed up at him, a gentle smile on her lips. "Let me guess. The fireflies got to you?"

"No. You did."

CHAPTER SEVEN

SHE GOT TO HIM? The idea boggled her mind. Or maybe it was the lasting warmth of his kiss. Either way, she couldn't take her eyes from his.

"You're quite the charmer."

"Not really. I'm big on the truth."

There it was. That one word alone was enough to sober her mood. "Well, then, here's a little truth for you. I'm starving."

"Those sandwiches we had at lunch were not very big."

"Or filling."

As the final glow of the setting sun wrapped the last of its tendrils around them in a warm embrace, Serena found it hard to leave this intimate sanctuary. It was as though everyone in town had secretly plotted to leave them alone in this romantic tableau, giving them permission to explore the budding attraction zinging between them. Her gaze moved to his lips and heat crept up her neck. She never allowed herself to let go, but the promise of the night and the curve of his lips had her contemplating throwing caution to the wind and kissing him again. She was tempted—that much she knew—to the depths of her soul, until common sense threw a bucket of chilly water over her intentions.

"The others are going to wonder where we are." With regret, she stepped away from him. Took one last look at the fireflies flitting away from them and held back a sigh.

Logan waited until she turned back to him and said, "Ready?"

She laid a hand over her growling stomach. "Definitely."

In a few minutes they were inside the rowdy and crowded Smitty's. Logan led her to the table where the gang, as she'd come to think of them, were engaged in a rousing conversation, their voices loud as they spoke over the clamor.

"It isn't baseball unless there's hot dogs and beer," Jamey explained to Carrie, who rolled her eyes.

"Or peanuts," Heidi added.

"Baseball?" Serena asked as she stopped beside her friend.

Heidi nodded in greeting. "The guys started talking smack about sports, Carrie asked why the big deal about baseball and it went down-hill from there."

"Look, either you're a Braves fan or you aren't," Jamey argued.

"I'm not anyone's fan," Carrie said, which started Reid and Jamey counting down the merits of rooting for the home team.

Logan nudged Serena with his elbow. She took the drink he offered her.

"Did anyone order Jamey's special?" Logan asked the group. As well as serving huge sand-wiches and delicious stews during the winter months, Jamey had added a beer cheese dip to the menu. Served with crusty pieces of toasted bread, it was a hit.

"We already went through one," his brother told him. Logan tapped Jamey on the shoul-der, stopping the pub owner's conversation with Carrie to order another appetizer.

"Coming right up," Jamey said, all smiles as he made his way back to the kitchen, call-ing out to regulars along the way.

Serena wrinkled her nose. "Beer cheese?"

"Do not judge until you've tasted," Logan ordered.

The pub was packed. Locals blowing off steam after a busy week. A rousing game of darts was happening in one corner, and a guy with a guitar was setting up in the other. It was noisy, the scent of the savory food hung in the air and, for once in her life, Serena felt like she belonged. She and Logan stood a small distance from the others, yet they were still included in the never-ending baseball debate.

"Do you have an opinion?" Logan asked.

"On sports? No. Other than my daily run, I'm not very athletic."

"We should go sometime."

"To what?"

"A baseball game." He chuckled. "It's America's favorite pastime."

"Then why are we talking about it in a pub?"

"Good question. I'd advise you not to mention that fact to Jamey."

She sipped her drink. Drank in the warmhearted camaraderie. She had friends here in Golden. For the first time in forever, she could let down her guard and enjoy herself.

Logan laughed at something Jamey said when he returned with the cheese dip. While everyone else dug in, Serena couldn't take her eyes from Logan. Never in a million years would she have imagined kissing him in the twilight. Yet she had. And she'd felt it all the way to her toes.

Warmth washed over her and she wondered why she'd let him close. She'd walled herself off from the world, keeping people at arm's length for so long, yet this man had breached her defenses. This man who made it very clear that if you messed with his grandmother, you'd answer to him. A man who'd dressed up in a suit and tie to attend a ladies' luncheon because his grandmother asked. In the short time she'd gotten to know him, he'd gotten under her skin. He made her feel special. Even though she'd hidden from personal entanglements—Serena against the world, for so long—he seemed determined to pull her into his world and make sure she had some fun along the way.

So caught up in righting the wrongs her father had committed, and her, by extension, she hadn't been living life. Hadn't stepped out from under the cloud of shame. She'd thought that with each name she crossed off the list she was one step closer to freedom. But what would happen when she paid back all the money? Would she really be free? Not if she didn't start engaging in life around her. She didn't know what that looked like, but Logan had changed her perspective. Should she reach out and grab her chance?

She could continue to cover up her past. Or was it time to trust people? Carrie and

Heidi had become more than just friends, yet she was hiding a huge part of herself from them. And Logan? After that kiss, how did she move forward knowing he valued truth? Right now she didn't have the answers, but she was determined to enjoy the night with these people who had rallied around her, the people who had become friends. She glanced at Logan. She was willing to take baby steps toward the truth for the man who was beginning to steal her heart.

"C'mon," Logan called. "You're missing out."

As her stomach growled again, she moved closer to the table. Logan held out a piece of pumpernickel bread, cheese on top, ready for her. "Prepare to be dazzled."

She opened her mouth, took a bite. Let the warm cheese slide onto her tongue and chewed the bread. "You're right. That is the best thing I've ever tasted."

Jamey took a bow.

"Aren't you supposed to be behind the bar?" Logan joked.

"My fans requested more of me."

The group laughed. Serena picked up a small, empty plate and filled it with bread and cheese, then munched away.

"I can't believe you've never had Jamey's signature dish," Logan remarked.

"To be fair, I've only been here for the Oktoberfest meetings. All business and no eating."

"You don't come here to unwind like the rest of Golden?"

She shrugged. "Usually I have paperwork to do. Or I'm busy sketching a new series."

He shook his head and tsked. "Miss Stanhope, you have got to learn to have fun."

"Sure. Right after I run the store, teach classes, pay taxes—"

Logan cut her off. "I get it. You're all about your business. But don't forget about the other wonderful things life has to offer."

He was right. She needed to get out more. And maybe with her friends, it was possible. When she looked up at him, it was easy to get lost in his coffee-colored eyes. There was something there, a strength she could learn from. Logan was not the kind of man to sit back and let life pass him by. Suddenly the future didn't seem as dire as she'd always viewed it.

She leaned closer to say thanks. His gaze moved to her lips and for one exciting moment she imagined he might kiss her. Here. In front of the people of Golden. But then she blinked and the look was gone. Embarrassed by her reaction, she turned away only to have Logan speak softly into her ear. "Yeah, I was thinking about stealing a kiss."

She felt the heat rushing up her neck. Was she that transparent? And if she was, what else could this man read about her?

A couple of people walked into the pub and cheers rose up from their table. Deke and Grace came over to join them. Welcomes abounded from all around, but Serena tensed. Deke had never been anything but cordial to her, but there was an undercurrent between them. Before she knew it, Deke and Logan had moved to the corner of the pub.

"I swear, Deke is always discussing business," Grace said as she slipped off her sweater, reached for a piece of bread and dipped it in the cheese.

Serena smiled at her friend, but it was an effort. Taking another taste of the dip, she watched the two men in deep discussion. That old feeling of needing to look over her shoulder engulfed her. Logan glanced her way, with the same assessing look he'd had on his face as when he'd first arrived in town and asked questions about her store and family. Was that what his undivided attention and kiss were all about? She hoped not, but after noticing the furtive looks the men sent her way, she fell back into safety mode. The taste of the dip turned to ash in her mouth.

They could very well be discussing the weather. Maybe making plans to attend a baseball game. Excuses ran through her mind, but the only common denominator she could come up with was her. And she didn't like it.

Placing her plate on the table, she was debating leaving when Carrie came over.

"You okay?"

"Sure. Why wouldn't I be?"

"Two minutes ago you were smiling and laughing, and now you look like you want to run off and hide."

Good grief. She really needed lessons on how to control her facial expressions.

"It's been a long day."

A sly smile tipped Carrie's lips. "You and Logan seem cozy. I noticed it took a while before you two showed up here."

"I had to close up the store and change."

"Nothing else?"

"Like what?"

"I don't know. A stroll through the park maybe?"

"We did stop there for a few minutes but it was no big deal." *Liar.*

"Then did somebody say something?" Carrie sobered and glanced around. "I bet it was Jamey, wasn't it?"

"No. It's nothing."

"But you'd tell me if something was wrong?"

Before Serena could reassure her friend, Logan and Deke returned. As Deke passed, he nodded at her, then slid his arm around Grace's waist. Logan walked her way and the warning bells in her head clanged louder than before. Where before Logan had been kind of flirty, now he was more serious. What had caused the change?

"So," he said as he stopped beside her. "Ready to order dinner?"

Fifteen minutes ago she would have said yes. Now she couldn't eat if she tried.

"Actually, I'm going to head home."

He looked at her closely. "Are you okay?"

"I wish people would stop asking me that."

He held up his hands. "Sorry."

She blew out a breath. "No. I'm sorry. Listen, I'm not good company tonight."

He paused, sized her up, then said, "Rain check on the meal?"

"Sure."

Waving at her friends, she quickly ducked out the door and jogged back to her apartment in the evening shadows. Maybe being part of the world wasn't as good an idea as she'd hoped. The one thing she knew for sure? Keeping secrets wasn't for the faint-hearted.

ON MONDAY MORNING, Logan still couldn't believe he'd kissed Serena. Where was his professionalism? His quest to dig deep and uncover answers? It had all blown away when she'd been delighted by the fireflies. Fireflies. He rolled his neck to relieve the tension. What was wrong with him?

"Planning on spending the day alone?" Jamey asked as he leaned in to wipe the neighboring table.

"If it's not a problem."

"Not for me, as long as you buy lunch." He tossed the towel over his shoulder. "Don't you have a perfectly good office in Atlanta?"

Logan scrolled through a search-engine list on the laptop screen. "Right now it's better if I stay up here. The commute's not cutting it."

"So what are you up to? You and Deke have been thick as thieves lately."

"Can't say."

He sent Logan an amused grin. "Or maybe it's because of a pretty store owner?"

Swallowing back a sigh because, yeah, he

didn't want to talk about it, Logan muttered, "Really can't say."

"Or don't want to?"

Logan sent his friend a scowl. "Are you gonna keep talking or can I get back to work here?"

Jamey chuckled. "You sound like Serena's friend. That woman knows how to put a man in his place."

"Then clearly I'm not as good at dealing with you as she is."

Jamey held up his hand. "I've got things to do in the kitchen."

Left in much-needed silence, Logan grinned. Seemed Carrie had made an impression on Jamey.

Just like Serena with you?

He shook off the thought. He had work to do, and since the pub didn't open until eleven for lunch, he returned to his task. He appreciated Jamey letting him hang out here during the week, but the interruptions weren't helping his peace of mind. Especially when he couldn't get the image of Serena's closed-off expression out of his mind. What had caused the light in her eyes to dim the other night? They were having a good time until Deke showed up. Could she be on to them?

The thought didn't sit well. So here he was

at square one, with little to start off the week with. Finding out who the Stanhopes were was getting tricky, kiss notwithstanding. He needed to get this case under control—which meant not being attracted to his subject—so he planned on stepping up his investigation. He owed Deke that much.

He logged on to a database to search the phone number he'd found at Serena's apartment. It had the same exchange as the area where Deke's mother lived. No one answered when he'd called. The blanks in both of their histories were proving to be challenging, but Logan was convinced that James had a direct connection to Serena. Now Logan needed to find the proof they were related, but hadn't dug up a birth certificate for Serena in Georgia. Could she have been born in a different state? Have a different legal last name? That had to be the key.

He was trying another background search, his fingers flying over the computer keyboard, when the heavy door to Smitty's opened, ushering in bright sunlight. Since it was still early, Logan looked up to see who was hitting the pub. He smothered a groan as his father strode over.

"Dad."

His father wrapped his fingers over the top

of the chair across from him. "What have you done, Logan?"

He cocked his head as he rattled off the list of his personal achievements. "Let's see. I graduated high school with honors. Joined the military. Started my own business." He met his father's angry gaze. "Need my résumé?"

"No. I mean what have you done to Reid?"

"I haven't done anything to Reid. When I left this morning he was getting ready to sand down the original wood floors in the house he's living in."

"Yes. I just came from there." Typical impatience laced his father's voice. "He informed me he's thinking about leaving Masterson Enterprises. Did you have anything to do with that?"

Logan sat back in the chair and crossed his arms over his chest. "Like I would ever tell Reid what to do. He's a grown man. He makes his own decisions."

"But you're staying with him?"

"I don't owe you an explanation, but yes. I have business here in Golden."

"So you're influencing him to get back at me?"

"Are you kidding?" Why did he expect anything different from this man? "It's not all about you, Dad. I'm supporting my brother.

I would think you'd find that an admirable quality."

His father pulled out the chair and sank into it. Loosened his tie. "Of course I do." He ran his hand through his hair. "Reid's leaving is going to create a hardship for the company."

"You should have thought about that before you ticked him off."

"This move will affect the business's finances. Even your grandmother's portfolio."

"Grandmother will be fine. She's made smart investment decisions."

A defeated expression crossed his father's normally strong features. "I don't know how many times I can apologize, Logan."

"I guess until I believe you."

In arguments before, Arthur Masterson always held the upper ground. Assumed he would come out the victor. Never once had he tried to see the past from Logan's point of view. Now he looked old and tired. When had that happened?

While you were gone, a voice that sounded suspiciously like his grandmother's said.

Logan moved around in his chair, an unfamiliar twinge of guilt making him uncomfortable—the first such feeling since finding the information that had totally changed his life.

Jamey approached, an eyebrow arched as he caught Logan's gaze. Logan shrugged in response.

"Can I get you anything, sir?"

"No. I'm headed back to the office."

His father rose, clapped Jamey on the shoulder and stared at his son. "I wish you'd see that I'm trying to make things right," he said, then turned on his heel and left.

Jamey blew out a low whistle. "Think that's the first time your dad has ever stepped foot in this place."

"If I hang around, I'm sure it won't be the last."

Jamey sized him up with curious eyes, then asked, "Need a refill?"

Logan glanced at his empty coffee mug. "No. Suddenly I need some fresh air."

Logan packed up his computer and folders, said goodbye to Jamey and pushed open the heavy door to step into the bright sunshine. He took his sunglasses from his shirt pocket and slipped them on, then stashed his belongings in his SUV. He needed to block out his father's accusations and figure out why Deke's case was so difficult. If he was honest with himself, the memory of his kiss with Serena was tripping him up. Maybe he should resign? Refer Deke to another PI? Because clearly he wasn't going to stop dwelling on Serena Stanhope anytime soon.

He set off to the bakery, thinking an apple fritter would improve his mood, when his eyes lit on Blue Ridge Cottage. Serena stood out front, dressed in a blue-and-white patterned dress, adjusting the sandwich board on the sidewalk. He'd surveilled her enough. Maybe some pointed questions would loosen her tongue.

He crossed Main Street and strode toward her as if he was on autopilot. The sun shone off her gleaming black hair. Her eyes went wide when she caught a glimpse of him. She stood still, waiting for the unexpected. He had to give her props for that.

"Serena."

"Logan."

A heavy silence followed.

"Do you have a few minutes?" he asked.

"For?" Her dark eyebrows rose.

He cleared his throat. "I'd like to ask you some questions."

"About?"

He opened his mouth to answer, but closed it when an older couple walked by, waving to Serena, who returned the gesture with a bright smile that didn't stick when she focused her attention back on him. He shoved his hands in his pants pockets. "Can we go inside?"

She glanced through the glass door. "It's not any more private in there."

"Humor me."

She shrugged and opened the door, holding it for him as she entered the store before him. Carrie and Heidi abruptly stopped talking, surprise written on both their faces. The two shot Serena a "what's up?" look before disappearing to the back room.

When Serena faced him, his gaze zeroed in on a print of a mountain scene on the wall behind her and he knew exactly how to remedy this rather clumsy encounter.

"Look, I know it's last-minute, but I'm going to drive up to Pine Tree Overlook. I was wondering if you would join me."

"Logan, I'm working."

He jerked his head toward the other room. "Looks like you have help."

She ran her palms over her dress. "Yes, but I can't leave on the spur of the moment."

"Sure you can," Carrie said as she walked toward them, not showing one ounce of embarrassment at her obvious eavesdropping. "You haven't had a day off in ages. Go. Heidi and I can hold down the fort."

"Yes. Go," Heidi shouted from the back.

"Well, I…"

"Grab your sketchbook. Make going off with Logan a working break."

Indecision clear on her face, Serena didn't move until Carrie rounded the sales counter with her purse. Heidi ran up front with the sketch pad, shoved it into Serena's hands, then returned to whatever she was *not* doing.

Serena gave up, the merriment in her eyes making his breath catch. "Looks like I've been overruled."

A satisfied grin curved Carrie's lips as she shooed them out. "Keep her for as long as you like, Logan. I'll be here all day."

Shooting her friend an "I'll get you later" look, Serena headed for the door, shoulders straight, head held high, and Logan's day felt increasingly brighter.

At his SUV, he opened the door for her, made sure she was safely inside and then took his place behind the wheel. Moments later they were driving along the scenic incline of the mountain leading to one of the more popular tourist spots in the area. After parking in the public lot, they strolled to the path leading to higher elevations.

Serena looked down at her flat shoes. "I'm not exactly dressed for hiking."

He thought she looked beautiful, but held

his tongue. He was here to interrogate, not flirt.

"Right. But there are benches all the way up. Just say so and we'll stop at one when you'd like to."

As they stepped beneath the trees, branches spread out in a wide canopy, the temperature dipped. A breeze rustled the leaves, a few drifting from overhead. The packed-dirt path was uneven under his feet, so he kept close to Serena to make sure she didn't tumble. That was his excuse, anyway, but she didn't seem to mind. A hint of lavender fluttered his way, mixing with the earthy scents around them.

They walked for a while before he found an empty bench. Birds chirped overhead. A calmness settled over him.

From this vantage point, the valley below was spread out before them, dotted with tiny houses and barns. The thick forest edged along the lowlands and the sun shone on the crystalline blue water of Golden Lake.

"What a lovely view." Serena took a seat, taking the pencils from her purse. "I usually go to out-of-the-way places, but I've certainly been remiss by not capturing this scene."

"Golden does have its moments."

She tilted her head as if deciding what to draw first, then settled on the lake.

As she doodled on the page, Logan spread his arms across the back of the bench. "I haven't been boating on the lake in years."

"How many?"

"About thirteen."

"Because you left?"

"Right after high school."

Muffled voices approached from the path.

"It must have been wonderful growing up around here." She tucked the pencil behind her ear and pulled out another. "So much to do and see."

"Looks like a treasure trove for you."

She smiled. "Sales are up. Every time I find a special place like this, it's pure gold." She chuckled. "Gold. Get it? Because we live in Golden?"

He laughed with her. "Like no one has ever made that joke before."

"What can I say? I'm always behind on the curve." She switched pencils again. "Your family seems entrenched here."

He shrugged, brushing her bare arm with the sleeve of his shirt. He recalled her soft skin and shook off the memory. Questions, he reminded himself. He'd come here to ask questions.

"You mentioned your mother the other night. Do you miss her?"

Her hand stilled on the paper. "Every day."

"I don't mean to upset you."

"It's okay. I was young at the time." She started shading the blue water again. "Now I keep the happy memories alive in my heart, so I don't mind talking about her."

"You were close?"

"Yes." A smile curved her lips. "I remember my mother presiding over grand tea parties with my stuffed animals. Or when my dad would take us out for ice cream. Mom would argue against dessert before dinner, but we'd end up in the car, off on another adventure."

"So you went on lots of adventures?"

"Until she got sick."

"So that bond…it never went away?"

She lowered the pencil and turned to him. "What's up, Logan?"

He'd been meaning to unearth information about her mother, but instead he revealed, "Bonnie isn't my birth mother."

Serena went still, then laid the sketch pad and pencils on the bench beside her. "I didn't know."

"I'm not sure anyone besides my family knows the truth." His heart felt heavy, like a rock in his chest. Why had he started this conversation? He should stop while he was ahead, but the compassion on her face kept him going. "My mother died shortly after giving birth to me. Bonnie raised me as her own."

Serena twisted around to face him. "Wow. That must have been hard."

"Maybe. Only I didn't find out until I turned eighteen."

"Your folks kept it a secret?"

He nodded, his throat thick. "I uncovered the truth when I went looking for my birth certificate. My dad handled anything that needed family records, but I was interested in joining the military and had started gathering information to sign up. I knew Dad would never go for it, so I went behind his back. I felt bad about that, until I discovered a different name than Bonnie Masterson listed as my mother."

He remembered the confusion at seeing *Linda K. Royal* on the line for birth mother. The signature had blurred before his eyes. Thinking it was a mistake, he'd reread the document. When he realized what the name meant, shock chilled his veins.

Serena's hand covered his arm, the light pressure reassuring. "What did you do?"

"Confronted my parents. First they were stunned I actually held the certificate in my hand. Then guilt flashed over Bonnie's face while Dad's cheeks turned red. Seems my dad had an affair with a woman in Atlanta and I was the result."

Serena's voice was gentle. "Oh, Logan."

"Bad enough I had to hear about it eighteen years after the fact, but my dad was not very apologetic."

"What do you mean?"

"He was more concerned about what people would think, instead of reassuring his son. Instead of telling me he was sorry, he railed at me, like *I'd* done something wrong." He let out a bitter laugh. "Like I was the guilty party for finding the birth certificate and calling him on it."

"I'm guessing that's when you left?"

"After a huge fight." He tried to make sense of it again, like he had that fateful night. And as always, he came up empty. "I'd looked up to my dad until then, but after he basically told me to get over it and move on, I was so furious I couldn't stay in his house a minute longer."

"Why on earth would he say that to you?"

"Because he was covering his tracks. They'd lied to me my entire life. He wanted to brush it under the rug, but I couldn't get over it."

She opened her mouth, then closed it.

"What?"

Hesitating again, she finally said, "From what I've observed, you still haven't."

"It's not like I would have rebelled my entire life if I'd known Bonnie wasn't my birth mother. My mom died in a car wreck. It was a freak accident, I found out later. But the secrecy is what really made me angry."

"Maybe he was trying to protect you?"

"Not me. Himself." Logan fisted his hands. "He and Bonnie were separated when she found out about my mother. Then I came along after my folks had reconciled. I have no idea how my mom fit in the picture, but when she died, my father took me in and Bonnie raised me. A few years later Reid was born."

"But I don't understand how the town wouldn't have known Bonnie isn't your mother. They must have seen she wasn't pregnant."

"She was gone for over a year, living south of Atlanta with her parents while they tried to work things out. Dad would go down there to see her. Since she hadn't been around for so long, folks assumed I'd been born while she was away, and my folks stuck to the story." He stood, unable to keep still as the weight of the past pressed down on him. "I don't blame Bonnie. She was as much a victim of my father's actions as me. But Dad? I can't forgive him. The way he brushed off my birth mother, as if she were of no consequence? It wasn't right."

"It sounds like everyone made mistakes."

"More like cover-ups and lies."

Her voice was steady when she said, "Sometimes people have valid reasons for keeping the truth to themselves."

He turned on her. "That doesn't fly with me."

She lowered her head and he couldn't read her expression.

"I'm sorry for dumping all this on you." What had he been thinking to bring this up? He never talked about his father's indiscretion with anyone, yet he'd spilled everything to Serena. Was it time? Maybe after learning she'd lost her mother, he felt he'd met a kindred spirit? Whatever the reason, he should be investigating Serena, not getting ensnarled in her spell. "I meant to... I don't know. Just hang out together. Not bring up the past."

Serena put away her pencils and slowly closed the sketch pad. "The truth is part of your past, Logan, whether you like it or not. We all have events in our lives we'd like to forget but can't change. It's what we do with the challenges that makes us the people we are today."

"You make it sound so easy."

"It can be. It's up to you. You either forgive your father or keep the anger bottled up inside. It's your choice, Logan." She stood. Met his gaze. "You either make positive changes in your relationships or stay mired in the past. Only you can decide."

Picking up her belongings, Serena started down the path back to the SUV. He watched her walk away, his chest so tight he could barely breathe.

Was it really that easy? The betrayal still burned like acid in him. But what would it cost him to stop the burning?

Maybe he'd been running from that answer long enough.

CHAPTER EIGHT

WEDNESDAY MORNING STARTED out as any normal business day. Calm. Quiet. At least until Serena's beginner's watercolor class arrived. Heidi had disappeared into the office to go over sales numbers and Carrie was upstairs working on her computer.

Behind the sales counter, Serena figured out her own math on a piece of paper, calculating how much she'd have to save a week to reimburse the next victim on her list. Hmm… if she cut down on extras, like coffee from Sit a Spell, or lowered her grocery bills, she might squeeze enough money into the fund. *Might* being the operative word. She ran the numbers again. She needed a new stream of revenue, besides investors. Even though she'd sent Mrs. M. an update of the proposal, she was thinking of abandoning that idea, anyway. But what else?

She gazed out the wide store window, her nerves soothed by the comforting scene outside. Golden was beautiful in the morning.

Residents hurried about on the sidewalks, running errands or visiting with friends. The first of October was here, ushering in a noticeable trace of coolness in the air. This had always been her favorite time of the year. Once tourists descended upon Golden for Oktoberfest, the colorful leaves would be at their peak viewing pleasure. She'd decorated the store in her favorite harvest shades of orange, gold and red.

Glancing back at the page penciled in with numbers, she knew sales would pick up between now and Christmas, but the promise of an increase didn't affect her calculations. The idea of a harvest-themed class started brewing. Once she pushed the worries aside, she hoped the creative part of her brain would work up an idea she could run with.

"C'mon," she encouraged her muse. "Don't fail me now."

"Talking to yourself?" Heidi asked as she materialized beside Serena.

"Giving myself a pep talk."

Heidi leaned over to peek at the paper. "You do know accounting is my job."

"Of course." Serena folded the paper in half, hiding the figures from Heidi's shrewd, but nosy, gaze. "I was thinking about adding a new harvest-themed opportunity to raise sales. With all the tourists in town, I want something different to grab the market."

"Another class?"

"I suppose. That does fit into my wheelhouse, but I wanted to do something more interesting to reach the tourists."

"The annual changing-of-the-leaves tours are pretty much a staple, so that's out. Oktoberfest is covered."

Serena tapped her temple. "It's right there. I need to focus."

The door opened and two chatting women entered the store.

"Your creative mind will have to kick into gear after class."

Ignoring the arduous weight on her shoulders, Serena straightened. Tucked away her paper.

"Full class today," Heidi commented, her head angled as she studied Serena.

"Yes, it is. It's always satisfying with more people."

Heidi rested a hand on her hip. "Why do I get the feeling you're worried about money? You do know the business is doing well, right?"

"I do, and I'm so thankful you've got your finger on the finances."

"Then what's up with you? You've been wound tight lately."

Arranging her features in what she hoped was a neutral expression, Serena smiled at her friend. "Have you ever known a business owner who wasn't worried about income? Or new ways to drive revenue?"

"No, but you're usually pretty even-keeled."

"Blame it on expansion."

"The investors? Any bites yet?"

"No, but I didn't expect overnight success."

Heidi put her hands on Serena's shoulders and turned her toward the women arriving for class. "Go. Enjoy your students."

A small part of the stress she'd been hiding eased as she viewed the women mingling around the table. "I honestly love my classes."

"And people love you. Have fun."

Logan's voice sounded in her head.

Fun. Right. She smoothed her navy-and-white checkered dress and greeted the women. Soon, the supplies had been passed out and Serena explained the goal of the class.

"Just have fun. When I'm painting or drawing, that's when I come up with ideas to personalize cards. Whether for a birthday or to say thank you, even 'get well' themes, I make sure to add my own special touch. This is what today is all about, your own personal creativity." As the women began dipping their brushes into the paint, Serena walked around the table, adding suggestions here and there.

One of the women, Andrea, a mother of two daughters in grammar school, called over Serena.

"I haven't been able to take your calligraphy class, but I'd love to in the future."

"That's my most popular class, so we run them quite frequently."

"Now that the girls are in school and I'm home during the day, I'm thinking about ways to fill my time."

Serena walked to the counter, picked up a current class schedule and returned to hand it to Andrea. "I'd love to have you."

Andrea pulled her long blond braid over her shoulder and sat back in her chair. "I have to say, I was inspired by your story. I was on your website to find class times, but then spotted your bio. Makes me think that maybe I could start a business."

"What kind?"

"I like plants and flowers. Maybe I could start a landscape design service."

Serena loved to encourage women who were considering starting a project of their own.

"Sounds like you've done some serious thinking."

Andrea grinned. "I'd love to make my own hours and be home when the girls finish with school for the day."

"Then write down your ideas," she suggested. "I'm not going to lie—it's a lot of work getting a business up and running, but once you do, it's very fulfilling. My friend Carrie was instrumental in helping me start Blue Ridge Cottage. She's in town for a while. Maybe you can get together and discuss your vision."

Surprise, then pleasure, crossed Andrea's face. "You'd introduce me to your friend?"

"Sure. Why not? Women need to empower each other."

"Hear! Hear!" said an older woman at the opposite end of the table. "I so wish I was starting out again. Young ladies today are not afraid to go after their dreams and I admire that."

Serena grinned at Andrea, then moved to help the other women at the table.

"Speaking of your website," said another student, "I love your picture. Whoever took the photo captured you perfectly."

Serena stopped in her tracks. "Picture? No,

I think you must be mistaken. I don't have a picture on my website."

The woman dabbed her brush on the canvas. "Oh, no, Serena. It was most definitely you."

A burning sensation closely resembling fear twisted in her stomach. Serena had refused to post a picture of herself, even though Carrie had tried numerous times to convince her otherwise. Yes, she was overly guarded, but hadn't that caution kept her secrets safe so far? No, she'd been firm with Carrie. This had to be a mistake.

The class time couldn't pass quickly enough. Keeping a smile on her face, she tried not to panic. Once the ladies left, with Serena promising Andrea she'd set up an appointment with Carrie, she ran to the counter to open her laptop. After a few keystrokes she pulled up her website. Went light-headed when she saw a picture of herself on the home page.

Carrie must have taken the shot. Serena sat on a bench in Gold Dust Park. Her head was down, and her face was obscured by her long dark hair falling around her shoulders as she sketched on a large pad in her lap. If you looked hard enough, you could sort of make out Serena's features, but that wasn't the point. It might not be a full-on image, but Serena had been firm when she'd told Carrie never to put any photos of her online.

She grabbed her cell phone and sent a quick text asking Carrie to come downstairs.

Serena paced as she waited. Tried to slow her rapidly building panic. Ignored the sense of betrayal simmering in her chest.

"Hey, I got your text," Carrie said as she joined Serena in the store a few minutes later. "What's up?"

Serena swung around to confront her. Anger fueled by fear slithered out of her. "You put my picture on the Blue Ridge Cottage website after I told you not to."

Carrie frowned. "You told me that when you first started out. I didn't think you were still stuck on remaining faceless."

She swallowed around the knot in her throat. "Carrie, I haven't changed my mind. Take it down."

"I don't get why you're so camera-shy. It's important for your customers to put a face with a name." Noticing the open laptop, Carrie moved the screen so it faced them. "Your visibility is growing. People want to connect to you and your story. You make it harder by refusing to add a picture."

"I get that you're the marketing guru. The expert." Her voice rose to being on the edge of hysteria. "But I want the image gone. Today."

Heidi stuck her head into the store. "Hey, what's up with you two? I can hear you clear in the back."

Eyes narrowed, Carrie said, "Your boss is being stubborn and not considering the big picture."

Reaching deep inside to calm herself, without much success, Serena stood her ground. "We've done fine without my customers knowing what I look like. It's Aunt Mary's story that draws them in."

"At first." Carrie waved a hand, indicating the store. "But then they look at your beautiful artwork and want to know more about the artist behind the creations."

"There is enough about me there now. We don't need more," she barked at her friend.

Carrie blew out a breath and glanced at Heidi. "She's being unreasonable."

Heidi eyed them with uncertainty. "Serena, I have to agree with Carrie. People feel more connected if they recognize your face."

"And what if I don't want my face out there for the world to see?" she shouted, appalled at her total lack of control.

A troubled silence blanketed the room. Serena felt her cheeks heat. Her friends looked at her like she'd lost her mind. Well, she had for a moment, hadn't she?

Taking a breath, she said, "Carrie, please remove the picture. I own this business. I don't have to give you a reason why. I want it done."

"I'll do it right away," Carrie answered in a subdued tone.

Did she sound as horrible as she thought? Gathering her jumbled emotions, Serena said, "Thank you."

The tension lingered. Trying to recover a little dignity, Serena walked past the women to pick up her sketchbook and bag of colored pencils. "I'm leaving for a while." She looked at Heidi. "Please cover the store."

"Sure. I, ah…"

Stopping Heidi before she could say more, Serena held up a hand. "I'll be back in a few hours."

Chin high, she exited the store, fighting the burning sensation behind her eyes. She'd yelled at Carrie. Carrie, of all people. The one person who'd been in her corner since she'd come up with the idea to start Blue Ridge Cottage. What was wrong with her?

Your past is catching up to you.

No. It couldn't be. She'd been so careful. No one knew she was the person repaying her father's victims. No one knew Aunt Mary was the figment of her imagination who had become the story behind the business. Her father had opened a door to all their secrets and seemed unconcerned about it. Everything she'd worked so hard to contain was unraveling. Suddenly it was all too much to bear alone.

But she was alone. She was in too far to confide in her friends now. They'd be hurt that she hadn't told them the truth from the beginning. Then there was her reputation here in Golden. What would Mrs. M. think if the truth came out? She'd grown so attached to the woman, it would break her heart if Mrs. M. looked at her with disillusionment in her eyes. And if she found out that Serena was the daughter of a con man, Logan would find out, too.

She never should have told Mrs. M. about her business proposal. Never should have chanced bringing investors into her life. She'd have to shut the door on that idea.

She blindly hurried along the sidewalk, unsure of her destination. Her labored breathing had her wondering if she was having a panic attack. Maybe going deep into the woods would calm her down. She'd find a place to sit and draw until her mind settled. Possibly she could find some peace. Discover a way to get her life back on track.

"Serena. Wait up."

She glanced up. Logan. Not now.

She already suspected that he was way too curious about her. She'd tried to justify not worrying about him. Hoped his interest came from her friendship with his grandmother. They had an attraction she couldn't deny, and he'd even kissed her in a way Serena had only imagined in her romantic daydreams. He was determined—that much she knew. And if he was looking into her past? She shuddered at the possibility.

She stopped. Closed her eyes. She didn't want to see him, not now, when she was tied up in knots. Peeking through parted lids, she saw his purposeful stride as he came closer and realized she didn't have a choice.

LOGAN WATCHED SERENA'S face go from troubled to resigned. Seemed she wasn't thrilled to see him.

"Where are you off to?"

She nodded in a vague direction over her shoulder. "To find a place to sketch."

"Business slow?"

"No. I just need...to sketch."

"Mind some company?"

She averted his gaze. "Actually I do. I work better alone."

What was up with her? Yeah, she could be prickly at times, but what he liked best was her usually sunny personality. Today she looked like she was stranded under a bank of storm clouds and he wanted to make the shadows in her eyes go away.

"How about a pastry before you get to work? Frieda always puts a few apple fritters aside for me."

"Logan, I'm not hungry right now."

"All you have to do is walk over to the bakery. Heck, walk *by* the bakery and you'll change your mind once you smell all the sugary treats inside."

When she finally met his gaze, he was surprised by her despair. "You aren't going to let this go, are you?"

He rocked back on his heels. "If you want me to."

After a pause, she said, "Okay, but I only have time for a quick visit."

If he wasn't a pretty self-confident guy, he might have changed his mind due to her less-than-enthusiastic response to his invitation.

He followed her as she marched down the sidewalk and had to hide a smile when she slowed near the bakery entrance. She lifted her head and he imagined she was inhaling the sweetened air, just like him.

"I only have a few minutes," she warned as they went inside.

"That's all I need." He wanted to bring a smile to her lips and had to ask himself why. He wasn't the type of guy who needed everyone around him to be happy, but for some reason the idea of Serena unhappy bothered him. Then he started speculating on what had put her in a bad mood and his suspicious mind wanted answers. Now he understood why women didn't want to date him when he peppered them with questions. Occupational hazard. Or in this case, getting to the truth.

Minutes later they were back outside, Logan holding a bag with their pastries wrapped in waxed paper. After a quick detour to Sit a Spell for coffee, they took a seat at a shaded wrought-iron bistro table on the sidewalk nestled under a tree. Long limbs spread overhead. Beams of sun sneaked through the gaps in the gently waving leaves, allowing flashes of light to dance on the tabletop. A few cars passed by. Voices drifted from the coffee shop.

As he removed the lid from his cup, he inhaled the heady coffee scent and then opened the bag to place a fritter on the napkin before her.

"Why do I get the impression you're having a challenging day?" he asked when it became clear she wasn't going to initiate conversation.

"Maybe because I am," she said before taking a bite. She closed her eyes as she chewed, and he almost chuckled, having experienced firsthand that delicious first bite.

"Is it the store?" he ventured. "Usually I don't see you out and about during business hours."

She lifted a shoulder. "The store is fine."

"Then is it your friend? The one who showed up unannounced on your doorstep?"

Her eyes flicked to the side before focusing back on her fritter. "Carrie is fine."

"Not used to having a roommate?"

She looked up at him. "I could ask Reid the same thing."

He sat back in the armless chair.

"I know you're staying with him," she offered.

"I forgot how fast the small-town rumor mill works."

"It's not a rumor if it's true."

He tapped a finger on the edge of the table. "Yes. I'm bunking at Reid's for a while."

Her panicked gaze flew to his. "Is your

grandmother sick? Is that why you're staying in town?"

"Grandmother is fine. Still considering your updated proposal."

Serena placed a hand over her chest. "Thank goodness. After her health scare, I worry."

"She told you about that?" He couldn't be more surprised. Grandmother had kept her condition quiet. As far as he knew, only family was privy to her condition.

"Yes."

"Huh. Doesn't sound like her."

She sat up straight in the chair. "I haven't told anyone else, if that's what you're worried about."

"No. That hadn't crossed my mind. Grandmother isn't usually that forthcoming with people."

"I suppose she likes me," she stated as she pinched off a chunk of the fritter and placed it in her mouth.

He chuckled at the starch in her voice.

"She does like you." He paused. "So do I."

Her eyes narrowed as she glanced at him.

"What? A guy can't pay a compliment?"

"Not if the guy seems unusually interested in my business," she accused.

"I told you, Grandmother asked me to read over your proposal. Nothing more than that."

Okay, that was partially the truth, but he couldn't ignore the guilt he felt at covering up his true motives.

Her snort said she didn't believe him as she ate another piece of the fritter.

"Did we have a falling-out that I don't remember, because you're awfully prickly today."

She finished chewing and swallowed. "Sorry. It's one of those days."

"What kind of day?"

"When everything seems to be piling up and you can't breathe under the weight of it all."

His pushing to make her reveal what was going on with her now seemed selfish. "Didn't mean to add to the pile."

"It's me. I guess I'm touchy."

At her dejected expression, his instinctive reaction was to kiss away the frown. He didn't think she'd appreciate the gesture, so he forced himself to stay put.

"Anything I can do to help?"

"Thanks, but no. Things will work out," she said with a shake of her head. Trying to convince herself?

The questions about Serena bombarded him again, but he refrained from voicing any of them. She wasn't in the best of moods to respond, and if he wasn't careful, he might alienate her completely. With each passing day, Logan realized he wanted to know Serena better, despite the fact that his doubts about who she really was and what she was up to grew stronger with every dead end he hit.

"How about we change the subject?"

At her nod, he sipped his coffee then asked, "So what do you hope to draw today?"

"I'm not sure. I'll know when I see it."

"The creative process?"

"Something like that." She folded the empty waxed paper. "Are you creative?"

"Not if you consider a poorly drawn stick man high-end art."

Finally, a glimmer of a smile. The warmth in his chest spread.

"I have other strengths."

Interest glinted in her eyes. "Such as?"

"I can be relentless, especially when trying to make a woman I like smile."

"I bet you say that to lots of women."

Oddly enough, he didn't. Serena was the first woman in a long time that he cared enough about to want to see smiling. "I'm too busy to notice, which doesn't sound good as I'm admitting it out loud, but is usually the case."

"You're polite to everyone."

"That's kind of you to say, but not always true."

Serena paused as she started to speak. She tilted her head, then said, "Why do I get the feeling you and Deke are checking up on me?"

Surprise rendered him speechless. The woman was more perceptive than he gave her credit for. A major miscalculation on his part. He searched his mind for an answer. He couldn't use his grandmother as an excuse in this case, so he tried to deflect. "Why do you ask?"

"The other night at Smitty's you two had your heads together in conversation. Then you both looked over at me."

Yep, perceptive. Was she naturally that way or was she observant because she had something to hide?

"Deke and I were discussing business, that's all."

Interest lit her eyes. "What kind of business?"

Before he could answer, his father strode into his peripheral vision. He'd never been so happy to see the man.

"Dad," he greeted as he jumped up.

His father's steps faltered.

"Serena, you remember my father, Arthur Masterson."

"Yes. Hello, sir." She rose and gathered up her sketch pad. "Logan, thanks for the treat. I need to run."

"Are you sure, because—"

"I'm sure." She nodded at them and walked away.

As he watched her head to the park, his father took her empty seat. "Logan, we must talk."

Distracted, he sat down. Serena would be all right, wouldn't she?

"What do you need, Dad?"

"Who says I need anything?" Arthur bristled.

"It's been my experience that when you come to me, you want something."

"I suppose you aren't completely wrong." Logan's eyebrows rose.

"I just came from the office. Reid is still MIA."

"Give him time," Logan said, then sipped his coffee.

"I need him. There are important deals in the works and he's involved in each one."

"The more you push him, the more he'll stay away."

His father blew out a breath. "He can be stubborn."

"Gee, I wonder who he inherited that trait from?"

"Are you implying I'm stubborn?"

Logan leaned forward. "Let me ask you this. In light of Reid's defection, were you hoping I'd fill his place?"

"I was hoping to revisit that conversation."

Sitting back, Logan folded his arms over his chest. "Once again, the answer is no. Find a way to make things work with Reid."

His father stared across the street. Long moments passed before he met Logan's gaze. "You're truly done with Masterson Enterprises?"

"I'd have to have been a part of the business to begin with and I never was."

His father nodded. "You're satisfied in your line of work?"

"Not only satisfied, but good at what I do."

"I'm not surprised. You did always focus on what you wanted, then went for it."

Logan didn't respond. Wasn't sure what to say at his father's rare praise.

"Even in high school you were motivated. If not, you might never have found your birth certificate."

He froze. Where was his father going with this?

"You told me you wouldn't accept my apology until you were sure I meant it. I want to prove to you that I'm sorry for keeping the truth surrounding your birth from you."

What was his game? This man didn't always play by the rules, using strategic moves to his advantage.

"You're going to be in town for a while?" his father asked.

"At least until after Oktoberfest."

"Good. Perhaps we can spend more time together. Your mother would like to have you home more often."

So he was doing this on Bonnie's behalf? Made sense. And proved to Logan he was still the same.

"I'll make sure to see her while I'm here."

"She loves you, son."

He knew that. Bonnie had made sure to tell him since he was a child. But his dad… that was another story.

"Are we done here?" Logan asked, not willing to be duped into helping his father's agenda.

"Not quite. Your grandmother has informed me that she has decided to invest in Serena's business."

Logan hadn't talked to her in a few days. "When did she decide?"

"She told me this morning. I read over the new proposal and I'm afraid this might be a risky undertaking."

His father took risks daily. What was it about Serena that bothered him?

"I tracked you down to see if you would check into BRC, Co."

This made the third person who wanted to know more about Serena. His case was getting crowded.

"You know Grandmother likes Serena. It may be more that she wants to invest in a friend."

"Your grandmother has a good heart. And while that may well be true, I wouldn't feel right advising her unless I know more."

Okay, here came the tricky part. Did he confide that he was already investigating Serena? He could brush it off, but knowing his father, the man would find someone else to uncover information. He'd fess up, but leave Deke's request about her background out of it.

"I'm looking into her company, Dad. Grandmother already asked me to."

Surprise crossed the older man's face.

"Grandmother is smart. She knows not to invest her money because of sentiment. Yes, she likes Serena, but she wants to be sure the company is solid."

"And is it?"

"From what I've discovered, yes."

His father nodded. "Very good. But, son, for your grandmother's sake, I'd like you to keep an eye on the woman."

He had every intention of doing just that. Because the more time he spent with Serena, the harder it was to deny his increasing attraction to her. An attraction he shouldn't acknowledge because of the job, but he found his feelings growing stronger every day. Talk about conflict of interest.

"I agree. And I will. I'll also talk to Grandmother before she gives Serena her final decision."

"One thing we can both agree on." His father rose. "Keep me updated."

Logan stood. Gathered up the pastry wrapping and empty coffee cups. "I will."

"Perhaps over dinner at the house?"

Yep, the old man was stubborn. "We'll see."

His father gripped his shoulder in a tight clutch. "That's all I can ask," he said, then headed down the sidewalk back to the office.

Logan dumped the trash into a nearby container. Thought about joining Serena in the park, then decided she wasn't in the mood to be interrogated, so there was nothing to gain by infringing on her solitude. Except spending time with her, which he enjoyed way too much. He found himself thinking about the next time he'd see her, which was very unprofessional of him, but Serena was getting to him.

It was all he could do to keep from walking to the park, but he was a man who knew how to play the long game. Unless he stopped using the job as an excuse and lost his heart to her instead.

CHAPTER NINE

THE FIRST DAY of Oktoberfest dawned bright and chilly. The leaves had obliged the festival by changing into glorious shades and deep rich hues of yellow, brown and red. As Serena ran her usual route early Friday morning, she tried to enjoy the autumnal vista and not let worries bombard her.

Logan had been absent for over a week, which made Serena hope that out of sight meant out of mind and would keep her from thinking about him, but nope, he was in the forefront of her thoughts, anyway. She couldn't decide if she was relieved or if she missed him, intrusive questions and all.

Carrie had kept a wide berth from her, even after Serena apologized for her outburst. Her picture was taken off the website, but what if someone had seen it? All she could do was convince herself it hadn't been up long enough for anyone to notice.

After finishing her run, she cooled down by walking to Gold Dust Park. Earlier this week the volunteer teams had set up the festival tents, readied the serving areas and hung multicolored lanterns in the trees. Once the sun set, the outdoor *biergarten* would come alive with music and dancing.

Tonight was the kickoff. Serena was scheduled to work as a server in the food tent, where visitors could sit at the long stretches of tables to enjoy authentic schnitzel, potato dumplings and red cabbage. As she calculated the calories in the food choices, she figured if she indulged, she'd burn off plenty of energy while working Golden's annual celebration.

Just before she reached her apartment, Lissy Ann Tremaine, town event organizer, stopped her on the sidewalk and handed her a sheet of paper. As usual, her clothes were trendy, her jewelry tasteful and her perfume expensive. Serena tucked the strands of hair that had escaped her ponytail behind her ears and smoothed her rumpled tank top.

"Here is your work schedule for the next three weeks," Lissy Ann announced. "If you have to rearrange your block of time, there's a number at the bottom to call and we'll make arrangements to switch."

Serena glanced at the paper. She was scheduled almost every night. Between working at the store during the day and serving tourists at night, she was going to be busy.

"These are a lot of hours."

"Aren't you committed to making Golden *the* tourist stop in north Georgia?"

"Sure, but I also have customers at the store."

"It's only three weeks."

Said the woman who didn't work regular business hours. And by the demanding expression on her face, this woman was not going to accept any excuses to get out of volunteering. But this was one of the things Serena loved about Golden, right?

"Any suggestions on how to keep up the pace?"

Lissy Ann grinned. "Get a good night's sleep, drink lots of water and stay away from the beer."

"Gotcha."

Serena had taken a few steps away before Lissy Ann stopped her. "Serena, I've been thinking."

Oh, no. Serena had lived in Golden long enough to recognize that gleam in the other woman's eyes. It meant more work and she already had a full load.

"Your store is quite unique. We should feature it during Oktoberfest. Not everyone who comes to town is here for the food and drinks, and besides the sightseeing, it might be a way to keep folks who aren't into the festivities interested in Golden."

Well, she couldn't complain about this suggestion, could she? "What did you have in mind?"

"Is there any way we can highlight Aunt Mary's story? I know she's passed—bless her soul—but maybe we can capitalize on her influence. Isn't the cottage on your logo the source of inspiration for you to start Blue Ridge Cottage?"

Not exactly. "Um, yes."

"That's the white cottage set off in the woods outside of town?"

"It is."

"Hmm." Lissy Ann's brow wrinkled. "Think about it and get back to me."

"I will."

Wiggling her fingers, Lissy Ann hurried off to complete her duties. Relief swamped Serena. Another lie averted. She pushed aside the story of Aunt Mary and focused her thoughts on her day. Until Logan strode into view. Attraction and dread warred within her. The butterflies in her belly assured her that attraction won the battle.

"Serena. Haven't seen you in a while."

He looked good, better than ever, wearing a tan button-down shirt, dark jeans and loafers. She blinked, thinking he would make the most amazing magazine model. The way his wavy hair picked up the sunlight just so, his high cheekbones and probing brown eyes, well, she'd certainly buy a copy of anything if he graced the cover.

"You okay?" he asked as she stared at him.

She didn't miss the humor in his tone. "Sorry." She cleared her throat. "You've been busy?"

"I was in Atlanta all week."

"But now you're back for the start of Oktoberfest?"

He held up a paper. "Complete with a work schedule delivered personally from Lissy Ann."

"She is nothing if not efficient."

He jutted his chin toward the park. "Are you working tonight?"

Why did the question sound so…personal? Could he be interested in her schedule because he was interested in her? Logan was making conversation, polite as always, but it didn't mean he'd missed her while he was gone. Not like she'd missed him.

"Serena?"

Right. He'd asked her a question. She

shook off her distraction. "Yes, and most every night after."

"Me, too. Lissy Ann has me on—" he chuckled as he read the paper "—security."

"Does she expect the festival to get out of hand?"

"Not to my knowledge. There might be a few folks who enjoy a little too much beer, but for the most part, things should be pretty orderly."

"How long has it been since you've volunteered during Oktoberfest?"

"Before I left to join the military."

"So you don't actually know how the crowd will behave."

"True." He sent her a sly grin, making her heart flip in her chest. She was walking a tightrope with Logan, an off-kilter sensation that didn't bode well for her purposeful plans. If she allowed herself to get too deep in her growing affection for him, she might fall off the tightrope and shatter her carefully constructed world.

"But I can guarantee," he continued, "that the Tremaines won't let the crowds get rowdy. All for the good of Golden."

The crowds might be manageable, but what about her feelings for Logan?

"Right. Look, Logan—"

His phone rang. He pulled it from his pocket and glanced at the screen. "I have to take this."

Slowly easing out a long breath, Serena welcomed the interruption since she had no idea what she'd planned to say, but had a sneaking suspicion it would have been to ask him to spend some time with her. "I need to get home, anyway. See you tonight."

His crooked grin warmed her from the inside out. "Definitely."

Shaking off her heated reaction to Logan, Serena jogged around the building then up the stairs to her apartment. As she entered, breathing in a whiff of freshly brewed coffee, she spied Carrie at the table, hunched over her computer.

"And you wonder why your back hurts," Serena teased as she opened the refrigerator for a cold water bottle.

"Huh?" Carrie looked up and blinked. "Oh, right, I know, but when I get involved in a project, I lose track of time and correct posture."

"What are you working on?" Serena asked as she joined her friend.

"An old client of mine needed a rebranding campaign, so I signed on to work freelance with her company."

"Are you ever going to tell me what happened at your old job?"

Carrie peered at her closely. "What makes you think I don't have a job?"

"The fact that you're camped out here in Golden, which is a far cry from the big city you claim to love. Also, you've been spending a lot of hours in the store, which leads me to believe you don't have any work on your schedule."

With a sigh, Carrie leaned back in the chair. "I had hoped to fix things before coming clean with you, but it didn't work out."

Serena pulled out a chair and sat down. "Fix what things?"

Carrie closed the laptop. "Remember six months ago when I told you about the big client the agency had landed?"

"Sure. You were excited because you were named account executive on the project."

"Which went great for about five minutes."

"What happened?"

"The client was difficult from the get-go. Critical of every idea I presented. Made noises that they could do a better job in-house than I was doing. I was a nervous wreck for weeks, hardly slept trying to prove to the client, and my bosses, that I could get the job done."

"You did look pretty worn out when you showed up here."

Carrie picked up the mug at her elbow and took a sip before continuing. "Long story short, the clients accused me of trying to sabotage their brand with my terrible ideas. Even though the higher-ups at the agency knew I was eating and sleeping this account, they were not happy when the client eventually walked away. They had to blame someone."

"And it was you?"

"Yep. I was on pins and needles for about two weeks after the client pulled out, waiting for the bottom to drop. They finally fired me. The clients had made sure to let any other company in the area who would listen to them know that I had messed up. Even with a detailed résumé, I couldn't land a new job."

Serena placed a hand over Carrie's. "I'm so sorry."

"I was embarrassed. Decided getting away might help me get over the debacle, so I came here."

"And you can stay as long as you like."

Carrie's expression remained unconvinced.

"Look, I know I apologized for lashing out at you, but there is no one on the face of this earth I'd rather have doing my marketing than you. You're good at what you do, no matter that those clients couldn't see it."

Resting her elbows on the table, Carrie dropped her chin into her palms. "I check job listings every day. Send out my résumé. Hear nothing." She glanced at Serena with such dejection that Serena nearly cried for her friend. "Am I washed up at twenty-eight?"

"Hardly. This is a temporary bump in the road."

"If you say so."

"Hey, you've gotten work from an old client who thinks you can help them. It can't be all bad."

"True. I'm not taking this job for granted, but, Serena, I'm worried."

Join the club, Serena wanted to say, but couldn't. Again, the guilt of not being truthful to her good friend assailed her. Carrie had confided her worst worries, yet Serena had never told Carrie the entire scope of her past. The feeling, that the truth was going to come back to bite her any day now, simmered just below the surface. If she was smart she'd try to do damage control now, but old habits of keeping secrets buried deep inside kept her from spilling it all to her friend. What was wrong with her?

Instead of divulging her past to Carrie,

Serena said, "You know, the chamber of commerce could use your expertise. The Tremaines are trying to make Golden a premier tourist destination, but sometimes I think they have too many ideas that end up overwhelming vacationers. I could talk to Lissy Ann. See if they could use your marketing skills."

"I don't imagine it would come with much of a salary."

"Probably no salary."

Carrie groaned and buried her face in her hands.

"But you're welcome to stay here for however long you need to and you can have hours at the store."

"Thanks," she replied, the word muffled by her hands.

"Maybe you could let the local businesses in on your services. I could put in a good word and you might drum up accounts that way."

Carrie lifted her head. "I had hoped to get a job before it came to this, but you're right. I can leave my information all over town and see what happens."

Rising, Serena pushed the chair in and squeezed her friend's shoulder. "Think positive."

"You do know who you're talking to, don't you?"

"My dear friend who is great at marketing even if she is hard on herself. And now I have to get ready for work."

Carrie lifted the laptop lid and gazed at the screen. "That makes two of us."

As Serena changed and then jumped in the shower, her pep talk rang through her head. Shouldn't she take her own advice? She had to trust someone and it made sense to start with Carrie since she'd known her for so long. Or even Heidi, at this point. Hopefully they wouldn't be ticked that she hadn't revealed her past before now, but honestly, could she blame them if they were?

And Logan. He'd looked so handsome when they'd run into each other on the sidewalk. There was no denying he stirred up feelings in her that she'd never allowed before. He was a good man. A man who valued the truth. If she started a relationship with him and he learned the extent of her past and how she'd hidden it, would she ruin their chance at a relationship before it even started?

Was it possible she felt more trapped than ever before?

The warm water rained down and she lingered in the shower, her head pounding. She shut off the stream and wrapped herself in a fluffy towel, turning her attention to what to wear today. As distractions went, it wasn't great in terms of keeping her thoughts off the disaster that would transpire if she did something stupid, like fall in love with Logan.

IF THE BIG crowd was any indication, opening night of Oktoberfest was a success. From his location under the stone archway at the park entrance, Logan kept a steady eye on the revelers. On the other side of the park, Jamey played sentinel at his post. Streams of people queued up for food and beverages or broke into dance as the band played a lively polka number. The savory scent of bratwurst had his stomach growling but he ignored it, keeping his attention on the job at hand.

Nearby, his grandmother manned a table selling meal tickets, chatting up tourists and encouraging them to visit local shops while in town. From his vantage point he could see into the food tent, and he caught glimpses of Serena as she served heaping plates of food to the happy tourists. He could make out her flushed face under the lights and decided she'd never looked lovelier.

He'd placed the Stanhope job on the back burner this past week while he dealt with bigger issues at his office. Spending some time outside of Golden had let him put his feelings for Serena into perspective. He still needed more background information on both Stanhopes, but found himself oddly reluctant to uncover Serena's life. If she had a hidden past like he and Deke suspected, did he want to know what it was? He prided himself on always getting to the truth of the matter, but somewhere along the way his heart had engaged and he wanted to look the other way. Impossible, but he couldn't deny that he'd considered it. In the end, the truth, no matter where it took them, was the ultimate goal. If he didn't find out what she was all about, questions would remain between them and he realized he wanted a relationship free and clear from any entanglements that would cause them pain down the line.

He shook his head. Relationship? When had he begun to think of them in those terms?

"Logan. Can you please come over here?"

His grandmother's voice snapped him into the present. "What is it?"

She indicated a bank bag by her elbow. "Could you make a quick run to hand this off to Carter Tremaine? I'm not comfortable sitting here with all this cash."

"On it." Bag in hand, he made his way

through the crowd to find his old schoolmate barking out instructions to the local high-school band, who would take the stage after the next break. Logan pulled him aside.

"My grandmother would like you to empty this."

Carter felt the heft of the bag and a smile split his face. "This is only from two hours in?"

Logan nodded.

"Wait right here."

Carter took off, to place the money some-where safe, Logan hoped, and returned a few minutes later. "Tell your grandmother thanks for working tonight."

"And miss all the action? She wouldn't be anywhere else."

"How about you. Need anything?"

Logan almost looked around to see if Carter was speaking to someone else. He wasn't used to his old classmate being concerned about anyone but Carter.

"I'm good. Thanks for asking."

He handed Logan the empty bag. "Don't forget, volunteers can eat once the crowds head home."

"Your wife informed me."

Carter looked away at the mention of his wife.

Okay...

"I'm heading back to my post," Logan said, but Carter had already moved on to the next volunteer needing his attention. Logan walked across the park, taking an unplanned detour to poke his head into the food tent. Serena walked by, loaded down with a tray full of dishes, her cheeks red from the heat pouring out from under the canvas. It had to be a good ten degrees hotter in the tent.

"Having fun?" he yelled over the din.

Her gaze caught his and a smile blossomed as she deposited the plates. She lowered the now empty tray and sidled up to him.

"I wish someone had warned me it would be this busy."

"The first night always draws the biggest crowd."

She scanned the packed dining area. "It's like no one has ever eaten before."

Logan chuckled.

"How is security going?"

"So far so good. No citizen's arrests."

A shout came from the kitchen area.

"I need to run. More hungry mouths to feed."

She took off before he could ask her to meet him when they finished up for the night. Disappointed, he made his way back to the entrance. Since only a few stragglers came into the park now, he stood beside the table after handing the bag back to his grandmother.

"Quite a night," she said.

"If you mean a good start to the festival, then yes."

"You don't seem very excited."

He sent her a raised eyebrow. "I never liked all the hoopla, even when I was a kid and we sneaked in for sample cups of beer."

Grandmother looked surprised. "Why didn't I know about this?"

"Because we never got caught. And because we never got caught there was no excitement, so we didn't bother again."

"Goodness. I should have known. You always were adventurous." Her eagle gaze swept over the crowd. "The high-school band is playing tonight. Please make sure none of the underage performers swipe any samples."

He pulled out the empty chair beside her and sat down. "I will do my sworn duty."

"Sworn duty?"

"Lissy Ann swore me in as part of the official Oktoberfest security staff and made me promise to keep things under control."

"I bet the police chief won't be happy to hear he has additional staff he didn't hire."

"I'm sure he'll appreciate the help."

They sat together for a long moment, watching the people enjoying the crisp October night. A little over a week into the month and fall had finally shown up. Logan could taste the change in the air, was happy to wear a jacket early in the morning. It was almost like he could breathe after living with the muggy temperatures of summer for so long.

The town had decorated accordingly, with haystacks, pumpkins and even spooky bats and skeletons in advance of Halloween. It reminded him of all the good years before he'd discovered the truth behind his father's actions.

"I always loved Golden this time of year," he said.

Grandmother turned in her chair to look at him. "You could love it again, you know."

"I don't see that happening."

"Really? And what about Serena? Could she make you love living here again?"

He sent a sideways glance to his crafty grandmother. "Not very subtle."

"I'm beyond subtle. I adore Serena. I see you two falling in love."

If only she knew he was halfway there.

"Don't push it."

She leaned in. "So there's a chance?"

"I'm not really sure where we stand."

"I am." Grandmother looked across the park. "I saw you watching her in the food tent tonight."

"You make it sound creepy."

She chuckled. "No, more like a lovesick puppy."

"Not much of a compliment. And if you say anything to Reid, I'll deny it."

"Would it be so bad? Falling in love?"

Would it? He'd never been there, so he couldn't say for sure. "You know I have trust issues, Grandmother."

She waved her hand through the air. "Please. Just because your father made an error in judgment doesn't mean every marriage is doomed. I was afraid when you went into your line of work you'd become jaded."

"C'mon. You know I've never wanted to walk in Dad's footsteps."

"There are other men of character in our family line to emulate. Why, your grandfather was the finest man I knew. I loved him from the first moment I laid eyes on him and I still do to this day."

"I know Grandfather was a good man. So is Reid. But I can't help wondering…"

"Because you and your father are so alike?"

He ran a hand down his face. "I can't believe I'm agreeing with you, but yes."

"Then you look at his mistakes and make sure you never repeat them."

Was it that easy? And why did he doubt himself? He'd swore never to be like Arthur Masterson. Wasn't that enough?

"Logan, look at me," his grandmother demanded. He turned, not missing the sheen in her eyes under the bright lantern lights. "Love is worth experiencing. Until you discovered your birth certificate, you never doubted your parents' love. Or mine."

"I never question your love, Grandmother."

Her lips curved down. "Bonnie and your father do love you."

"Your point?"

"You can't deny your heart forever, Logan. There is a woman out there who is waiting for your love. And you for hers."

"And you're along to, what, accelerate the process?"

"I may tease about wanting you to marry before I die…" She paused. Frowned. "Okay, I mean it, but have I ever really pushed one particular woman on you? No. I've moved you in the general direction. Until now. Until Serena."

"Why are you convinced she's the one?"

"Why are you convinced she isn't?"

If his grandmother had posed this question a few weeks ago, he'd have had solid answers. Now he wasn't so sure. The line had grown fuzzy and he wanted to be with Serena, secrets and all, but he still had cold feet.

"How about I promise not to close the door on the possibility of love."

"You know, for all your bravado, you sure hesitate putting your heart on the line." She took his hand in hers, the touch of her soft, wrinkled skin comforting his uneasy mind. "Give love a chance, Logan. I promise it's worth the effort."

Uncomfortable by how much he wanted to believe her, he untangled his hand from hers. "Enough talk about relationships. I'm falling down on the job." An amusing thought occurred to him. "Maybe Lissy Ann will fire me."

"Our Lissy Ann? Oh, heavens, no. She's too softhearted for that."

He recalled the dynamo handing out detailed orders at the volunteers' meeting. "Are you sure?"

"I'm sure." She grinned at him. "About everything."

As a group came up to the table to buy tickets, Logan returned to his position while his grandmother got to work. He couldn't get their conversation out of his head, because like it or not, his grandmother was usually right.

A few hours later the crowd thinned out, leaving mainly volunteers in the food tent taking advantage of the empty chairs in order to put up their feet. His heart double-timed as he came upon Serena and her friends.

"Please tell me tonight is the busiest night," she pleaded.

"Every night is busy," Heidi answered.

Dropping her head back, Serena saw him and jerked upright. He pulled out a chair beside her and sat down.

"Don't tell me you're tired," he teased.

She recovered by straightening in her seat. "Tired doesn't begin to cover it. Did you see all the plates of food I delivered?"

"That we all delivered," Carrie corrected.

"My shoulders will be achy tomorrow," Serena grumbled.

Jamey ambled in from another direction and sat down. "Tonight was a breeze."

Three pairs of female eyes speared him.

"What did I say?"

"I believe the ladies are lamenting the size of the crowd as it correlates to their duties," Logan said.

"Not me," Heidi said. "Instead of people I see dollar signs."

Serena gaped at her. "That's horrible."

"And typical given her love of numbers," Carrie added.

Heidi shrugged. "I call it like I see it. And if we want to turn Golden into *the* vacation spot Lissy Ann keeps going on about, we need money to promote how awesome we are."

Logan didn't miss the exchange between Serena and Carrie. Of course, he didn't miss much of what Serena did. Now, who she was… that was another story.

Heidi didn't miss their look, either. "What're you thinking?"

"I told Carrie to offer her services to the chamber of commerce."

Heidi perked up. "Would you? That would help so much."

"I guess I could stop by tomorrow."

"We'll hold you to it," Jamey said.

Carrie lifted her chin. "I don't need you to tell me what to do."

Jamey merely smiled, making Carrie get up and stomp away. Logan leaned close to Serena. "What was that all about?"

"I have no idea." She turned and their gazes caught and held. After a drawn-out moment she said, "I should head home. I want to soak my feet before I go to bed."

Logan rose. "I'll walk with you."

"I don't want to put you out," Serena said, grimacing as she stood beside him.

"Think of me as your personal escort. If you need an arm to lean on, I'm here."

She turned and waved to Heidi and Jamey. "See you tomorrow."

"We'll be here," Heidi said with a knowing grin sent in Logan's direction.

Within minutes they were out of the park, heading down Main Street toward her apartment. The bright lampposts lit the way, the stores around them dark. Few folks lingered on the sidewalks at this late hour, as the locals went home after a busy day at work and the tourists did the same after their sightseeing.

"So, what did you think about volunteering for Oktoberfest?" Logan asked.

"I didn't realize it would be so painful." She sent him a scowl. "Why don't you look the least bit worn out?"

"Probably because I wasn't delivering platters of food all night."

"I get this is all for a good cause, but I sure hope I can keep up the momentum for three weeks."

"It'll get easier."

They moved on in silence for a few moments.

"Are you back at your brother's place?" she asked.

"For the time being."

As they passed under a lamppost, Logan looked down at her. Being this close, he felt his heart race like he'd set off a trip wire. His grandmother's words echoed in his head. *Take a chance.* Before he realized it, they'd reached her building and made their way to the back stairs. She paused at the bottom.

"Thanks for seeing me home. It was very gentlemanly of you."

"My pleasure, but I have to admit, I have an ulterior motive."

Her brow wrinkled. "You do?"

He moved into the space between them. Surprise lit her eyes, and then a slow smile curved her lips. He inhaled her lavender scent. Placed his hands on her hips. Leaned down and whispered, "There are no fireflies."

"That's okay. I think we can make our own magic."

She lifted her hands to his shoulders and stood on tiptoes. He lowered his mouth to hers, brushing her lips with his, once, twice, before settling in for a long kiss.

If caution bells rang, he chose to ignore them. Savored her instead. He'd never felt this way with a woman before. With Serena he could be himself and that was enough.

She finally broke the kiss and stepped back. Brought her fingertips to her lips. "Wow. That was…"

"Just the beginning?"

"You're pretty sure of yourself."

"I know a good thing when I see it."

"So do I." She stood on her toes and gave him a quick peck. "Not to get ahead of yourself, but I think we should call it a night."

He grinned.

"You don't have to look so happy about saying goodbye."

"I'm already thinking about kissing you again tomorrow."

With a laugh she dashed up the stairs, leaving him to wonder if all his concerns about them starting a relationship were for nothing.

CHAPTER TEN

THE FIRST WEEK of Oktoberfest blew by like a whirlwind. By the following Saturday afternoon, Serena was thinking twice about the busy schedule she'd been maintaining. Burning the candle at both ends wasn't ideal, although the side benefits were worth it.

Logan walked her home from the festival every night after the dinner shift. They'd spent more time together and there was no denying that she was seriously falling for him. They talked about the town, her classes at the store and how the holidays were fast approaching. What they didn't discuss was family. Either of theirs. Yes, it bothered her that she couldn't reveal her past. The day they'd sat on the bench together at the mountain outlook and he'd told her how his father had lied about his birth mother, she'd responded by saying people had reasons for keeping the truth to themselves. Hadn't she lived her life that way? Keeping her secret deeply buried to cover her shame? But when

Logan said that excuse didn't fly with him, she was convinced this spark between them would be extinguished if he discovered her family history.

Leave it to her to fall for a guy who valued the truth above all else.

So she pushed that fact from her mind. Tried to be clever and witty. Looked forward to stopping at the bottom of her apartment steps to indulge in lingering kisses that heated up the increasingly chilly nights.

Despite her reservations, she found herself looking for Logan in a crowd and wishing her childhood had been different. She still couldn't bring herself to come clean about her father's activities and her part in them. But what if he confessed that he had feelings for her? Just like she had for him? That would change everything and she suspected she'd tell him the truth.

The front door of Blue Ridge Cottage opened and a group of women entered. Serena called out a cheery hello. Due to the increase in tourist traffic, the store was bustling with daily activity. She had a new class later today that had filled up right away when she'd posted it on the website. If sales and class participation kept up this way, her money worries would be put to rest. She'd have enough income to pay back the next victim on her list without investors in the business and her secret would remain safe.

After Carrie had posted her picture on the website, Serena had started backpedaling in her quest for investors. Dumped all of her sleek proposal materials in the bottom drawer of her desk. She didn't want anyone poking around in her business. She also hadn't heard from her father despite multiple attempts to contact him. Putting her plans on hold for the time being seemed the best course of action.

On a positive note, she had friends now. Believed she could trust them. So maybe it wasn't a question of whether she should reveal her past. More like, was she willing to share her shame? She wanted to. So desperately. She was tired of carrying the load alone. But fear held her back. She didn't know if she could handle the disapproval she was sure to see on their faces. Especially Logan's.

A short line had started at the counter. Serena rang up sales while Heidi assisted customers on the sales floor. Yes, Serena convinced herself, with the rise in earnings, things would be fine.

The front door opened again and in came Mrs. Masterson, a big smile on her face. She waved at Serena as she crossed the room, all brisk and businesslike.

"Thank you," Serena said as she handed a bag to a customer before turning to her friend. "Mrs. M. How are you today?"

"Quite well, my dear." She glanced around. "I see you're busy, but may we speak? It will only take a moment."

"Certainly." Serena called Heidi, who took over the register, then led Mrs. M. to the small office.

"Would you like to have a seat?" Serena offered, pulling out the rolling office chair.

"No. Like I said, this will be quick." Mrs. M. opened her large handbag, removed a check and handed it to Serena with a flourish. "For your expansion. I've decided to invest."

Serena glanced at the amount. She should be excited but only felt dread. It had been a while since she'd resubmitted the proposal and assumed the woman had decided against investing. Why now, when Serena had changed her mind?

"Oh, Mrs. M., I appreciate it, but maybe we should put this off until after the holidays." She tried to hand back the check, but Mrs. M. shooed her hand away.

"Serena, I studied your revised proposal and I want to be a part of the growth of your company."

"I, ah…"

Mrs. M. sent her a curious gaze. "Don't tell me you've had a change of heart."

The kind woman was giving her a way out and she latched on to it. "This tourist season has increased revenue. So perhaps I was a bit hasty to look for investors."

"Nonsense. You're a smart businesswoman. Expansion in your case makes sense."

And the door of excuses closed.

"I know you've been spending time with my grandson. He hasn't discouraged you, has he?"

She pictured Logan, his teasing smile, his coffee-colored eyes when they grew heated before he kissed her. She held back a shiver. "We haven't talked about my business. Not the financial end, anyway."

"Then there's no reason not to go forward with your plan." Mrs. M. took the check from Serena's hand and placed it on the desk. "You hold on to this. Seriously think about what you might be giving up if you rethink things. I'm available as a sounding board anytime you need me."

"Thank you." Serena glanced at the check then back to Mrs. M. "I'll consider everything."

"Wonderful. And speaking of my grandson—"

Serena held back a grimace. They hadn't been, but he was never far from her thoughts.

"He isn't one to rush into relationships, but he definitely has his eye on you. I understand he's been escorting you home when Oktoberfest shuts down for the night."

The memory of his kisses and laughter filled her head. "That's true."

The older woman's eyes lit up with a matchmaker's gleam. "Then there's hope."

For who? she wanted to ask, but pressed her lips together. Hope that Logan would fall in love with Serena and overlook her past if it came to light? Hardly. She knew he wasn't wired that way.

She wanted love. A family. The freedom to live her life without looking over her shoulder. But that wasn't her reality. Keeping her secret locked away meant keeping her friends, and Logan, at arm's length. Mrs. M.'s generous investment reminded her of that.

"Serena?"

Blinking back stinging tears, Serena forced a smile. "I have a feeling you'll find your feet on the ground floor of many growing businesses, Mrs. M. If I decide to rethink my strategy, I'm sure you'll understand."

A quick flash of disappointment crossed Mrs. M.'s face. "Your store is quite unique, so my offer remains."

Before Serena could argue, Heidi popped her head into the room. "Need help," she squeaked, then disappeared.

"Duty calls," Serena said, thankful for the reprieve.

"I won't keep you." Mrs. M. closed her purse. "Stay in touch."

"I will."

Serena walked Mrs. M. to the front of the store and said a final goodbye. Her words were tinged with regret, she noticed before answering a shopper's questions.

The rest of the day passed quickly. At four, a group of women in their twenties assembled for a greeting-card class. As Serena handed out supplies, the chatty group discussed retro ideas for vintage cards. Serena encouraged their designs and the girls decided the session was definitely cool.

"This is way more fun than texting," one of the group said, followed by agreements. The hour flew by, and before she knew it, Serena was asking them to finish up.

One of the older women pulled Serena aside.

"This is going to sound odd," she said, "but you look very familiar. Have we met before?"

Serena had noticed this woman sending her questioning glances more than once during class, but she didn't recognize her.

"I don't think so," Serena said quickly as her stomach twisted.

"It must be your eye color. That shade of blue is very memorable."

Just what Serena had been afraid of when Carrie posted her photo. "I'm afraid you're mistaken."

"Hmm. I'm usually pretty good at remembering faces." The woman tapped a finger against her lips. "Maybe it's the story of your aunt Mary that is playing with my memory."

Serena scooped up the woman's project with trembling fingers and slipped it into a store bag. "Be sure to let me know if you figure it out," she said, trying to usher the woman out of the store without looking obvious.

Before long all the customers were gone and Heidi locked the door. Serena's shoulders sagged with relief as she gathered the leftover supplies from the class.

Heidi let out a long breath. "I don't know about you, but I'm tempted to call in sick tonight. The idea of delivering heavy trays of food to hungry tourists is more than I can endure."

"You don't honestly think Lissy Ann will approve time off, do you?"

Heidi frowned. "She's tough, no denying."

"I'm with you, though." Serena dropped down into a chair at the craft table. "Maybe we could organize a strike."

"Which Lissy Ann would ignore. She'd talk us right back into volunteer duty."

Serena chuckled. "We have an hour before the shift starts."

Heidi wandered over and joined Serena at the table. She glanced around the room and said, "As much as I love customers, this is the first time all day it's been quiet in here."

Serena tossed markers into a bin. "It is pretty awesome."

Heidi took a marker and rotated it between her fingers. "So, want to tell me why you were in such a hurry to get that last group out of here?"

Serena's head jerked up. "What are you talking about?"

"Ever since you went ballistic over Carrie putting your picture on the website, you get jumpy whenever someone thinks they know you. Why?"

She tried to stall. "It's weird. I don't want people thinking they know me."

"You're the face of the business."

Serena looked away. "I don't want to be."

"Then let Aunt Mary's memory take over."

Closing her eyes for a second, Serena drew in a breath. Too many secrets were piling up, and Heidi was much too perceptive. Hadn't her friend witnessed her meltdown over the website picture? And truth be told, the secrecy was weighing on Serena. Maybe she could let this one fib go.

"There is no Aunt Mary. There never was."

Heidi sat back in the chair, her eyes wide. "Come again?"

"I made her up."

Heidi blew out a breath. She leaned forward, resting her elbows on the table. "Tell me."

"It goes back to college."

"Your infamous business model?"

She nodded. "One of the things I learned was that people love a story. Think about some of the successful brands we know. They all have a backstory."

"So you made up Aunt Mary?"

Oh, yes. She'd learned a thing or two from her con-artist dad.

"She sort of came to me as I was preparing

for the project. I guess you could say she's a compilation of women I remember from when I was a child." She hesitated, then unburdened herself. "My mother was a storyteller, delighting my father and me with worlds she'd created to entertain us. Her best friend, Mary, loved to draw and used to come up with scenes for the stories. When she noticed my artistic talent, Mary encouraged me to draw. After my mother died, I lost touch with Mary, but I remembered the hours we'd spent immersed in our art projects."

"So then she really isn't a lie."

Serena cringed. "She wasn't my aunt."

Heidi looked away, but not before Serena caught an odd glint in her eyes. "Sometimes close friends become your real family."

They did, but they couldn't in Serena's case. "I needed a theme and Mary's artwork came to me. The idea sort of mushroomed from there. My professor assumed Aunt Mary was real and encouraged me to make her story part of my business proposal. I guess I got caught up in the excitement, especially when I started selling items online."

"Now I get why you didn't want your face on the website."

"I know people like the idea of Aunt Mary inspiring me. I suppose I should ease away from it, focus more on my own talents, but to be honest, she's been with me from the start."

"I get it. She may be a story, but she's your story."

"Yes."

The room went silent. Serena folded her hands. She'd done it. She'd unburdened a lie she'd lived with for years. Why didn't she feel better?

"Can I make a suggestion?"

Serena met her friend's solemn gaze.

"Keep Aunt Mary alive. Even if she's made up, she's important to you."

Tears blurred Serena's vision. "Thanks," she whispered.

Heidi reached out to place her hand over Serena's. "We all have secrets."

Serena glanced up, wondering what Heidi's secrets were.

"Yours are safe with me."

It was all Serena could do not to slump in relief. Being honest with Heidi had been a huge step. It didn't diminish the shame she felt at having duped families with her father, but it made her feel that maybe, just maybe, she might be able to figure out a way to reconcile what she'd done and still maintain relationships with those who were becoming important in her life.

Logan Masterson topped that list.

DINNER AT MASTERSON HOUSE hadn't been as excruciating as usual, a bright spot in Logan's busy day. Reid had declined the invitation—again—but at least his father didn't harp on it during the meal. Or blame Logan for his brother's defection. Grandmother and Bonnie carried most of the conversation, highlighting such topics as the next Golden Ladies' Guild project, the crowds swarming the town for Oktoberfest and the delicious meal Alveda had prepared.

He kept waiting for his father to hound him about joining the family business, and was pleased when an entire evening passed by without a word. Could he have finally come to terms with Logan's decision?

After he'd said goodbye to Bonnie and his grandmother and was about to escape to the town park, his father stopped him in the foyer.

"Logan, a word."

Holding back a sigh at losing his chance to slip out of the house, he turned to face his father. "I have to get to my shift at Oktoberfest."

"It will only take a minute. My study."

Resigned to the fact that he wouldn't take no for an answer, Logan strode down the hallway to his father's inner sanctum. He'd come to hate this room after the truth about his birth was revealed here. They'd argued and shouted at each other until Logan had stormed from the room. He could still hear the front door banging off the wall after he'd gone, fueled by hurt and anger. Remembered disappearing into the night, then sitting by the calm lake, where he came to a final decision to join the military.

His father closed the ornate office door behind him and motioned for Logan to have a seat in a leather armchair. Logan tensed as he tried not to let the events of that time long ago color their discussion tonight.

"What's so important?" Logan asked as his father took a seat behind his massive mahogany desk.

"Your grandmother."

Logan sat forward, fingers gripping the chair arms. "Is she ill?"

"No. Nothing like that. Her health is fine." His father rested his forearms on the desk. His gray hair gleamed in the light pouring from a nearby floor lamp. "She informed me today that she wrote a check for Serena Stanhope's business."

Grateful that his grandmother wasn't experiencing health problems, Logan sat back. He wasn't surprised by his grandmother's decision. He'd expected it, especially in light of her friendship with Serena. "And you have a problem with that?"

"Your grandmother is business-savvy, but as I said, I have questions."

"Which Grandmother didn't want to hear."

"As usual, she's made her mind up and there is no swaying her."

Logan allowed a small grin.

His father cleared his throat. "Have you learned anything new?"

Logan squared his shoulders, sure the old man wouldn't like his answer.

"You did the background check on BRC, Co.?" He raised a hand as if to hold off Logan's response. "I simply want to make sure the proposal is legit. We don't need another episode of tenants taking advantage of your grandmother."

Logan rose and walked to the bookshelf. Studying the neatly shelved books with worn covers, he weighed the wisdom of how much information to reveal. He glanced at his father. Just like their discussion at Smitty's,

Logan couldn't ignore the impression that life had worn down Arthur Masterson. The lines on his face and the rounded shoulders were more pronounced than usual. His father still maintained a larger-than-life presence, but he looked every bit his sixty years.

His mind flashed to the conversation at the park with his grandmother. How Logan had admitted that he and his father were alike. Did he really want to resemble a man he didn't admire? Once again he wished that his father had handled things differently in the past. Hadn't blown off the truth that had torn apart Logan's world. Instead he had marginalized events and their relationship had suffered. That didn't, however, mean they couldn't look out for the woman they both loved.

"Since Grandmother hired me to check on Serena's business, nothing has changed."

His father's eyebrows rose. "I guess I shouldn't be surprised. You are thorough." He paused. Met Logan's gaze. "So why are you still in town?"

Logan couldn't answer, not without revealing the entirety of his investigation.

When he looked away, his father tried a different tactic. "Can you be more specific about Serena?"

"Blue Ridge Cottage is in good financial shape. No bankruptcy issues. Not behind on vendor payments. I believe her vision to expand the business model is her only motivation." While he still had questions about the Stanhopes, could Logan swear that Serena would never intentionally mislead his grandmother? He hoped she wouldn't, especially in light of his growing attraction for her.

The woman had started and grown a very successful business. Logan admired her and found it hard to believe she could be a con artist, like they suspected her father to be. She seemed to be on the up-and-up. Was sensitive, kind and fun. He'd laughed more with her than he had with anyone in a long time. And if he was totally honest, she stirred up strong romantic feelings he'd never experienced with another woman. As much as he had no control over his growing regard for her, he sure hoped she didn't prove him wrong.

"Hmm." His father tapped a finger on the desk blotter. "You're still here because of your interest in Serena?"

His father may look tired, but he was still sharp as a tack.

Logan leveled his tone. "Why would I discuss my reasons for staying in town with you?"

His father waited a beat. "Fair enough."

Logan didn't expect that answer. He was too used to his father telling him what to think or do.

Talk about a dilemma. Did he engage in this personal side of the conversation? It all boiled down to how much he wanted to reconnect with his father, if at all. In the few weeks he'd been in town, he couldn't deny how much he'd missed his family. Yes, he'd been shocked and hurt by his father's betrayal and handling of the truth, but he was a man now. He was weary of carrying the anger he'd let define his life for so many years. It was time to either forgive his parents or keep perpetuating this schism with no productive outcome.

"To be honest, I've enjoyed catching up with family," he admitted. "Staying with Reid has been like old times. And I'll always come when Grandmother calls."

"Unlike your mother and me?"

Logan gritted his teeth.

"Unfortunately I know the answer to that." His father rested his elbows on the arms of his chair. "I've been pleased that you've come to the house for dinner." He paused again before emotion crept into his voice. "Your mother has missed you."

Hearing the unspoken "I've missed you, too," Logan tried not to cringe. He loved Bonnie, but she'd been part of the cover-up as well. She was trying hard to draw him back into the family, but was that enough?

His father continued in a hushed tone. "We all get to a certain age when the mistakes of the past are too much to bear and must be rectified."

Logan met his father's gaze. Saw the sincerity reflected there.

He returned to the chair and sat. Since his father was in a mellow mood, Logan decided to take the risk. "Can I ask you something?"

His father nodded.

"Tell me about my mother."

Surprise flickered in the older man's eyes. As he gathered himself, the only sound in the silent room came from the steady tick of the mantel clock. Finally, he said, "She was a good woman. Pretty. Kind to everyone she met."

Logan noticed a hint of sadness on his father's face, but it was quickly gone.

"I was leaving a meeting in Atlanta. As I hurried out of the building, we collided. It was on the tip of my tongue to tell her to watch where she was going, but she stepped back and sent me the most beautiful smile. I stopped in my tracks. She asked where the fire was and I started laughing. To apologize for my behavior, I took her to a nearby coffee shop. We spent the afternoon talking. Her sunny personality was infectious, and as our conversation continued, about everything and nothing, her positive outlook on life encouraged me." He met Logan's gaze. "It was easy to be smitten by your charming mother."

Logan swallowed around the knot lodged in his throat. "You became involved?"

Arthur rose and stalked to the window. Stared out at the rapidly approaching nightfall. Logan could just make out the stars in the sky over his father's shoulder.

"I'm not the easiest man to get along with." He shot Logan an amused glance before sobering. "Bonnie and I had...marital problems and I was too full of myself to consider her feelings. After we separated I met your mother and we...clicked. The attraction was sudden and strong and I allowed it to get the best of me. When she discovered she was pregnant and I refused to divorce Bonnie, your mother left."

"Did you look for her?"

"To no avail. She contacted me after you

were born. Then the accident transpired and Bonnie and I decided to raise you together."

His voice tight, Logan asked, "Why not tell me the truth from the beginning?"

His father ran a hand through his thick hair and returned to his seat. "Pride." A ghost of a smile moved his lips. "When your mother died, I asked Bonnie what we should do. She took one look at you and declared she was your mother. I guess I thought that would be enough. Why tell you about my sordid past when I could cover it up, like it had never happened?"

"But it did." Logan paused. "I wouldn't have been angry with you."

"That's what you say now." He sent Logan a sad smile. "You looked up to me and I'd kept this huge secret for years. As you got older, it seemed smarter to never reveal the truth."

"You know the truth always comes out. It's one of the fundamentals I've learned since becoming a private investigator."

"I realize that now. And why being honest is so important to you."

Both fell silent again. Logan ran a hand over his chest. "I'm mostly angry over the way you handled the situation when I found the birth certificate."

"Again. My narrow thinking. I'd decided what was best, regardless of your feelings. Thought I knew better. Didn't give your reasonable reaction any validity. I could have listened to your point of view. Taken into consideration your shock. I was too stubborn to do otherwise. I'm sorry."

Finally. A real apology.

Whenever they'd discussed this topic before, his father had been haughty and belligerent. Tonight, he seemed remorseful. Could his father finally, after all this time, truly be sorry?

"So where do we stand?" Logan asked.

"The ball is in your court, son. I'll always be your father, so I must ask again, do you forgive me?"

Did he? He'd carried the anger around like a tight-fitting coat for so long, he wasn't sure how he'd feel devoid of it.

"We're family, Logan. For better or worse."

His father was right. It was time to accept the olive branch, but it would still take a while to repair their relationship.

"Apology accepted." Logan rose. "In the meantime, I'll continue to watch Grandmother's interactions with Serena. Make sure everything is legitimate."

"Thank you."

"And a word of advice?"

His father nodded.

"Lay off Reid. He's got to figure out his life on his own."

"Point taken."

Logan closed the door behind him and started down the dim hallway. He hadn't expected the conversation to go the way it had, but the usual tightness in his chest after spending time with his father was missing. It felt good to finally reconcile the past.

He stepped into the foyer when his grandmother appeared.

"I thought you'd left."

"Dad and I needed to speak first."

"And…?" One perceptive eyebrow rose.

He sent her a reluctant grin. "We made progress."

His grandmother rushed over to hug him. He inhaled the familiar perfume, savored the love she wrapped around him and felt more a part of the family than he had in thirteen years.

She pulled back, tears shimmering in her eyes. "You know this is what I've wished for."

"I know."

She patted his arm. "You're such a good boy. Now you'll fulfill my next wish."

"Next wish?"

"For you to be married and give me great-grandchildren."

He held back a groan.

"I mean it, young man. You'd better get serious before some other discerning man swoops up Serena."

"You're rushing things."

"Am I?" she asked, all fake innocence.

He kissed her cheek and stepped into the dark night, focused on Serena. Because his grandmother had mentioned her?

No, an inner voice taunted. *She was already on your mind.*

CHAPTER ELEVEN

THE FOLLOWING WEDNESDAY, Logan jogged into Gold Dust Park thirty minutes late for his Oktoberfest shift to find Deke manning the station. He slowed his steps, happy to see his friend for two reasons. One, he'd never hear the end of it from Lissy Ann if he was late and hadn't found a replacement to cover his post, and two, he had good news on the Stanhope case.

"Thanks, man," he said as he reached the park entrance.

"No problem," Deke replied. "But I have to ask, what kept you?"

Logan glanced toward the food tent, catching a glimpse of Serena delivering a tray of items to hungry visitors, then returned his gaze to Deke. His excitement was tempered by the fact that his discovery might affect his relationship with Serena, but he had to move forward. "I finally got my first concrete lead on Stanhope."

Deke's eyebrows rose. "Credible?"

"I'll let you know in a few days, but I think so."

Deke pushed away from the stone archway he'd been leaning against. "Care to share the details?"

Logan made sure to angle away from the ticket table. No point in allowing the chatting ladies to be privy to the conversation. He stepped closer to Deke and in a low voice said, "I haven't found a social security number for Serena, which is a whole other problem, but discovered early in the investigation that she does have an employer ID number. That got me thinking that Stanhope might have applied for a number if he was running a business scam. It took a couple of hours, but I found an employer number attached to the name *Stanton*."

"A close variation of Stanhope."

"Correct. There were different types of businesses listed, but they all closed up years ago. I ran the names through a fraud database and found a complaint. I'm going to talk to the couple who filed it and see what information they can provide me."

"What kind of business?"

"A savings and investment firm. Something called Tomorrow's Solutions. From what I could gather, the company was meant to help people save money or increase their investment funds through deals and other projects."

"Only they never received the money when they needed it? Or any money, for that matter."

"Bingo."

When Logan had first made the connection, he was pumped. Putting in the hours was necessary when hunting a good lead, and his patience had paid off. James Tate, Stanton or Stanhope had covered his tracks, but all it took was one solid lead to uncover all sorts of secrets. Logan was sure that checking into the complaint would help him make progress on the case.

But after thinking about what he was doing—digging into the life of a woman he was involved with to get information on her father—he couldn't quell his doubts. Serena took him at face value, having no reason to believe he was a PI delving into her family history. Sure, it seemed like a great case for his agency, but on a personal level, he had mounting reservations about his deception, because Serena would certainly look at his actions that way.

"Want me to tag along when you question the couple?" Deke asked.

"I know you're champing at the bit, but it's

best if I talk to these folks alone. I want them to feel comfortable enough to confide in me. If you're hovering, it may add stress to the situation. This time, I go solo."

Deke nodded. "When are you leaving?"

"I'm heading into Atlanta to my office first thing tomorrow morning. After setting up an appointment, I'll drive out to see the family."

"Do you want me to inform my brothers?"

"Mind holding off until I have real answers? I may be close, but you know things can go sideways in an interview."

"I can wait." Deke jerked out his chin. "As long as you have results."

Logan grinned. "Doubting me?"

"No, but Stanhope has been more slippery than we expected."

"The best con men are."

Deke glanced across the park. Logan followed his line of sight. Serena. He refused to acknowledge the regret twisting in his stomach.

"I'll keep working on the fraud end. I have a few ideas, but let me run with the information I have first."

His friend looked back at him. In the evening shadows Logan almost missed the censure in his eyes. "I gotta ask, Logan. What happens if Serena is up to her pretty little neck in all of this?"

It wasn't like Logan hadn't pondered that very question himself. He'd spent sleepless nights asking why he'd allowed himself to become intrigued by a woman with a hidden past. It still didn't stop him from spending time with her, walking her home after her dinner shifts, stealing kisses under the harvest moon. If her con-artist dad finally got nailed, would she hate Logan? He had it bad for Serena, and if this lead panned out, it might do serious damage to his heart, and hers, but he was in too far to back off now.

"I'll be honest—I'm not sure."

Deke's gaze pierced his, steady and unrelenting. "Do you have feelings for her?"

Oh, yeah.

The need to be with her every day had sneaked up on him, surprising him by the intensity of his emotions. When he'd started this job, he expected an easy case, no messy entanglements. He'd been prepared to spend time with Serena to get results, but that had backfired big-time. She'd ensnared his heart so completely, with her winsome smile and encouraging words, he would never be the same again.

But he couldn't admit that to Deke. Was

having a hard enough time coming to terms with the realization himself. "Nothing I'll let hinder the case."

Was that pity he spied in Deke's eyes? He surprised Logan when he muttered, "There's something about these Golden women."

"Which is why when this case is over, I'm headed back to Atlanta full-time."

"Think it'll be that easy?"

No, he didn't. It would take everything in his power to walk away from Serena and Golden.

Logan considered his friend. "I take it you're speaking from experience?"

"I haven't left, have I?"

True. Deke and Grace were solid. Logan didn't know if he and Serena could ever be that concrete. Not with all the questions piling up. He'd never come up against personal stakes in a case until now. Didn't like the ramifications. This entire situation could become messy and painful, but he was duty-bound to see the investigation through. He'd do everything in his power to shield Serena from the worst of the fallout and be there for her in the aftermath, if she'd let him.

Deke leaned over to clap Logan's shoulder. "Good luck, my friend. You're going to need it." Then he walked into the crowd.

Truer words had never been spoken.

Expelling a deep sigh, Logan moved into the shadows to watch the activity in the park. As he stood there, Deke's words echoed in his head. Did his friend offer him luck for the case or because of his rapidly growing feelings for Serena? Probably both. He ran a hand over his face. He should be rehearsing what he'd say to Serena when he told her he'd been investigating her to get to her father. He owed her that much.

Unable to do anything at the moment, Logan settled in for his shift. The first hour crawled by, but the second picked up. He broke up a brawl between two teenage boys, arguing over a girl. Surprise. Then he escorted an overzealous festival guest back to his hotel. He still wore a button-down shirt and jeans, but now there was a tear in his sleeve. By the time he returned to the park, the crowd had cleared out and the volunteers gathered under the tent for a bite to eat and a recap.

His chest squeezed tight when he met Serena's gaze. Her hair was pulled up in a messy bun. Long strands had escaped confinement and framed her pretty face. As soon as she noticed him, she flashed a smile so bright it hurt. She pulled out the chair beside her and nodded to the heaping plate on the table. She'd brought him dinner? After serving others all night?

"Braised brisket and potato dumplings tonight," she said as he took his seat. The food smelled great and his stomach responded with a long growl.

Serena laughed. "Hungry?"

He picked up his fork. "Got caught up in work today and lost track of time."

"This will fill you up."

Her arm brushed his and her lavender scent invaded his space. If he'd actually expected to put some much-needed space between them until he finished his job, he was sorely mistaken.

Conversation flowed freely after Lissy Ann gave her nightly report. He had to admit, getting reacquainted with friends and hanging out together while doing his part for Golden hadn't been as smothering as he'd expected. He liked living in Atlanta because of the job prospects, but the feeling of belonging here was hard to ignore. Not just with his friends, but his family as well. Could he have experienced this sense of being a part of something bigger than himself if he'd come home sooner? Too late to tell now, but he was happy with the personal strides he'd made in the past month.

"You're awfully quiet tonight," Serena said after he finished his meal. He wiped his hands on the paper napkin and tossed it on the plate.

"Long day."

Her deep blue eyes shone in the subdued lighting. "So you said."

Yeah, this was harder than he'd imagined. He didn't like deceiving Serena when there was a distinct possibility her father was deceiving them all. He was all about truth, wasn't he? At least that was what he said. Could he carry this through until the end?

He needed the next few days out of town to straighten his head.

"Serena. I have a lot on my mind right now."

He ignored the sting when her sunny expression turned to uncertainty. "I didn't mean to bother you."

"You're not..." He blew out a breath. What more could he say?

She scooted away from him, taking her warmth with her. He missed it immediately. When he glanced across the table, Deke, who sat with his arm around Grace, looked at him questioningly.

Serena jumped up and started clearing away the empty plates. He joined her, not wanting her to take on the burden alone.

After dumping the paper plates in the trash bin, Serena stepped around him for a pitcher of iced tea to refill glasses.

"Let me," Logan said, reaching out to help.

"I've got it." As she swung away, tea splashed over the rim. She stopped and steadied her grip.

"You're making a mess."

She shot him an annoyed look and tried to walk away, but he grabbed her hand. "Serena."

Long seconds passed before she looked up.

"I'm sorry," he said. "I'm acting like a jerk and you deserve better than my bad mood. Can we start over?"

She considered him for a long, drawn-out moment and finally said, "Hello, Logan. How was your day?"

He released a breath. "Productive. Yours?"

"Lots of sales at the store."

He nodded to the table. "Why don't we take our seats."

He followed her back to the others to find only Deke and Grace remained. At Deke's scowl, Serena hesitated before sitting.

"So, Grace," Logan said to cut the tension, "how is the vacation business?"

Grace perked up. "Deke has been busy, so I'm not complaining. The festival is drawing all kinds of crowds." She glanced at Serena. "Your store must be busy as well."

"It is." Serena's gaze darted from Grace to Deke and back. "Super busy, in fact."

Grace glanced up at her boyfriend. Elbowed him in the side before rising. She turned to Serena. "Mind coming to the restroom with me?"

Serena jumped up, sending a shaky smile to Logan and completely ignoring Deke.

After the women walked away, Logan rested his elbows on the table. "Dude, why don't you hold up a sign saying you don't trust Serena?"

"Blame it on your earlier news. I keep picturing my mother with that con artist and it makes my blood boil."

"Well, stop it. You're going to spook her and then I may never get to the bottom of your case."

Deke ran his hand down his face. "You're right."

Logan leaned back and crossed his arms over his chest. "I'm always right."

Deke chuckled. "I'll weigh in on that after you bring me results."

Yeah, Logan thought, there was the pesky

need for results. To wrap up this case once
and for all. Worst-case scenario meant losing Serena, the most honest, real thing that
had ever happened to him.

SERENA WASHED HER HANDS, meeting Grace's
gaze in the mirror over the sinks. "Something
is going on, isn't it?"

Grace quickly looked away to pull paper
towels from the dispenser. "Everyone is tired.
It's week two of Oktoberfest and we've all
been pulling multiple shifts."

Serena took the towel Grace offered. "You'd
tell me if there was, right?"

Something resembling sympathy flashed
in Grace's eyes.

Serena slumped against the sink. "It's bad,
isn't it?"

"It's not my place to say."

"I knew Deke was glaring at me." She
crumpled the towel and tossed it in the trash.
"Why?"

"Maybe it's not about you. I know he's
worried about his mother."

Oh, no. Had her father decided to tell the
entire Matthews family about his past? Because if he had, they'd discover her part, too.

"Serena, I really like you. If there's anything that might be…questionable in your

life before you moved here, now would be the time to fess up."

Her eyes grew wide. They knew. Somehow Logan and Deke had discovered her father's scams. But how? "What do they think I need to confess?"

"The guys are probably wondering where we are," Grace said, trying to make her wobbly voice lighthearted but ignoring the question.

"You go on." Serena took her phone from her back pocket. "I forgot to return a text earlier."

Grace gave her one last long look and left. With shaky fingers, Serena pulled up her father's number and dialed. Right to voice mail. Biting her lip, she quickly sent him a text informing him that she was afraid Deke and Logan were on to them and she needed to speak to him pronto.

Taking one last peek in the mirror—and cringing at her haunted appearance—she exited the restroom. There were only a few park lights still on. An odd silence had settled over the festival area. She took a few steps before noticing Logan, leaning against a nearby tree. Waiting for her.

"Everyone cleared out," she commented as she joined him.

He pushed away from the tree. "It's late."

She hadn't noticed, not with her mind awhirl.

"Ready to head home?"

She nodded, making sure there was plenty of space between them. As much as she craved his steady strength, tonight she was afraid his intensity might make her start spilling her secrets.

Conversation lagged as they walked under the stars back to her apartment, this journey so different from previous nights, when they'd talked for hours. Once they reached the steps, she wanted nothing more than to run upstairs and hide behind closed doors, but she stayed put. Took a seat on the bottom step, where Logan joined her.

"Something is wrong, isn't it?" she finally said.

"Why would you ask that?"

"You've been…distant tonight. And Deke? He was staring bullets at me when we sat across the table from each other." She swallowed hard. "Why?"

"Family issues."

"That's what Grace said, but it feels more personal."

He went still. "Why would you think that?"

How much should she tell him? They'd

gotten this far in their relationship without spilling their secrets. Or hers, anyway. Would he believe her side of the story? Understand her dilemma? And if she decided to unburden herself, where would she start?

"You've mentioned how much the truth means to you," she began, knowing this would be a stumbling block between them. "Because of what your parents kept from you."

"That's right."

Her heart thudded in her chest. "What if I were to tell you there are things I haven't revealed about myself."

A flicker of emotion flashed over his face before he contained it. "I wouldn't be totally surprised."

Was she that transparent? She rubbed the tattoo on the inside of her wrist, wishing her mother was here to tell her what to do. She'd never wanted to risk all her secrets over a man, but that was what she'd be doing if she told Logan the truth—risking her livelihood. Her plans. Her future.

But he was worth it.

She angled her knees until they brushed his leg and took his hand in hers. Absorbed his quiet strength. "When you were a kid, before the falling-out with your father, did you think he could do no wrong?"

"Sure. He was bigger than life." He paused. "I didn't see any flaws until I got older."

"I never talk about my dad. He was…all I had after my mother died. But he couldn't cope. Got tangled up in things that weren't in his best interest."

"Did you know about it?"

"Not until it was too late."

Logan stared into the night.

"He got sick when I was in high school and I feared I might lose him, too. Thankfully he recovered, but it was a wake-up call. He got on the straight and narrow afterward and stayed there."

Logan sat back, resting his elbows on the steps behind them. "Why are you telling me this?"

"Because no one is perfect, Logan. Sometimes life deals us a hand we can't win."

He looked at her, his eyes shadowed by the dark, but remained quiet. "What did your father do, exactly?"

"It's not my place to say. I don't want…" She glanced at him, her voice pleading. "I've built a good life here. And I want to stay."

He sat up. "You're thinking of leaving?"

"No, I mean… My business may grow bigger than I expect and I'll have to adjust as I expand."

That wasn't even remotely what she meant, but she didn't know how to come clean with Logan. If her past caught up to her, she'd have to leave. She needed more time to pay back her father's victims before she could start a real life. A life with no regrets hanging over her head. A life with a man like Logan.

He broke the thick silence. "You know you can trust me."

"Can I?" Years of self-preservation warned her to be cautious. To convince Logan to keep taking a chance on her until she could unburden herself without lasting repercussions. "I'm sure everyone trusts you, Logan."

"But not you?"

He was much too sharp. Unable to answer him truthfully, she broke their locked gaze. Blinked into the darkness as her eyes stung and a lump settled in her throat.

He untangled his hand from hers. Stood. She slowly rose beside him.

"I'll be out of town for a while," he informed her. "You'll be here when I get back?"

She nodded, struggling to find her voice. "I have the store, so…"

Not what he was asking, but she couldn't reveal any more of herself tonight. It hurt too much and she was already buckling under the strain.

"Then I'll see you in a few days."

Logan strode away, shoulders straight, then turned into the alley to take him to Main Street. No kiss, even on the cheek. No promises of missing her while he was gone. No charming smile or jaunty wink goodbye.

What if she'd just ruined the best thing to ever happen to her by opening the door to her past even the slightest bit?

Either way, keeping the truth from him or telling all, she'd probably lose him anyway.

CHAPTER TWELVE

THURSDAY, SERENA FOUND herself bone-tired. Since Logan had left she'd been on edge, waiting for the truth to come out. She'd been awake before dawn and found herself dragging by late afternoon, so she left Heidi in charge and drove up to the overlook. Even sketching couldn't provide a diversion that would get her mind off Logan. She kept reliving her last conversation with him. She wondered where he was. When he'd be back. What the state of their relationship would be when they spoke again.

When she returned, Heidi had closed the store for the night. Serena carried her art supplies with her up to the apartment, hoping for a few hours of quiet. When she opened the door, her gaze landed on Carrie, who jumped up from a chair at the kitchen table.

"Hey, Serena." Carrie held a hand out to her side. "You have visitors."

Serena's eyes went wide as her father hurried over to wrap her in his embrace. She hugged him back, eyes filling with tears as she drank in the familiar scent of him, his solid arms ensuring her she wasn't alone in this mess.

She pulled back. Let her gaze take in his beloved face, then asked, "Daddy, what are you doing here?"

"After your message last night I couldn't stay away. We got in the car this morning and drove up here."

"All the way from Florida?" she asked then stopped, noticing the other person in the room. "Daddy?"

"You needed us, so we came."

He gestured for the attractive older woman to join him. She stood tall and regal, her skin tanned, with dark hair that had streaks of gray in a bob style and sharp brown eyes that led Serena to believe she didn't miss a thing. Her father took the stranger's hand and a slow smile curved the woman's lips. "Serena, I'd like you to meet Jasmine."

The love of his life, no doubt.

Jasmine held out a hand. "I've heard so much about you."

Serena shook her hand, feeling a little off-kilter by this surprise visit. "I wish I could say the same."

Jasmine sent her father an "I told you so"

glance. "I'm so sorry. I told your father we should have met before this, but he refused to listen."

Red crept over her father's face.

Serena swiped at the moisture on her cheeks. "I appreciate you coming here, but it may be too little, too late."

Her father tugged her into another tight hug, his eyes suspiciously wet when he stepped back.

Jasmine came closer, wrapping Serena in a sophisticated scent. "Your father couldn't rest after your text, so we're here to do what we can."

This was too much. First Logan's mood last night and now this. "I need to sit down."

As she moved to the couch, Carrie sidled up beside her. "What am I missing here?"

Serena said wistfully, "It's a long story."

Carrie read her expression and nodded. "Which you are going to tell me?"

Serena's shoulders sank. "Yes."

Carrie looked at the guests, then back to Serena. "I'll be in my room if you need me."

Serena grabbed her hand and squeezed. "Thanks."

After she sank into the sofa, Jasmine eased down beside her. Her father took a seat in the armchair, concern wrinkling his brow. "What happened to make you so upset?"

Serena shot a glance at Jasmine.

"Since she knows all about my past, Serena, you can say anything in front of Jasmine and it will be held in strictest confidence."

She looked to the newcomer. "No offense, but I don't know you."

"No offense taken, honey. But after everything your father has confided, it seems you've held on to quite a few secrets for long enough."

A sob bubbled up in her throat and years of fear and shame escaped in a torrent of tears. Once the storm had passed she leaned forward and wiped her eyes.

"Sorry for the outburst."

Jasmine dug in her purse for a tissue that she handed to Serena. "We all need a release once in a while."

After drying her face, Serena readied herself for the news she'd have to share with her father. "I believe someone has been looking into your past, Daddy. That he may have caught on to you. And me."

"Oh, dear," Jasmine said, sending a worried glance in her father's direction. "I'm afraid that might be my fault."

"My father told me you have sons in law enforcement."

She returned her gaze to Serena. "Sons who have hovered over me since I became a widow. I kept mum about James, so it doesn't surprise me that they'd send someone here to ferret out the past through you."

Her mind went straight to Deke. Jasmine's explanation made sense. Like Deke scowling at her or why he'd pulled Logan into his confidence. The intense conversations between the two men added up now.

Serena laced her fingers together in her lap. "I don't know what to do."

Her father had been quiet to this point. He leaned forward to rest his arms on his knees. "What makes you think anyone would look into your involvement?"

Guilt? The constant fear of being found out? "People have been asking questions. The timing, I guess."

He nodded.

Jasmine tapped a finger against her thigh. "James, this has gone on long enough. I'm summoning the boys here to clear things up once and for all."

Summoning? One look at Jasmine's fierce expression and Serena didn't doubt the woman would do just that. And succeed.

The panic on her father's face mirrored her own. "I'm sorry to both of you. Your sons won't be happy, Jasmine, and I've put you in an untenable position, Serena. I still need to decide how to address all of this."

He was right. He shouldn't have involved her in his schemes, but he was her father. She'd always protect him. She reached out to take his hand. "I love you, Daddy."

"I love you, too."

An uncomfortable silence hovered in the air.

"How would you like a cup of tea?" Jasmine suggested. "I find tea goes a long way in settling nerves."

Was this woman as nervous as Serena? "Sounds like a good idea."

Serena led the way to the kitchen to collect cups and tea bags. She opened the refrigerator door to find she didn't have any milk. "Oh, no, I hope no one wants milk in their tea."

Her father walked over to Jasmine. "You always take a splash in yours."

Jasmine patted his arm. "It's okay."

"How about I run out to the store? Give you two some time to get to know each other."

Serena saw the uncertainty on Jasmine's face and said, "That's a wonderful idea, Daddy."

He grinned. "On it. I'll be back in a jiff."

"He's a good man," Serena said as the door closed behind him.

Jasmine took the kettle and filled it with water. "I couldn't agree more."

Once they'd each completed their task, they stared at each other.

"This is awkward," Serena said.

"It is." Jasmine leaned back against the counter.

After another silence, Jasmine said, "You look exactly the way your father described you."

Self-conscious, Serena ran a hand over her hair. Smoothed the wrinkled skirt of her navy shirtdress.

"Your father is very proud of you. Why, the first time we met, he couldn't stop telling me all about his successful daughter and the life you've created here."

"Thank you." Serena wasn't sure how to respond. This was so surreal.

"The first thing we had in common when we met was the fact that we had grown children. Over time, talking about you slowly led him into talking about his past."

"I can't believe he told you." Serena shook her head. "And you still stayed with him?"

"I couldn't help it. I fell in love."

The light in the other woman's eyes spoke

volumes about her feelings. Serena understood. She had worries about telling Logan the truth, but she'd fallen in love with him, regardless. Probably that day in the store when he'd come to town to champion his grandmother. She placed trembling fingers over her stomach. Asked the question that had been dogging her since she first met Logan.

"But the cons. It didn't bother you?"

"It did, at first. I was shocked. Until your father explained how he couldn't deal with life after your mother passed. I understood because I didn't know how I would ever be happy again after my husband died."

"My dad was lost and made a lot of bad decisions." The kettle whistled. Serena poured steaming water into each cup.

"That's why I stayed with him. Encouraged him to unburden himself so we could start our relationship based on truth."

Truth. Everything that Logan expected. The one thing Serena hadn't given him.

The door opened and her father made his way back into the apartment, brushing colorful leaves from his shoulder.

"My prince," Jasmine teased, but Serena saw the real affection in her eyes. Her father brought over the carton and proceeded to add a bit to her cup before they moved to the living room to sit. Her father sat beside Jasmine on the couch. Serena took the armchair.

"James told me how close you were to your mother," Jasmine said. "How much you suffered after her death and how much you missed her. He regrets not being stronger for you."

"Daddy, you never told me this," Serena said, starch in her tone.

"I was ashamed."

A Stanhope family trait.

"But I want to set things right. That's why we're here."

Serena met the older woman's gaze. "Aren't you afraid your sons will try to haul him to jail?"

A fierce expression crossed Jasmine's face. "They wouldn't dare."

"But it's their job."

"Once we explain everything, they'll come around to my way of thinking."

Even after an hour of talking to her father and Jasmine, she was still worried. The woman had a way of making the dire circumstances less daunting, but Serena couldn't believe that things would be fine.

Carrie came out of her room a little before seven, dressed in her serving clothes. "I'm off to the festival. Should I tell Lissy Ann you won't make your shift tonight?"

"Please."

"Your shift?" Jasmine asked.

"Golden hosts an Oktoberfest celebration every year," Serena explained. "We all volunteer."

"How exciting," Jasmine gushed. "We've come to town at the best time."

Was there ever a good time to unearth old secrets?

"You and dozens of other visitors." Carrie sent Serena a final glance. "You okay?"

"I'm good." For now.

Carrie nodded, said goodbye and left.

After talking over the situation and getting the truth out in the open to some degree, Serena was a bit calmer than when the couple had first arrived. She hugged her father again, to reassure herself that he was here, safe and sound with her.

"Where are your bags?" she finally asked. "It'll be crowded, but we can all sleep here."

"We can't impose," Jasmine said. "I booked rooms at the Nugget Bed-and-Breakfast. Seeing as how there's a festival going on in town, I'm surprised we were able to get rooms on such short notice, but they must have had a cancellation."

"Are you sure? I don't mind the company."

"I wouldn't want to put you out." Jasmine smiled. "Besides, we have work to do while we're here."

She didn't miss her father's grimace, but also a sense of purpose she'd never seen him exhibit before. Maybe Jasmine was exactly the woman he needed.

Just as she was realizing she needed Logan.

Her father asked her about the store. Since Blue Ridge Cottage was a favorite topic, Serena filled them in on her new classes.

"Your website says you create specialty items," Jasmine said, sending Serena a sly glance. "Like wedding announcements?"

Reaching out to pick up her cup, Serena's hand froze in midair. "Wedding?"

Jasmine grinned as if she hadn't dropped a bomb. "Oh, yes. Your father and I are getting married."

Serena's father laughed as her mouth fell open. When she recovered, she said, "Um, wow. Congratulations, I think."

"Jasmine does love the dramatic," her father said, smiling at his future bride.

"I'll remember that." Serena took a sip of tea then asked, "I take it you haven't told your sons?"

"We actually decided on the drive up here."

Serena closed her eyes, waiting for more. There was always more.

"We'll tell them when they arrive."

The nerves that had finally settled down kicked right up again. No way was she getting a good night's sleep.

"I'm happy for you, Daddy."

"So you'll come to our wedding? Stand up beside me?"

"I'd be honored."

As long as the repercussions of the past didn't yank a knot in their celebration plans first.

DARK CLOUDS GREETED Serena when she woke the next morning. She dressed for work, purposely keeping as quiet as possible to not disturb Carrie, and made it downstairs in plenty of time to open the store for business. To her surprise, Jasmine stood outside, a bright smile on her face despite the gloomy day.

Serena ushered her inside. "Jasmine, I didn't expect to see you so early."

"Are you kidding? After your father gushed about your store, I wanted to arrive first thing and take it all in." She glanced around at the displays. "It's just as I pictured it."

Serena went to the coffee maker to get it started. "Where is Daddy?"

Jasmine waved a hand. "He's having breakfast. I was in a rush to see your store, but I told him to meet me here so we can take in the town."

Before long the fortifying scent of freshly made coffee filled the air.

"I can't believe how talented you are," Jasmine commented as she studied Serena's inventory.

A pleased glow warmed her. For some reason, this woman's opinion meant so much.

Jasmine circled the room again and came to the counter, a smile on her face. "I can't stand this a minute longer. I have to tell someone."

Serena raised an eyebrow.

"My son Dylan finally got engaged."

"How...wonderful?"

"I love his fiancée. And truth be told, I've been waiting for my sons to marry for quite a while now."

She sounded like Mrs. M.

"I'm... Why are you telling me?"

"Why wouldn't I? I realize you haven't met the boys yet, but you'll be their sister soon enough."

"Sister?" Shock had her tumbling over the

word. "I only just met you and you're welcoming me into the family?"

"We haven't had time to get to know each other, but I already feel like you're the daughter I never had."

Overwhelmed, Serena swallowed hard.

"I would never presume to take your mother's place," Jasmine assured her. "But I'm hoping you have room in your heart to look at me as a second mother."

Serena placed her hand over her mouth, holding back her emotions.

"Am I coming on too strong?" Worry eclipsed Jasmine's face. "My boys always tell me I have the tact of a steamroller. I didn't mean to rush, but from the second I met you, Serena, I knew we would be friends."

"But…you know my part in my father's schemes."

"You were a child. How could you know any better? And you are genuinely sorry for what happened, same as your father." Jasmine reached for her hand. "Besides, that is the past. From now on we are working on building the future."

This couldn't be happening. She'd been alone for so long, carried her secrets for what seemed like forever. And now she had a family? The only daughter of a con man?

"Oh, dear. I am coming on too strong." Jasmine hurried around the counter to wrap her arms around Serena. "I've had time to think about this, but it's all so new for you. Forgive me for pushing, but I'm thrilled."

This woman was excited to have her in the family? Knowing what she'd done? It didn't compute, yet the proof was in the warmth of Jasmine's hug and the sincerity sparkling in her dark eyes. This woman knew her father's faults and loved him just the same. Was it too much to hope she'd love Serena, too?

And if this gracious woman could look past her father's mistakes, was it possible that Logan could do the same and fall in love with her? Telling him the truth was a gamble, but she needed to lay it all on the line. Hinting around at a troubled past wasn't enough. She had to be forthright, no matter the outcome.

Jasmine took both of Serena's hands in hers. "Give us time, honey, and we'll have you feeling like family in no time."

The door opened and her father strolled in, looking well rested compared to the sleep-deprived stress Serena felt sure was reflected on her face.

"There you are, James. I was welcoming

Serena to the family. And I told her about Dylan and Kady."

Jasmine beamed and her father watched Serena with pause. He looked different today. Before, the years of guilt over his actions had weighed him down, but he seemed more at peace with himself. His love for Jasmine was clear. How could she not have given him her blessing when they'd announced they were getting married?

"I'm sure the wedding will be in Florida, but you'll be invited. And you are more than welcome to bring a date."

Serena almost laughed out loud. First, that was a big assumption since she hadn't met Dylan yet. And two, the only date she'd even consider bringing was Logan, and after the truth came out, she wasn't sure they'd ever see each other again.

THE DRIVE FROM Atlanta had been brutal—Friday-night traffic—but once Logan pulled onto Main Street, he breathed easier. He wasn't looking forward to the report he had for Deke, but that was part of the business.

He parked a few blocks from Serena's store and got out to walk. He'd missed her while he was gone. Wanted to see her smiling face.

Apologize for leaving her with questions the night before he left. He arrived to find Heidi in the doorway.

"I was closing for the night."

He peered into the recesses of the store. "Is Serena here?"

"No, she left a while ago."

"I see. Is she at the park?"

"No. Visitors stopped into town, so she went to dinner with them."

Visitors?

"Tell her I stopped by."

"I will."

Heidi closed the door and the lock clicked into place. Logan looked down the street to find a light still on at Put Your Feet Up. He crossed to the other side of Main Street and went inside. Grace sat at the desk, focused on the computer. She looked up, her quick smile slowly disappearing.

"You look like the bearer of bad news."

"Not bad, but not great." He scanned the office. "Deke around?"

"He's not back from a trip to Bailey's Point. I don't expect him to return for a few more hours."

"Then pass on the news that I'm in town and need to speak to him."

"I will." She tilted her head. "Are you okay? You look worn out."

He hadn't slept well in days, so yeah, he was pretty tired. "I'll be fine once I get something to eat."

"Smitty's had a pretty good slow-cooked pork special for lunch. If you're lucky, Jamey might have some left for dinner."

"Thanks. I'll check it out."

He stepped out to the sidewalk, the accordion-and-brass polka music drifting his way from the park. He really wasn't in the mood for dancing and heavy German food, so he took Grace's suggestion and walked the few more blocks to Smitty's. Since Oktoberfest had started he hadn't had a meal there. As he grew closer and inhaled the savory scents coming from the pub, he perked up. A decent meal and some small talk with Jamey might pull him out of his funk.

He opened the heavy door and stepped inside the pub, feeling right at home. The place was crowded, music booming from the speakers, loud voices and laughter rising to the rafters. Logan headed to the bar and grabbed an empty stool. Jamey came out of the kitchen with two plates, saw him and grinned.

"Let me serve these and I'll be back."

When the bartender came his way, Logan ordered a beer. After the last couple of days, he wanted to wind down.

"So," Jamey said as he took up his post behind the bar. "The prodigal returns."

"I was working."

"Is that what you call it?"

Logan reached over to snag a handful of peanuts from the bowl. "I'm not in the mood for your lame attempt at joking."

"It's only lame if it misses the mark."

"Trust me, you're missing by a mile."

"Sour grapes," Jamey replied, not at all concerned about Logan's comments. "Where have you been?"

"At the office."

"I thought you were using my place as your office?"

"My real office. And thanks, by the way. I know I don't talk about work or much about my life in Atlanta."

Jamey grabbed a towel and wiped down the shiny wood surface as the bartender delivered Logan's drink. "You will when you're ready. But let me guess. Problems with the job?"

"How did you come to that conclusion?"

"I played baseball with you in high school.

You got the same look whenever you struck out."

"When you're right, you're right."

Logan had contacted the family who'd filed the fraud complaint. Went for the interview. The family recognized Stanhope's picture, or Stanton, as they remembered him, and swore he was a representative for the company that had scammed them. He was a single father trying to make a life for his young daughter and he was so sincere and honest, they wouldn't believe he'd been the one to actually steal their money. Logan tried to explain that he suspected Stanton to be behind the con, but they surprised him with the revelation that all the money they'd lost had been returned to them in full after they'd filed the fraud claim. They had no reason to believe Stanton had stolen their money.

"So what happened?"

"Right lead. Bad timing."

"That's why I own a pub. Less stressful." Jamey placed a laminated menu before him.

"Grace said you featured a slow-cooked pork for lunch. Any chance I can get a box to go?"

"Coming up, my friend. This is sure to cure the blues."

Logan doubted it, but he was hungry. Once he got his dinner he would head back to Reid's to eat and then try to get a good night's sleep. He'd deal with everything else—talking to Deke and catching up with Serena—tomorrow.

As he waited, he swiveled around on the stool. He envied folks having a good night while he had to bring his friend and client disappointing news. He'd been convinced that an interview with the family would prove that Stanton/Stanhope had been involved in a con, just as the Matthews brothers had suspected. He took a sip from his mug and caught sight of Serena seated at a table in the back.

Longing kicked him swift and hard in the gut. Under the overhead lights, her hair shone and her smile took his breath away. There she sat, owning his heart while he was out digging up dirt on her family. For the first time in his career he felt scummy, even though what he was doing was right.

"Food'll be out in ten," Jamey said from behind him. "We're backed up in the kitchen."

Logan turned around and placed his mug on the bar. "I'm going to talk to a friend."

Jamey looked over Logan's shoulder and chuckled. "A friend. Right."

Tossing a few bills on the bar, Logan made his way through the crowd until he came to Serena's table. He barely contained his shock when the man he'd been investigating sat with her.

"Serena, honey, you have company," a woman he didn't recognize announced. Serena looked up and her smile faded.

"Logan. I didn't know you were back."

"I returned a short while ago."

She stood, as did the man at the table. She wore another of her signature blue-and-white dresses—this one made her look incredibly attractive. Her high-heeled shoes put her on eye level with him. "Logan, I'd like you to meet my father, James, and his girlfriend, Jasmine."

James reached over to shake Logan's hand. "Pleased to meet a friend of my daughter's."

Logan nodded, too stunned to react. He finally turned to Serena. "I stopped by the store. Heidi said you had visitors."

"Surprise visitors," Jasmine added. "Please, join us."

He glanced at Serena, trying to decipher the unease on her face.

"Thanks, but I'm waiting for takeout." He

leaned toward Serena and said in a low voice near her ear, "But I wouldn't mind a few minutes if you can spare the time."

She bit her lower lip, clearly uncertain.

He added, "We can step outside if you'd like."

She nodded, then told her father she'd be right back. Logan took her hand and they wended their way through the crowd to exit into the cool night. He steered her to the side of the building, where they could have privacy.

"Did your trip go okay?" she asked, running her hands up and down her arms for warmth.

"I've had better." He stepped into the space between them and cupped the nape of her neck with his hand. Strands of her silky hair caressed his skin. "But I couldn't stop thinking about you."

Her eyes went wide at his declaration and he decided to do the one thing he'd been thinking about for hours. He lowered his head, catching the affirmation in her eyes, and kissed her long and hard. Her hands ran up his chest to land on his shoulders as she steadied herself. His free hand tangled in her luxurious hair until he slid his fingers to her cheek. He savored the kiss, her lavender scent, the fact that she was in his arms.

When they finally broke the kiss, Serena's hands drifted down his long sleeves and her eyelids slowly lifted, her gaze steady as she met his.

He realized then that he was well and truly lost to her.

Inhaling her scent, he rested his forehead against hers. Tried to slow his breathing but his chest kept rising and falling like he'd run a marathon.

"I missed you, too," Serena finally said. "Didn't exactly expect this welcome home greeting after the way we left things the other night."

"I'm sorry about how I acted. I was concerned about my trip and—"

She placed a finger over his lips. "No need to explain. You're here now."

He was and didn't plan on leaving anytime soon.

"There are things we need to talk about," she continued.

At her words his heart froze.

"After my guests leave."

"Serena, I should probably tell you—"

She stopped him again. This time she

whispered against his lips. "Can't we have this night? Before everything changes?"

"Before what changes?"

She brushed her lips over his and he continued the kiss in earnest, trying to disregard her plea. He wanted this time with Serena, the woman of his dreams, before she found out he'd been investigating her. Before her affection turned to anger, because he hadn't been up-front with her. Never mind he couldn't tell her at the time, but that wouldn't matter. Not in the end.

They kissed for what seemed like an eternity and still that wasn't enough. She stepped back, her eyes dewy, her smile sweet.

"I should get back."

He nodded, his throat tight.

"But we'll sit down and talk soon."

She stepped close, kissed his cheek and went back inside the pub. Logan fell back against the building, resting his head against the solid wood structure. What a mess this job had turned into.

Shaking off the feeling of despair, he turned the corner just as Jamey came out of the door.

"There you are." He handed over a bag. "Dinner is served."

Logan reached into his jeans pocket for

more money. "Thanks. How much do I owe you?"

"By the look on your face," Jamey said, clapping him on the back, "this one's on the house."

CHAPTER THIRTEEN

"ARE YOU READY?" Carrie asked as Serena straightened the coffee cups she'd placed on the kitchen table, along with small plates and napkins, then angled the pastry platter and a bowl of freshly sliced fruit in the center. She wanted everything to be perfect.

"Coffee is brewing. Pastries are out." She tucked her long fall of hair behind one ear. "My soon-to-be family will be here in minutes." As she said the words, reality overwhelmed her. She grabbed Carrie's hand, panic-stricken. "Brothers. Four of them."

"I'm still getting used to the idea of meeting your father after knowing you for all these years," Carrie said dryly.

"There's so much…" Serena swallowed. "I have so much more to tell you."

"Good thing I'm patient."

"I owe you so much—your support, your advice, but most of all your steady friendship all these years."

"Yet you never talked about your father."

Serena grimaced. "It's complicated."

Humor flashed in Carrie's eyes. "The best stories are."

"I'm going to reveal everything, I promise. I owe you and Heidi that much." She rubbed her palms over her denim skirt. "But first I need to meet the Matthewses."

Carrie strolled to the couch to pick up her purse. "I would love to be a fly on the wall for this get-together, but I need to open the store." She walked toward Serena and pointed at her. "But I want all the nitty-gritty details, got it?"

"I do."

Tough talk over, Carrie pulled her into a hug. "They're going to love you. Just like everyone else who knows you loves you."

"I don't know about everyone."

Carrie stepped back. Sent Serena a knowing glance. "Logan?"

"I need to tell him the truth, too."

"You're starting to freak me out," Carrie said. "Are you some kind of criminal?"

"Close." Serena choked over the word.

"I did not just hear that."

Serena placed her hands on her friend's shoulders and turned Carrie toward the door. "Later. If I start talking now I won't be able to stop, and I need all my wits about me when Dad and Jasmine arrive."

"Now you've got me thinking the worst."

"I'm hoping it'll be fine."

Carrie turned back to look at Serena. "Do you really believe that?"

"I have to." She waved her hand in a shooing motion. "Now go."

Shaking her head, Carrie left the apartment. In the ensuing quiet, Serena rearranged the cups and plates on the table, plumped a few pillows on the couch and paced. She stared at the coffee maker with longing, desperately yearning for a bracing cup of coffee, but was afraid to drink too much caffeine in case she became jumpy. No, she needed to be calm.

"Where are they?" she asked the room, stopping before a wall mirror for one last look. Dressed in a long-sleeved, lacy cranberry-colored blouse, black denim skirt and boots, she hoped her style said girl-next-door. Sister-worthy. She'd gone through almost all her clothes last night trying to decide on the perfect outfit, finally opting for dressy casual.

A solid knock thudded against her door and she whirled around. Pressed her hands against her stomach, then walked over to greet her guests.

Jasmine barreled in. "Thank goodness we beat my boys. I wanted to get here first to create a good atmosphere, and they're running a few minutes late." She viewed the table and nodded. "How lovely, Serena. I see you've gone to a lot of trouble for us."

James entered and closed the door behind him, a smile on his face. "Good morning, Serena," he said, kissing her cheek.

"Hi, Daddy."

"Now, one last time before they get here," Jasmine said. "Derrick is a skilled interrogator. He can squeeze information out of a rock. Dylan is fair, but overly protective. Dante is—"

A knock came from the door. As Jasmine hurried over to answer, Serena leaned into her father. "That's only three sons."

He grimaced. "Relax."

She shot him a glance. "Like you?"

"Okay, I'm nervous, too. I've only met Dylan briefly."

"This is a train wreck," she whispered.

Her father took her hand. "We've weathered worse," he whispered.

They had. And life went on.

Serena met his gaze, knowing they were both thinking about her mother. She straightened her shoulders. Watched as, one by one, the tall, dark-haired brothers came into view.

"Dante," Jasmine said as the first man pecked her cheek.

"You're in trouble with the others," he said, hooking his thumb toward the door as he sauntered into the apartment, curiosity written on his face.

Another brother entered. "That's because we don't like secrets."

"Like you don't have any, Derrick," Jasmine accused, playfully tapping his arm.

"I do. I'm just better at keeping them than you."

"Believe me, Mom's been pretty close-mouthed," said another. The third brother gazed across the room and latched on to Serena's father. She moved closer, as if to protect her dad from what was about to happen.

Jasmine said, "Dylan, you remember James." She went on to introduce Serena's father to the brothers he hadn't met, who greeted him with hard stares.

Through the open door Serena heard boots thudding up the stairway and soon the final brother loomed in the doorway. "I knew you'd figured it out, Deke."

"Hello, Serena," he said, face chagrined as he closed the door behind him.

"I knew… I mean…"

"It's okay. Deke has that effect on people," Dante quipped.

"Why didn't you just ask me about my dad?" she questioned when she could get her voice to work.

"It's called surveillance."

"Hmm, you might want to rethink your technique," Serena countered, appalled at her remark. She placed a hand over her mouth.

Derrick swiped a bagel from the pastry platter. "I like her."

"Let's hold off on a verdict until we hash this out," Dylan said.

There they stood, a wall of brothers sizing up her father. Instead of letting them get the upper hand, she returned their stares, looking *them* over.

She already knew Deke, but the brothers all had similar characteristics. Tall. Varying degrees of dark hair. Blue-eyed, but different shades. There was no mistaking that Jasmine was their mother. All good-looking, but not one could hold a candle to Logan.

Logan. Oh, no. She had to muster up the strength to face him. Tell him her truth.

"Please," she invited. "Everyone, get a cup of coffee and some food."

Now that the introductions were over, the Matthewses all filled plates or settled for coffee.

"Why don't we sit," her father said.

When he took the cozy chair, Jasmine perched beside him on the arm, and Serena took the chair next to his, hoping they presented a united front. Derrick and Dylan took the couch, while Dante and Deke pulled table chairs into the circle.

"You must know why we're here," Dylan started, obviously the spokes-brother of the group.

"You don't like me dating your mother," James replied.

Jasmine huffed.

"It's more than that." Dylan didn't blink as he stared at them with his gunmetal-blue gaze. "Who are you? Really?"

Serena grabbed her father's hand.

"My name is James Stanhope. Serena is my daughter. My wife died when she was a child."

"Then why go by Tate?"

Her father flinched but answered. "I have a checkered past."

Serena looked across the group to catch

Deke's gaze. Not one bit of surprise on his face. Seemed like he already knew this.

"You have to understand—" Serena began, but her father stopped her.

"It's time, Serena."

She nodded and let him explain.

"I was involved in some less-than-legal business endeavors years ago. Unfortunately I brought Serena, unwillingly, into the mix. I sold bogus insurance plans and ran a few other moneymaking enterprises."

"You're pretty brave telling us all this," Derrick said, his deceptively smooth tone serious.

"I love your mother," her father stated, simply and with force.

Serena felt the testosterone in the room flare.

"And I love him," Jasmine said in return, her look sincere when she glanced at James.

"You knew?" Dante asked.

Jasmine nodded. "Of course I knew. Just because I'm a widow doesn't mean I've lost my head."

Serena hid a grin at the varying looks of guilt and frustration on the brothers' faces.

"I can make decisions without all of you going behind my back to find information on James."

"How did you—" Dylan began.

"You came in, guns blazing—excuse my metaphor—then suddenly the questions stopped. I grew suspicious, but when Serena called her father in a panic—" she shot a glance at Deke "—I knew you were butting in."

"Mom, this guy is a criminal," Derrick argued.

"Actually I'm not," James responded. "I was never arrested."

"And you're proud of that?" Dylan countered.

"There is nothing to be proud of. I stopped after a few years, not liking the direction of the scams I'd started. The example I was teaching Serena. I went legit."

"It's true," Serena said, adding to her father's defense.

"But the thing that bothers me most," her father continued, "is you going after Serena like she was guilty, too."

Four pairs of eyes settled on her. Under the weight of their scrutiny, she blurted, "I've made sure to return the money. Well, most of it, anyway. It's still a work in progress."

Her father gasped. "Serena?"

She shifted to look him in the eye. "I found the old notebook, Daddy. The names, the families… I couldn't let what we did affect them forever. So I started putting money aside until I could pay back each person, one at a time."

Her father stared at her, aghast. "For how long?"

"Since college."

"That explains the extra jobs you had while taking classes. You worked far too much and you were really paying back our…my victims."

"I had to."

Her father ran a trembling hand over his brow.

The room grew quiet.

"Tell her," Jasmine said in the thick silence.

Her father blinked at her, as if not seeing anyone in the room but Serena. "I've put money aside for years to pay back the families. I went to the storage unit to get the book, but couldn't find it. Or any of the incriminating paperwork. It was all gone. I've been trying to re-create the list of names for years, ready to return every cent I took."

Tears blurred Serena's vision. "You were going to make things right?"

"Of course I was. It wasn't until I mentioned it to Jasmine that I started putting a better plan together, but the money is sitting in a savings account, ready to go."

"Where is this book?" Dylan asked.

Serena lifted her chin. "In a safe place."

"Which I don't think we're going to find," Dante said and took a bite of a sticky bun.

"Or other paperwork that might tie my father to any fictitious businesses. I destroyed it all." Serena leaned forward as she spoke. "My father lost his way after my mother died. I know that's no excuse. My mother knew how he could be and kept him on the straight and narrow. After she died? He couldn't see another way." She looked at him and smiled. "But he's been a wonderful father and I won't let you ruin him."

"You realize you could have simply told us all this," Deke said in his calm, logical tone.

"You're law enforcement," Serena pointed out, trying to control her high-pitched voice. "I wanted the money paid back before anyone discovered the past."

"We can be discreet when it's warranted," Derrick said, rising from the couch to refill his coffee cup. "You've made restitution to the victims. Most, anyway, and if James pays the rest back, there really isn't any point in digging up ancient history."

Dylan stood, his face dark. "Are you kidding me? Are you suggesting we give this guy a pass?"

"What do you suggest we do, Dylan? Arrest him without evidence? Investigate a crime that happened years ago? Track down all the victims for a statement without complaints or a paper trail? And what about the people who got their money back? Do you want to remind them of their lapse in judgment again?"

As the brothers began to argue, Serena's father rose. "Dylan. Derrick. Please stop." The two men glanced in his direction. "If you need to arrest me, I understand."

"But we need the book," Dante chimed in. He focused on Serena. "Somehow I think that's going to be a problem."

Serena stood. "I won't give it to you, so you'll have to arrest me, too."

Dylan ran a hand through his hair and started pacing.

"My sons are very honorable," Jasmine said. "They'll do the right thing."

Her comment started another argument. Serena moved aside as the brothers debated the situation. She rubbed a finger over the angel wings at her wrist, unsure of what to do. When Deke started in her direction, she wanted to run.

"I think I owe you an apology," he said.

Surprise rendered her speechless.

"I don't like this, but I get why you kept quiet."

She nodded.

"You've really been paying the victims back?"

"I have."

A small smile curved his lips. "No wonder Logan's got a thing for you."

As Deke sauntered away, Serena closed her eyes.

Logan had a thing for her? She wasn't quite sure what that meant, exactly, but she took it as a good sign, because she most definitely had a thing for him. Now that the truth had come out, they'd have a chance, wouldn't they? Logan wouldn't be pleased when she told him everything, but she wanted to give their relationship a shot.

Her father came to her side.

Serena wrapped her arm around his waist and hugged him. "I have a feeling Jasmine will get her way here."

"And what about you?"

She thought about her answer for a long moment. "I've been waiting for this moment for years. Nothing can be worse than the weight of the secrets and the shame we've both been carrying."

"I'm sorry that I put you through this. That you took it upon yourself to repay my marks."

Resting her head on his shoulder, she said, "I'd do anything for you, Daddy."

"But it should have been the other way around." His voice went tight. "I'll reimburse you every penny for the amount you've already paid out."

"You don't have to. Just take over the payments."

"I insist, Serena. I'm the one who got us into this mess to begin with." He went still for a while. Then he asked, "This has affected your business, hasn't it?"

"No." She moved away to face him. "Blue Ridge Cottage is doing well," she assured him. "I was worried about when I could save up enough to pay back the next name in the book."

"It's not your responsibility any longer."

It wasn't. And for that she was grateful. She hugged her father. "I love you."

He kissed the top of her head. "I love you, too. I'll take care of things, no matter what happens."

Freedom. Was this what it felt like? No secrets? No more shame over hiding the past? Only moving forward for Serena now.

"With our new family?" she asked.

"About that."

She didn't like his tone. "What?"

"Jasmine and I decided to keep the news of our engagement quiet for now."

"Daddy, no more secrets."

"I think today was about all her sons can handle of me for a while. We're not changing our minds, just going to announce it at a less stressful family gathering."

Serena watched the men. "Somehow I doubt there'll ever be a more chaotic visit with this group."

She felt her father's chest rumble as he chuckled.

"And the young man who stopped by the pub last night? He seemed to only have eyes for you."

Serena bit her lower lip. Spoke from her heart. "He's special to me, Daddy. But I haven't told him."

"Make sure you do it now." His gaze drifted to Jasmine. "Don't lose him."

Her father had found love. And decided to tell the truth to keep that love. For the first time ever, Serena thought maybe there was hope where she and Logan were concerned.

Could it be true that love conquered all? She took a deep breath, ready to find out.

THE LIVELY MUSIC from the park drifted down Main Street, along with the scent of festival food, as Logan escorted his grandmother to Blue Ridge Cottage. It was a typical fall day—there was a welcome chill in the air, the scent of smoke on the breeze and a carpet of colorful leaves that lined the sidewalk. Since it was Saturday, the Oktoberfest celebration started at noon. One week left of the big party and Golden would return to normal.

Logan couldn't recall what normal felt like.

"You didn't have to come with me," his grandmother insisted as Logan kept his hand at her elbow. Serena had called and asked her to stop by the store. Grandmother wouldn't tell him why and, intrigued by the mystery, he'd said he'd drive her. "I'm not helpless."

"No one would ever mistake you for being helpless."

"Don't patronize me. I know you're up to something, Logan Masterson."

He was, but very soon it was all going to come to an end. Once the job was finished, he planned on pursuing Serena with every fiber of his being. She didn't know it yet, but Logan was going to come clean about the job

Deke had hired him to do. Once the truth was out in the open, he wanted to start afresh. A new beginning. Even ground, which he hadn't allowed them so far.

Kissing her last night had been cosmic. He'd never felt that way with a woman before. Couldn't imagine having these kinds of feelings with anyone other than Serena. She'd said she wanted to talk—about her past, he assumed. He wanted her to tell him freely, but he had to let her know he knew the truth. Had all along. But that didn't change how he needed to be with her, like he needed air to breathe.

"You're moving too fast, young man," his grandmother said sternly. He slowed his pace, still impatient to get to Serena.

"What is wrong with you today, Logan?"

"It's a beautiful fall day. I'm with my favorite person in the world and we're going to Serena's store. What could be better?"

"I knew it," she crowed. "You have feelings for her."

He pushed up the sleeves of his charcoal sweater. "I do indeed."

She threw up her hands. "Finally!" Then she smacked him with her purse. "Took you long enough."

"You know I don't rush."

"I don't care. I'm glad you saw the light."

A light that grew brighter with every step closer to Serena.

Before they reached the store, Deke and a group of men approached them. When Deke nodded at him, he said, "Grandmother, why don't you go inside. I'll be there in a minute."

His grandmother assessed the men and sent him a wary glance. "Why doesn't this look good?"

"Everything is fine."

She didn't seem convinced but went on to the store without him.

He waited for Deke. "Your brothers?" he asked in greeting.

"All of them." Deke made the introductions.

"So we have you to thank for getting to the truth about James?" Dylan asked.

Logan downplayed his confusion. "I haven't given Deke my report yet."

Deke explained that Logan had gone to meet a couple whom James had scammed.

"Turns out they weren't any help."

"Like the meeting with Mom and James," Dylan grumbled.

Logan watched the exchange with confusion. They'd met with Serena's father?

"James and Serena just came clean. Told us everything," Deke informed him.

Surprise floored Logan. "But...how? Why?"

"I'm sure our mother had a hand in the decision," Derrick said, putting on his sunglasses.

"What did you learn during your interview?" Deke asked Logan.

"The couple didn't believe Stanhope had anything to do with the bogus investment fund. And they've been paid back in full."

The brothers looked at each other.

"What aren't you telling me?" Logan asked when the silence went on too long.

"You'll have to ask Serena," Deke said. "Seems we misjudged her."

"You're being awfully cryptic."

Dante walked by and clapped Logan on the shoulder. "Gotta go, dude. Oktoberfest is calling."

With that, three of the brothers walked away. Logan stopped Deke. "That's all I get after the time I put into this investigation?"

Deke looked him straight in the eye. "I don't want to say more because you need to hear her side. Understand her reasoning."

"I'm on the clock here. Fill me in."

"No. As of today, the case is officially over. Send me an invoice."

"Just like that? With no explanation?"

"Work things out with Serena. Then we'll talk." At Logan's frustrated grumble, Deke said, "I see the way you look at her. I know how that feels because it's how I look at Grace. You can't leave town until you set things straight."

"That's all you're going to tell me?"

"It's all I need to say."

Logan watched his friend stride away to catch up to his brothers, helpless to quell the confusion swamping him. What was going on here? After one final glance at his retreating friend, Logan continued his journey to the store.

He entered, immediately searching for Serena. She wasn't to be found. Heidi came around the counter.

"Looking for your grandmother?" She pointed across the room, where Grandmother was carrying on an animated conversation with Carrie and a group of older women. "She's visiting with some friends, taking a painting class."

"And Serena?"

"She had an appointment this morning and hasn't—" The back door opened and closed. "That's probably her."

"I'll go meet her."

An amused grin crossed Heidi's face. "You do that."

He made quick tracks to the back room. Serena's face lit up with surprise and pleasure when she saw him. Gone were the shadows that usually darkened her eyes. "Logan. What are you doing here?"

"I brought Grandmother to see you."

"Oh, good. Thanks. I need to talk to her."

He watched her for a long moment.

"What?" she asked, tossing her hair over her shoulder.

"I don't know. You look different."

"That's because I've had a good day." She walked over and gave him a quick kiss. "Which has gotten better since you're here."

Despite his curiosity about what had transpired with Deke and an uneasiness in his gut warning him there was trouble ahead, he couldn't resist wrapping his arms around Serena's waist and tugging her close. She twined her arms around his neck and whispered, "I'm really getting used to this."

Ignoring that internal warning system, he kissed her. Lost himself in her lavender scent and soft lips. Right now the future could wait. It was so unlike him, to push aside the facts in favor of uncertainty, but since meeting Serena much about him had changed.

He needed to reassure himself that holding her close wasn't a fantasy. That she was real and they had a chance together, because he couldn't imagine his life without her in it.

He broke the kiss, grinning at her heavy-lidded eyes. "I suppose we'll have to make this a daily occurrence."

"Deal."

"But first, we should talk."

She slid from his embrace. "We should. Probably should have done so sooner."

He cocked his head.

"I haven't told you much about my family," she said, not meeting his gaze. He ignored the caution buzzing in him. "But after today, it's okay."

"It wasn't before?" he asked even though he knew the answer.

Her cheeks went pink. "This is going to sound silly, but I thought someone was digging into my past. I know why and who, now."

She did? And didn't call him on it?

"My father and Deke's mother, Jasmine, have been dating each other. There was some confusion about my dad and the brothers wanted it straightened out. That's why Deke came to town."

Relief made his knees weak. He still had time to tell her about his part in the investigation. "He told you that?"

"Not in so many words, but it makes sense. Whenever he came into the store he was always questioning me. Sending me strange looks. I knew something was up."

"It also explains why you were jumpy talking about yourself."

"I'm sorry about not being up-front."

He ran a hand down his face.

The expression in Serena's eyes grew troubled. "Logan, what's wrong?"

He heard his grandmother's voice coming closer and knew he didn't have much time to confess.

"I haven't been completely up-front with you, either."

"Sure you have. You told me about your parents and what they kept from you. You get that family isn't perfect."

He did, but he wasn't sure if she'd agree. "It's not about family. It's about my job. About you—"

"Heidi said I'd find you back here," his grandmother said as she briskly walked up to them.

When Logan let out a low groan, Serena sent him a questioning glance.

"I hope my grandson is finally wooing you," Grandmother said, amusement in her tone.

At Serena's laugh, Logan said, "No one says that word anymore, Grandmother."

"Well, they should. It's quite acceptable. And fitting."

"I like it," Serena said, hooking her hand through the crook of Logan's arm.

His grandmother smiled. "You do know I approve," she said with a wink.

Serena looked up at him and smiled. "That means the world to me," she said, then shook her head. "Oh, before I forget, I have something for you."

She hurried to the small office and returned to hand a check to his grandmother.

"Thanks, Mrs. M., but I don't need any investment money."

"Are you sure, my dear? You seemed quite convinced when you first told me about the proposal."

"I got the money I need from a different source."

"And who is that?" Logan asked.

Serena's eyes went wide at his sharp tone.

"Logan," his grandmother cautioned.

"It's okay." Serena faced him. "My father."

None of this was making sense. The Matthews brothers letting the investigation go. Stanhope showing up, giving Serena money. What was he missing? "Grandmother, could you please excuse us?"

"No, I will not." She opened her purse and dropped the check inside. "Serena has made up her mind and I, for one, accept her decision."

He gritted his teeth. "I only need a few minutes."

"Which I don't have," Serena said. "My class already started without me."

"You see, Logan. Serena has work to do. Why don't we leave her to it?"

"I'll see you later," Serena said, stopping to give him a quick kiss before walking to the sales floor.

Logan leveled his tone, not wanting to lash out at his grandmother. "I wanted to talk to Serena."

"And spill the beans? I could see you were going to. She doesn't need to know I asked you to check into her business before I decided to invest in the store."

"It's so much more than that."

His grandmother must have sensed his distress. Her expression softened. "Let's go outside."

They walked toward the exit, Grandmother

waving before they left. Then she led Logan a few feet away from the door.

"What is going on, young man?"

"You aren't the only one who hired me to get information on Serena."

His grandmother's eyes widened. "Why, who else is interested in her?"

"It doesn't matter. The truth is, I've been investigating her without full disclosure and now I have to tell her."

"And you're afraid she won't like it?"

"Would you?" he asked, sounding as contemptible as he felt.

"I see your point."

He spoke his deepest fear out loud. "What if she doesn't want to see me again?"

"Then you apologize and beg her forgiveness," his grandmother advised, her words filled with passion. "Don't lose her, Logan."

"I don't plan on it."

As he battled with his conscience, trying to come up with the best way to reveal the truth, he said, "It's ironic. Here I'm always talking about truth. How it's so important in a relationship, and I wasn't forthcoming with Serena."

"Doesn't seem like it would have worked to your advantage when you were investigating," his grandmother pointed out.

"In the beginning, no, but once I started to fall in love with her? What was my excuse then?" He blew out a breath. "I'm as bad as my father, hoping to cover up my part in all this so I didn't have to face the consequences."

"But you always planned on telling her."

"I did, especially once I realized how important she's become to me."

"That has to count for something."

Did it? He'd find out soon enough.

He glanced across Main Street and saw James Stanhope sitting at a table outside Sit a Spell.

"Grandmother, I'll meet you at the car."

"Where are you off to?"

"To get some answers."

CHAPTER FOURTEEN

LOGAN CROSSED THE street in long strides, itching to make some sense out of the day. He wanted to hear Stanhope's story. Felt he'd earned it after all the time he'd put into the investigation.

"You owe me an explanation," he said as he approached James Stanhope. The older man frowned at first. Then his expression slipped to recognition.

"I was wondering when we'd speak."

"You expected me?" Logan asked as he came to a stop on the other side of the bistro table from Stanhope.

"I didn't convince people into handing over their hard-earned money by not being able to size them up." Stanhope angled his head. "We only met briefly last night, but when we shook hands, I realized you knew about my past. Or suspected, anyway."

"How could you?"

"The blatant way you appraised me. The way in which you carry yourself. Police?"

"Ex-military."

"Now?"

"Private investigator."

The older man's jaw clenched. "I see. And you made sure to find any and all pertinent facts concerning my past?"

"As much as I could," Logan said. He hated to admit the guy had outsmarted them. "You covered your tracks well."

Stanhope gave a careless shrug. "It's something you learn to do."

"But your past still caught up to you."

"Indeed, it has." Stanhope took a sip of his coffee. Changed tack. "You haven't told my daughter yet. Why is that?"

Perceptive. Logan wasn't sure he liked that trait. "I was still on the job."

"Sounds like a convenient excuse."

Logan gripped the iron chair before him, Stanhope's words fueling the anger in him. Anger mostly focused on himself. "I'll tell her."

"She won't be happy."

"I don't expect her to be."

Stanhope regarded Logan for a long moment. "Did you report to the Matthews brothers?"

"Deke specifically."

"I see." Stanhope moved his mug around on the tabletop. A breeze kicked up and dried leaves fluttered at their feet. "You'll want to touch base with him. We had quite an enlightening conversation this morning."

"I saw Deke earlier. You know they ended the investigation."

"I didn't for sure. Until now."

"They were concerned for their mother."

"Which is their place. Jasmine and I had always planned on telling them the truth of my past. You and Deke accelerated the timetable."

Logan tried to control his temper. "They should have known from the start."

Stanhope's eyes narrowed. "It wasn't their business."

Logan thought about his grandmother. Of the lengths he'd go to protect her. He understood why Deke and his brothers wanted to know all about Stanhope and he wouldn't hesitate investigating a case like this again. "I disagree."

Stanhope gave an angry jut of his chin. "What you think doesn't matter. We told the boys."

"And you'll get away with cheating those people?"

"Aren't you off the case?"

"I am."

"Then, again, it's none of your concern."

Stanhope was right. It wasn't any longer Logan's concern. Sure, he could continue the case with the information he'd gathered. If Deke and his brothers decided not to pursue Stanhope's past, Logan could still override them. The only hiccup in the plan was Serena.

"You'd be wrong. I'm worried about Serena."

Voices carried from the coffee shop, and the owner, Delroy, stepped out of Sit a Spell. He waved to Logan but thankfully walked off in the opposite direction.

"So tell me," Stanhope said moments later. "Do you have feelings for my daughter?"

"I do." Logan pulled out the chair and sat down.

"I see. You aren't very good at hiding it."

At this point Logan didn't care if the whole world knew how he felt about Serena, as long as he could explain himself to her before she heard it from Deke or one of his brothers.

"She's a very caring person, my Serena. Always had a tender heart."

This wasn't news to him. Logan thought about the way Serena had befriended his grandmother. How she'd listened to him tell the story of his parents' betrayal and comforted him. She took in her friend Carrie when she showed up on her doorstep, no questions asked.

"She thought she was protecting me, you know."

The anger returned. "You're the parent. It should have been the other way around."

"I won't argue that point, but you have to understand that I wasn't in my right mind."

Logan snorted. Someday when he had a family he'd never let them carry the burden of his decisions.

"When I lost my wife my world ended. I loved Serena, but I couldn't see past the grief. My wife had always been my guiding light and when she was gone? I was thrust into darkness."

"Now who's making excuses?"

"Ask me that when you lose someone you love more than life itself. It's not an excuse—it's fact. I'm not proud of myself, but I'll make it up to Serena."

"By investing in her store?"

Stanhope looked startled. "She told you?"

"Too little, too late, if you ask me," Logan scoffed.

"Then you don't know the entire story."

Tourists strolled around them, soaking up the afternoon sun, bags full of souvenirs and goodies from the local stores and Oktoberfest booths.

Life went on around them as Logan sat here, trying to make sense of why Serena's father would put her in such a problematic situation. As far as he was concerned, there was no good reason. The only point he could agree with was how bereft he'd feel if he lost the woman he loved, because it was a distinct possibility that Serena might walk away after she learned the truth.

"Let me ask you this," Stanhope said. "What made you enlist in the military?"

Logan was suddenly on guard. Where was he going with this? "Why does it matter?"

"Humor me."

After debating whether or not to say anything, Logan finally said, "To leave Golden."

"It can't be that simple."

Logan got the distinct impression that Stanhope was reading him much too well. He'd always prided himself on remaining neutral in an investigation. He never gave away his cards. But facing Stanhope, he could see why people would fall for his scams. Especially when he found himself responding to the man's statement.

"To serve my country."

"That's it?"

"I—I needed to get away for personal reasons."

A pleased grin curved Stanhope's lips. "Ah, now we're getting somewhere."

"I don't have to tell you my motivation."

"No, you don't. But whatever happened to you in the past set the course for your future. Brought you to this place and time, whether you had control over your situation or not."

"I had no control," Logan said tightly.

"Neither did I. My wife died and I lost my way. I didn't choose a noble path, but I got out before permanently damaging Serena."

"I'm supposed to respect you for that?"

"I want you to try and understand. For Serena's sake, not mine. I accept what I've done. Will pay the consequences. Serena deserves better."

Logan thought of what he was keeping from her. "She does."

"She has a way of making you think everything will be fine, even when it isn't. She's been like that since she was a little girl, trying to make sense of her mother's death and convincing me that we'd carry on after. I believed her…for a time."

Logan could envision a young Serena comforting her father, a little girl dealing with an adult problem, all the while hiding her worry from the man who was supposed to shield her. How it must have hurt her, to encourage her father and not have him respond. Logan had seen the lingering shadows in her eyes firsthand. But also the strength.

He'd been the recipient of her sound advice. He'd confided in her and she'd listened. He knew deep in his soul that she got him. Hadn't she encouraged him in her own way to make things right with his father? If she didn't understand the power behind family secrets, she never would have affected him. She had an insight into family pressures because of what she'd experienced. So how could he be so judgmental about her family when he hadn't built bridges with his own?

Stanhope looked over Logan's shoulder. Sat up straight. "I love my daughter."

"So do I."

"Then you know what you have to do."

Behind him, he heard Serena's voice. "What does Logan need to do, Daddy?"

Dread washed over him. It was time to face the facts.

Logan stood. Gazed at the woman who had come to mean everything to him. He nodded to Mrs. Matthews, who stood beside her, but his attention navigated back to Serena. When he didn't answer, her smile slipped.

"We need to talk, Serena."

She visibly tensed. Her gaze darted to her father and back again. "Why don't I like the sound of that?"

"You need to go with him," her father said. Her eyes went wide and Logan could see she was getting nervous.

"Daddy, you didn't tell him, did you?"

Stanhope shook his head. "I didn't need to."

Her shocked gaze flew to Logan. He swallowed hard. Took a step forward. "I know everything, Serena."

One hand flew to her mouth. Tears sparkled in her eyes. "How?"

He ran a hand over the nape of his neck. Wished he'd been up-front weeks ago.

"I'm a private investigator. Deke and his brothers hired me to find out information on your father."

She dropped her hand. "Through me?" she whispered.

At her expression, a sharp pain flared in his chest. This was a million times worse than he'd anticipated. "Yes."

Her face went pale and she whirled around, dodging traffic as she ran across Main Street.

Logan followed, his breath lodged in his throat as they managed to weave between cars without being hit. He followed her down the alley to the back of her building, catching her before she ran up the stairs to her apartment.

"Serena. Wait. I can explain."

She turned. Straightened her shoulders, eerily calm.

SERENA WENT COMPLETELY NUMB. A surreal type of frozen. Then an ache swept over her, walloping her with a punch so massive it was all she could do to keep from doubling over.

She gripped the handrail. "Information retrieval?" she asked, finally managing to say something.

Logan shifted his weight but his gaze never left hers. "Yes."

"Wow. I just… Wow."

"I wanted to tell you this morning."

"How decent of you." The sarcasm came unbidden from her tongue. "It would have been nice to know the real extent of your business when we first met."

"That wasn't possible."

"Right. The truth puts a damper on surveillance."

Logan grimaced.

A heavy weight, sure to crush her heart,

settled on her chest. "Makes me wonder what else you haven't told me."

"I never intended to deceive you, Serena."

"But you did."

"Other than to do my job, I've been honest with you, which is a lot more than I can say about you."

Serena rubbed the inside of her wrist, wishing her mother was an actual angel who could intervene right now. "You're right. I have no excuse."

They stared at each other, at an impasse, here in the shadow of the building that housed her life's dream. A chill crept over her skin. Mere feet away the bright autumn sun shone down on the paved alleyway. From the sidewalk she could just make out the voices of tourists laughing and enjoying their visit to Golden while her life came crashing down around her.

Yes, Logan was only doing his job. But what bothered her the most was that he hadn't been honest with her, after their relationship had progressed to where her feelings for him outweighed her concern about being discovered. He could have been straightforward with her, trusted her once the professional and personal lines became blurred. She didn't think she could be with a man who deceived people, period. It had taken a long time for her to get past what her father had done.

And that was when Serena recognized the door closing on her relationship with Logan. Already started grieving the end. What a mess the best time of her life had turned out to be.

She recalled the encouragement in her father's eyes moments before. "Tell him your side," he'd mouthed soundlessly. She shut her eyes as if she could shut out the gravity of the situation. She'd finally fallen in love and now her past and Logan's actions were going to ruin the hope she had for happiness.

She lifted her lids. Took in her surroundings. Wished she was anywhere but here, getting ready to ruin what Logan might feel toward her. She wanted to run to the park, her safe place, but right now Gold Dust Park was overflowing with tourists enjoying Oktoberfest. She briefly thought about her friends working their shift at the festival. Once she told Logan the truth, she'd have to be honest with them, too.

Sinking onto the nearest step, she nearly groaned out loud. Thankfully she wasn't going to hash this all out with Logan in public. Still, the shame she'd desperately wanted to shed returned with a vengeance. She'd have to deal with the fallout of her secrets, but she could only handle one revelation—no, make that two—in one day. Her friends and fellow business owners would learn soon enough and she'd deal with it.

Nervous now, Serena looked up and met his hooded gaze. "I love Golden," she said as a way to start. "Wanted to begin a new life here."

"A life based on lies?"

Her inner armor barely withstood the hit. "I should have put two and two together. I suspected you might be interested in me for all the wrong reasons, but I chose to ignore what was right in front of me. Instead I'd hoped you were interested in me because of your grandmother's matchmaking."

Logan averted his eyes.

"You really got everyone to keep quiet. Even Mrs. M. didn't spill the beans about your business." Now she could see the error in her thinking. At the time, she'd been so swept away by Logan, falling more in love with him every day, she hadn't wanted to face the truth. Any truth. Seemed old habits were hard to kick. "But you didn't volunteer, either. I guess that made looking into my life easier," she said, not ready to take all the blame for the secrets between them.

"I needed to be able to connect the dots," Logan said.

Her heart raced. Sure, he'd figured out every story she'd ever told. He was good at his job. "You know about Aunt Mary?"

He blinked in confusion and her stomach sank.

"She's not real?" he prompted.

At his flat tone, Serena inwardly cringed. Well, she'd stepped into that one, hadn't she? Stuck now, she went on to explain how she'd made up the imaginary aunt as a way to brand her company. "If you were doing a background check on me, didn't you figure it out?"

"The only thing I uncovered was the information in your bio. I was more focused on your father."

Logan crossed his arms over his chest. The action pulled his sweater tighter over his broad shoulders. The shoulders of the man she'd hoped to lean on, not defend herself to.

"You're talented, Serena. You didn't need her story."

"In the beginning I did. People connected to her, then to me."

"So the cottage. Outside of town. Another story?"

Tears welled in her eyes.

At the censure in his eyes, Serena saw any chance of making Logan understand her actions slip away. "No. Carrie and I drove past the cottage once when we visited the area. I fell in love with the place. It's the type of home I would have loved to have grown up in." The type of home she'd daydreamed of sharing with Logan one day. "I guess I wanted it so badly…" She met his gaze head-on. "Another story, I'm afraid."

Logan winced. "How many are there?"

Direct hit. She knew he'd be angry, but this was worse than she'd foreseen.

Before she could address his question, Logan said, "While you're being so up-front, explain why there are years where I couldn't find any background information on you." His voice rose. "I can't even find a birth certificate."

Panic knotted in her stomach. "That's because you were searching Stanhope as my last name."

A flicker of surprise crossed his face but quickly vanished.

Heat crawled up her neck. "My last name is Lee. My mother's maiden name."

His lips pulled into a grim line.

"In light of my father's early exploits, my

mother kept her maiden name after they married and decided to make it my legal name as well."

"So you aren't even who you say you are."

She swallowed, hurt combining with outrage at his accusation.

"Technically I am. I dropped Lee years ago but everything I've done in business is legit."

He was unmoved. "Doesn't make it right."

"I was a child, Logan. My parents did what was best at the time."

"You're an adult now."

She stood, his accusations making her blood boil. Could she get involved with a man who made a living uncovering other people's secrets? Someone who dredged up pain when there were times people had good reasons to keep those secrets? She grabbed on to the anger because it was better than the pain.

"And you think it makes the decisions they made any easier? I've had to live with the secrets all my life. Cover my humiliation when I couldn't have easygoing relationships with friends because I was afraid they'd discover who I really was. Afraid they'd look down on me like you are right now."

He, of all people, should understand why

she'd acted as she did. Especially since they'd both lived through trust issues with their parents. They'd dealt with those issues in different ways, yes, but the more they debated, it was becoming clear that the divide between them was too great to cross.

When he didn't speak, she unleashed her frustration. "Look at your own family, Logan. You can't escape that history any more than I can put aside mine. I'd think you'd at least understand how the actions of our parents influence us. Even now."

A muscle in his jaw twitched. "My family is not on trial here."

"No, but the facts remain the same," Serena argued. "What we went through as kids makes for messy family dynamics."

The tension in her chest grew tighter. Instead of softening, Logan was becoming more distant. He was reverting to the man who'd first come to town, full of questions and suspicions, to dig up dirt on her family. She wouldn't let him hold her shame over her head.

"Have you talked to Deke?" she asked.

He nodded.

"Judging by the intense conversation you were having with my father when Jasmine and I joined you, I'm assuming he told you my part in all this?"

"I know it all."

She leaned back against the railing. "I don't think you do."

"Enlighten me."

"My father scammed people. Took their money." She waited a beat. Then her heart hammered as she said, "I've been paying them back."

The shock on his face should have made her feel better. It didn't.

"So that's why Deke dropped the case," he reasoned out loud.

"I can't say, but if he and his brothers had decided to pursue it, Jasmine and I would have made it difficult for them."

She nearly missed the uptick of his lips.

Was there a chance he might be seeing her side of things? "What my father did was wrong, Logan. I tried to make up for it so I could at least have some semblance of peace somewhere down the road."

"The money from your father?"

"He's paying me back and continuing what I started."

Logan let out a long rush of breath. "You two have it all figured out, don't you?"

Disappointment nearly made her knees buckle.

The funny thing was that she and her father had never had it figured out. Far from it. Not until now, when he discovered that she'd been paying back his victims. Now, when everything had changed. When she'd met a man she wanted to share her life with, hoping he'd accept what she'd done, and love her just the same. By the rigid set of his body and frown on his face, she realized she'd lost.

"Where does all this leave us?" she asked, hating the quiver in her voice. The vulnerability it betrayed. "I swear I was going to tell you everything, Logan."

Logan ran an unsteady hand over his jaw. Apparently he was as affected by all this honesty as she was. "I was going to confess as well."

She heard the hesitation. Braced herself. "But?"

"The lies you kept between us." He blew out his cheeks. "How can we overcome this?"

She stilled. "The lies I kept?"

He nodded.

She stared at him. He thought this was all one-sided? Hot pressure built up behind her eyes.

"I knew all along that I was wrong to keep the truth from you, Logan. Especially when you made a point of letting me know how important the truth is to you. Which I get. I truly do. Ironically, probably more than anyone. But I've been living a life of secrets for too many years." She placed a hand over her heart. "I didn't know how to broach the subject. How much to reveal without giving my father away."

She swallowed back a sob of regret that constricted her throat. "Yet all along you knew. Knew I was keeping a large part of my life from you. And still you pursued me romantically. Kissed me. Gave me hope that there might be something real between us." She backed up and bumped into the first step, arms flailing. When he reached out to steady her, she shoved his hands away.

"Is that how you get information in your investigations?" Her voice sounded bitter to her ears. "Pretend to care for your target? Let them return the feelings, and then when they hope for more, pull the rug out from beneath them?"

"No. This—you—was different. I never wanted to hurt you."

But he had. "How could I have been so stupid?" she whispered.

He reached out for her but she dodged his grasp again. "No, Serena. Never. I...let you believe what you wanted to see."

A biting laugh escaped her. "That you were interested in me for me and not because it was your job?"

He looked uncertain now. "It started as a job, but over time my motivation changed. I got to know you, Serena. The real you."

"Yet you still kept quiet."

Tension radiated from him. "No matter how conflicted I became, it was wrong." He moved toward her, then decided against it. "Serena, I never confided in anyone about my family. Not until you. I thought you'd understand. And you did." His voice grew rough. "When I opened up to you I began to see us in a different light. Then I couldn't stay away. There were so many times I almost blurted the truth, but my word to Deke got in the way."

"You chose your word to someone else over me?"

"Yes."

She guessed she could understand his dilemma. She'd never told anyone the truth of her past because she wanted to protect her father. Still, his honesty hurt. "Despite the investigation, you couldn't find a place in your heart to put me first?"

His silence said everything.

Outrage spent, only sadness filled her now.

"I've come to care about you, Serena," Logan said in a steady tone. "Despite the past, the secrets and the way we met."

She loved him, but even in his declaration, she sensed hesitation. As if he wasn't truly convinced they could make a go of a relationship. And deep down, she agreed. The trust they needed to make a relationship work was too much to ask in this situation. Made the future uncertain.

If he truly cared for her, she wanted a relationship without reservations.

"Can you see a future together?" she asked.

"Right now, I don't know."

Seemed they were both finally on the same page. The truth was too much to overcome and that broke her heart.

In the end, all the things she'd tried to control, the secrets and the stories she'd told to cover her shame, hoping for a positive future, were all for naught. She'd never have Logan or a family. From this point on she'd be living down the aftermath of her secrets. Alone. Just as she'd been before she met Logan.

"Then I don't think there's anything left to say," she told him.

CHAPTER FIFTEEN

SUNDAY MORNING DAWNED gloomy and cold, a perfect reflection of Serena's mood. She dressed to go for a run, but when she stepped outside, a light drizzle greeted her. She turned around, went back inside and changed into a baggy sweatshirt and flannel pajama bottoms. After making a pot of coffee, she nestled under a soft blanket, sipping the warm brew that did little to warm her insides.

Last night, after she realized there were no words to bridge the impasse between her and Logan, Serena had retreated to her bedroom. Carrie knocked once to check on her, but Serena didn't have the energy to face her friend. Not after the maelstrom of tears that had physically drained her. She had stayed in her bed, staring at the ceiling, wishing she and Logan could have come to some sort of middle ground. A place to start the healing process. But she'd walked away and he hadn't stopped her.

So much for love.

Now, after distancing herself from Logan, she understood why her father had spent days on end mired in a fog of depression after her mom passed away. Loss, whatever kind, was hard to work through.

But she would get through this. Had no choice, really. Not with a business to maintain. Whether it was located here in Golden or somewhere else, she wouldn't lose Blue Ridge Cottage. It was all she had left.

Sighing, she blew on the steam rising from the mug. Though she and Logan were over, there were still people in her life whom she needed to explain herself to. Reaching over, she picked up her cell phone from the table and texted Heidi. Once Serena had her two friends in the same room, she'd tell them what had gone on the past few days. Strike that—for most of her life. Fresh tears burned her eyes. She hoped her friends wouldn't abandon her. She didn't know how much more pain she could take.

Thirty minutes later Carrie emerged from her room, feet dragging as she made a straight shot to the coffee maker. She filled a mug then flopped down in the armchair. Her blond hair stuck out at crazy angles, and her eyelids were drooping.

"What're you doing up so early?" Serena asked.

"Couldn't sleep," Carrie mumbled, sending Serena a pointed look over the rim of the mug. "You?"

"Didn't sleep."

"Are you ever going to tell me what's going on?"

"As soon as Heidi gets here."

Carrie sat up, no longer bleary-eyed. She opened her mouth but Serena stopped her.

"I can't do this twice."

Carrie nodded and settled back to wait.

Soon after, a knock sounded. Carrie jumped up to answer the door, then dragged Heidi inside.

"Hold on," Heidi ordered as they bypassed the coffee maker. "If I'm going to come over here at the crack of dawn on my day off, please let me have caffeine first."

Carrie relented and turned her in the direction of the kitchen. Heidi removed her outerwear, filled a mug and, moments later, took a seat on the opposite side of the couch from Serena. She ditched her shoes and pulled up her feet, grabbing the end of the blanket to cover her legs.

"It's cold out this morning."

"It's even colder in here," Carrie muttered, taking another sip.

Heidi glanced at Carrie, then back to Serena. "Something is going on."

"Now you can start," Carrie said. "From the beginning."

Gathering her scattered thoughts, Serena started talking. From her mother's death, to her father's con jobs, to the day she decided to pay his victims back. Why she created Blue Ridge Cottage and Aunt Mary. At Carrie's frown, she kept going, explaining why their friendships were so very dear to her. She took a bracing breath and told them about her father and Jasmine, her future brothers and the fact that Logan was a PI who had been hired to obtain information on her father—through her.

Heidi sat silent and wide-eyed. Carrie put down her mug and came to Serena's side, not so gently shoving her over so she could snuggle beside her. A long silence, which was a bit comforting, if Serena was honest, settled over them.

"You've been carrying around a lot," Carrie finally said.

"Sheesh. I thought my childhood was bad," Heidi said. "You might possibly have me beat."

"I was afraid you'd both walk out the door when I told you the entire story."

Carrie laid her head on Serena's shoulder. "Are you kidding? You need us right now."

"But I lied to you."

"Yes, and I'll have to process all that later, but after hearing your story, I can see why. You were worried about your dad. How all the things you'd done would come back to you one day."

"It's not an excuse."

Heidi shrugged. "No, but it makes sense. Why you didn't want your picture on any branding materials. Why you were always so close-lipped about your past. And your finances. Don't think I forgot about that."

"My dad is making it right," Serena told them.

"Good." Carrie sat up. Met Serena's gaze. "I knew you weren't exactly up-front in college. You were a good friend and I overlooked some of the warning signs."

"Warning signs?"

Carrie held out her hands. "How you'd get all weird if your father called and I asked questions. You wouldn't tell me about where you used to live or what your family was like." She shrugged. "We all have family issues, so I didn't mind because you were the best friend anyone could ask for."

Serena's eyes grew hot again, and before she knew it, warm tears rolled down her cheeks.

"You're not very good at hiding your emotions," Heidi added, "but I'm with Carrie. You are a good friend."

"So you aren't going to disown me?" Serena swiped at the tear trail. "Walk away? Because that's what I deserve."

Carrie's hand covered her heart. "Why would you think that?"

"Because I kept so much from you both." She folded in on herself, crossing her arms over her stomach. "I'm ashamed."

The cushions moved as Heidi shifted her weight. "I don't talk about my past. Ever," she said. "I understand your motivation behind keeping quiet. Secrets are not ideal, but sometimes necessary." She rested her elbows on the armrest behind her. "And to be honest, I'm a little peeved that you'd think we'd desert you because you made a mistake."

"She's right," Carrie said. "You had so much you were worried about, but you took me in when I showed up without calling first."

"And you gave me a job at the store while I build up my accounting business," Heidi added. "You have a generous heart."

"What about the rest of Golden? Will they feel the same way?" Serena sniffed.

"Who cares what they think," Heidi scoffed.

"I do."

Carrie hugged her again. "Look, I'm sure they'll find out. So you weather the storm, with us, and life goes on."

"It's not like everyone in town hasn't made a mistake a time or two," Heidi said.

"But they all believe Aunt Mary's story," Serena said. "Maybe they'll boycott Blue Ridge Cottage."

"I keep trying to tell you Aunt Mary is just a part of the brand," Carrie said. "I'll begin a new campaign, featuring more of you, starting on Monday."

"I'm sorry I never told you."

"Me, too, but we'll fix this."

"And I've told you the store is good financially," Heidi added. "You don't need Mrs. M.'s or anyone else's money to keep the doors open."

At the mention of Mrs. M., Serena's eyes filled up again. She raised a hand to her mouth to cover a sob.

"Hey, you didn't try to rip her off. She'll be fine," Heidi assured her, awkwardly patting Serena's leg.

Serena tried to speak, but couldn't utter a word.

"Are you worried about what Mrs. M. might think?" Carrie asked. "She seems pretty cool."

"But she's Logan's grandmother," Serena finally said.

"So. If Logan's okay with you, why shouldn't she be?"

Serena looked away.

"Logan's not fine with things?" Carrie asked.

"We don't exactly see eye to eye," Serena said.

"Wait. Did he end things with you?" asked Heidi.

"It was mutual." Serena blew out a gust of breath. "He was not happy I lied to him. I was hurt that he was investigating while pretending to care for me." She shook her head. Wished they'd figured out a way to repair the broken trust. "It won't work between us."

Heidi looked confused. "But he's crazy about you."

"Really? Which Logan? The PI with a job to do or the town's favorite son who would never accept the daughter of a con artist."

"In case you haven't noticed, Logan doesn't care what people think," Heidi said, deadpan.

"He cares about the truth," Serena said.

Indignant, Carrie asked, "Um, did he miss the part where he willingly misled you?"

"No, he feels bad about that, but his job came first."

Carrie and Heidi exchanged looks.

"But not bad enough to work things out?" Heidi leaned back and grimaced. "Then I guess you're better off without him."

"How can you say that?" Serena asked, sitting up, more life in her voice than she'd had since the conversation started.

Carrie grinned. "Looks like someone has it bad."

Heat flushed Serena's face. "Don't make fun of me. I gave my heart to Logan but this is too much for us to overcome."

"I'm not laughing. I'm stating a fact. You are in love with him, right?"

"Yes."

"Then we need to come up with a plan," Carrie countered.

Heidi sat forward and rubbed her hands together. "Oh, a caper. I love a good caper."

"He's probably back in Atlanta by now," Serena said, the thought depressing.

Carrie tapped a finger on her chin. "Then we have time. Let's find a way to get Logan and Serena back together."

"I doubt it'll work," Serena warned.

Carrie batted her arm. "What? You don't even want to try?"

"I don't know if it'll work and I don't want to get hurt all over again."

Heidi yelped and jumped up. "I need to go."

"Right now?" Carrie gaped at her. "We haven't even put on our thinking caps."

"Some of us don't need a cap. We're that good."

Serena groaned. "You came up with something, didn't you?"

Heidi crossed the room and shrugged into her jacket. "They don't call me a miracle worker for nothing."

"No one calls you a miracle worker," Carrie countered.

"Well, they should."

And with that, Heidi opened the door and left.

Serena stared at the door. "I'm going to regret this, aren't I?"

"Probably," Carrie said as she picked up her mug and went to the kitchen for a refill. "But you won't be alone. At least Logan will be included in her plan."

"That's what I'm afraid of."

LOGAN STOOD BEFORE the dining room window, taking in the lush property of the Masterson

House. The rain had let up and in the distance a sliver of sunlight tried to escape the dark clouds. A chill hung in the air. The thermal shirt did little to protect him from the drafty old house.

He supposed he should return to Atlanta. There wasn't any reason to hang out in Golden any longer. The job was completed. He'd spoken to Deke again last night, and he reiterated that he and his brothers were not going after James Stanhope. At least not right now. So really, Logan could leave at any time. Jump in his SUV and head south. He wanted to, but he couldn't.

Because of Serena.

A sharp ache lanced his chest. Did he really think he'd recover quickly after she walked away? They might have mutually agreed things wouldn't work between them, but he couldn't get past the irrational feeling that she'd bailed on him.

You didn't fight for her, either.

He squelched the inner voice, annoyed with himself. He'd been so broken up over the silent agreement that they were finished, he'd stood at the bottom of her stairs for a long time, trying to make sense of what had just happened. Bottom line? They couldn't find a way to forgive each other and he had to move on.

He was realizing it was not going to be easy.

Footsteps echoed on the wood floor in the hallway. He turned from the window, waiting to see who would be the first to breakfast. Bonnie walked in, stopping short when she saw him.

"Logan. I didn't know you'd be joining us."

"Grandmother invited me."

A pleased smile crossed her pretty face. As usual she was dressed up, today in a gold sweater and black pants, with not a hair out of place. She hesitated before crossing the room to him, and for the first time in a long time, he was thankful to see her. When she stopped in front of him, he pulled her into an embrace, inhaling the sweet perfume he remembered from when he was a boy.

She eased away, letting out a surprised laugh. "My goodness. To what do I owe the hug?"

"Can't I be happy to see my mother?"

Her smile slipped. "You haven't called me your mother and meant it in years."

"I'm sorry about that."

The confusion on her face mingled with surprise. "I'm thrilled, of course. Can I ask what brought on the change?"

He slipped his fingers into the front pockets of his jeans. "I've been doing a lot of thinking since I've been in Golden." He shot her a serious glance. "I've been out of line for a long time."

"It isn't like you didn't have your reasons."

He thought that was all the motive he'd needed to cut her out of his life. He'd been wrong. "True, but it didn't make how I treated you right."

"Your father told me he's been trying to apologize."

"I haven't been easy on him." He rolled his shoulders. Sorting things out with his father was still a work in progress. "But I realized something this visit. I've missed my family. Problems and all."

Her finely arched eyebrows rose. "My, that's a pretty significant conclusion, coming from you."

He admired Serena. She'd admitted that her father had been wrong, but at least she had a relationship with him, unlike Logan and his father. The truth stung.

"Your father and I aren't perfect," Bonnie admitted. "We made mistakes early in our marriage. And then you came along." Her sunny smile returned. "I took you in my arms and you captured my heart. No matter the circumstances around your birth, I vowed from the first time I held you that I'd be the best mother I could be." She paused, visibly gathering her composure. "When I sided with your father the night you confronted him about your birth, I broke that vow and I'm sorry."

"You have nothing to apologize for."

"Logan, you must realize that your father was embarrassed by the affair. And then to have a child? He thought if everyone assumed it was our child, you'd never have to be weighed down with the cruelty from close-minded people."

"Did you agree?"

"No. I wanted to tell you when you were old enough to understand, but your father wouldn't have it. The night you came to his study, angry and hurt, I realized the depth of our transgression, but the two of you argued and I never had a chance to explain. Later, you wouldn't let me."

"So the secret didn't bother you?"

"I told myself no, but as I watched you grow up, I wished we'd handled it differently."

Was that how Serena felt now? Wishing she'd handled things differently? She thought she was doing the right thing at the time, just like Bonnie.

He looked at his mother. Over the years fine lines had started to form around her eyes even though her skin was still smooth. For the first time he noticed a sadness about her. What would have happened if life had gone differently for the Masterson family?

"I love you, Logan. I always have. I always will." She laughed again and he realized he'd missed the sound. "You're stuck with me."

Placing his arm around her shoulders, he tugged her close. "I'm afraid you're stuck with me, too."

As they stood gazing out the window, Logan could finally see a future with his family. It would take work, but as Serena had once told him, no one was perfect. Everyone had their stories to tell or, in some cases, hide. She'd chosen to conceal her past, but as the facts of her story sank in, he realized she'd done the best she could and the results had snowballed on her. Despite her fears, she'd finally confessed, and that had to count for something. The hard truth was, he'd fallen in love with her and didn't want to live his life without her.

Another set of footsteps sounded in the hallway. Logan removed his arm and said, "I'm ready to work things out."

Bonnie reached up and cupped his cheek, tears glistening in her eyes. "So are we."

The moment was broken when his grandmother entered the room.

"Logan. You're here."

"I believe you summoned me, Grandmother."

She waved a hand. "You make me sound like a general."

He raised an eyebrow.

"Okay, I can be bossy, but I'm pleased you're here." She glanced around the room. "Reid?"

"Not today." He glanced at Bonnie, not missing the distress on her face.

"He's only been gone a few weeks but I miss him," she said.

"Give him some time," Logan suggested. "Not as much as you gave me, but a little more than he's taken."

Bonnie patted his arm and moved to the sideboard to fill a cup with coffee from the silver urn.

His grandmother sent him the stink eye. "I have to say, Logan, first you go off finding yourself, and now your brother's off figuring out his place in life. You're both cutting into my timetable."

"Sorry to inconvenience you," Logan replied dryly.

"Is there any progress with you and Serena?"

"We've hit a snag."

She glared at him. "Then you'd better fix it."

"I don't know if I can."

His grandmother dropped the outraged act and studied him closely. "Oh, dear. Is this serious?"

"We're not sure we can be together, Grandmother. We both kept things from each other and now I'd say we're…wary of going forward."

His grandmother pressed her lips tightly together, then said, "I knew I should have intervened sooner. Why I—"

Her tirade was cut off by the doorbell.

"Who on earth could that be?" Grandmother said, then turned to answer the door.

When she left, Bonnie approached him, concern in her eyes. "Is there really no way to fix things with Serena? Granted, I don't know her well, but you seemed happy."

"I misjudged Serena's motivations." Logan ran a hand across the back of his neck. "Thought I knew better. I was wrong."

"Then I'm inclined to agree with Gayle Ann. Only I'd suggest you try to fix things out of love, not because your grandmother wants you married."

Logan chuckled. "Thanks for the advice."

Moments later his grandmother reappeared, Heidi beside her.

Surprise kicked in, then alarm. "Is Serena all right?"

"No," Heidi answered, sending him an impressive scowl. "Her heart is broken thanks to you."

He cringed. In the light of everything that had happened since the first time he met Serena, he supposed he deserved that.

"I was just telling Logan to fix things," Grandmother said.

"I'm not sure..." Logan began.

"Well, I am," Heidi said. "You two love each other and there's nothing that's happened that can't be fixed."

Bonnie sent him a pointed look.

"So we need a plan," Heidi continued.

"Oh, I love plans," his grandmother cooed.

Why did Logan feel like he was losing control here?

"I really think you can work things out," Heidi said. "We need the right place for you to apologize."

His eyebrows shot up. These women were plotting his future now?

Heidi and his grandmother began to brain-storm ideas. Unable to stop them, he was relieved when Bonnie spoke up. "It's quite simple, really."

Everyone stared at her.

"The cottage."

Grandmother's eyes went wide. It looked like it was all she could do to contain her-self. "Why didn't I think of that? She won't be able to resist. I knew that girl had poten-tial from the first moment I met her."

"What's going on here?" Logan asked.

"The cottage outside of town? The one on Serena's logo? I own it. Why else would I have let her use the cottage for her brand?"

"You kept it a secret? From all of us?"

Grandmother shrugged, unrepentant. "Not everyone. And besides, sometimes we keep people in the dark for good reason."

"True," Heidi agreed. "And in this case, the cottage is the only thing that makes sense."

His grandmother looked up at him. "Can you do this, young man?"

For the first time in days, he actually felt lighthearted. "For Serena I can."

JUST AFTER ONE in the afternoon, Serena's cell phone rang. She'd finally gotten off the couch to take a shower and had dressed in a forest green pullover and black jeans. She'd tugged on boots, not really sure where to go, but she needed to get out of the apartment. The sun had finally broken through the dismal cloud cover and it looked to be shaping into a pleasant autumn day.

She scooped up the phone to see Mrs. Masterson's name in the caller ID. Stomach dropping, she swiped the screen.

"Mrs. M. Is everything okay?"

"Of course, my dear. I do have a request, though."

How could this woman be so nice to her? Could it be she hadn't heard that Serena and Logan were no longer together? That Serena had lied to everyone in town, including Mrs. M.?

"Um, go ahead."

"You know Aunt Mary's cottage outside of town?"

She inwardly cringed. Yeah, she needed to get rid of that story. "I do."

"I have the perfect idea on how to use the cottage to your advantage. Can you head over there?"

"I—"

"It's important."

She couldn't say no to her friend. "I'll leave right now."

"Splendid." Mrs. M. abruptly disconnected.

Sure this was a bad idea, Serena slipped on a fawn-brown suede jacket and grabbed her purse. She locked the door and hurried to her car, curious now. What kind of idea could Mrs. M. have come up with?

Ten minutes later she pulled up to the cottage, stopped in the driveway and parked. As she exited the car, she took in the scene around her. Her heart pinched, as it always did every time she viewed the white cottage nestled among the pines. It had always looked a bit run-down, nothing that a little TLC couldn't fix.

Shaking off her fantasies, she started up the path and noticed a tall figure rise from a rocker on the porch. When he moved to the steps her heart nearly stopped.

Logan.

The air rushed out of her. He looked wonderful. Tall and lean, his wavy hair lifting in the breeze. He wore a black leather jacket over a cream-colored thermal shirt, worn jeans and boots. He looked as handsome as the first time she'd met him. Maybe more so now that she was in love with him.

Love. There was nothing that was going to change how she felt about him. Ever.

"Serena," he said as he made his way down the steps.

She nervously glanced around to find them alone. "Your grandmother said she'd be here."

"No, she asked you to head over. She never said she'd be here."

Suspicious now, she asked, "And how do you know this?"

"Because I'm part of the plan."

Heidi had been successful?

"This place is important to you," he said.

"You know it is."

"Well, I happen to know the owner."

Serena swallowed. Where was he going with this?

"I've made an offer on the cottage," he said as he walked closer.

"I didn't know it was for sale."

The corners of his lips tipped up. "I have connections."

He was going to buy her dream cottage? Wait… "You're staying in Golden?"

"Can't see much reason to leave now."

She frowned.

"I love you, Serena. And despite how we left things, I firmly believe the only way to move out of the past is to walk toward the future together. Can we give us a second chance to get it right?"

Hope welled in her chest. Was it possible? Did she dare take that chance? If they trusted their hearts, and not their circumstances, would it be that easy?

"I don't like the secrets, Serena, but I think I can better understand why keeping quiet was the best course of action. I'm sorry I made things so hard for you." He paused. "For us."

She bit her lower lip, then said, "Me, too."

Logan finally stopped before her, his citrus cologne enveloping her. When he lifted a finger to caress her cheek, she contained the shiver of awareness. His voice was quiet when he said, "Wasn't I lying to myself when I was convinced I didn't need my family?"

Her breath caught. "Are you sure, Logan?"

He twined a strand of her hair between his fingers. "As sure as I'm standing here."

"I love you, too," she whispered, confident her heart wasn't leading her wrong. Logan was the only man for her.

His eyes went solemn and he lifted her chin. Leaned down and brushed his lips over hers and she knew she'd come home. For good this time.

When he pulled away, she sighed. Then a thought occurred to her. "Who owns this place?"

He smiled. "Grandmother."

"What?" she yelped.

He chuckled. "My grandmother saw potential in you, Serena, from the very start. She let you use the image of the cottage and the made-up stories for your products because of your genuine affection for the place and what it represents—love and family."

Serena shook her head, dismayed. "She is one wily woman."

"There's no denying that. And just so you know, when she and Heidi plot together, it's effective."

"Heidi knew about the real owner of the cottage, too?"

"Not until today. We both found out together."

"This town is full of secrets."

Logan looped his arms around her waist, tugging her closer. "Which are everyone else's problems. Right now, all I want to know is if we have a future together."

She leaned into him. He was the man

she'd always wanted. All her hopes and dreams rolled into one. And she was never letting go.

"I'm all yours."

"To starting over," he said, smiling, then sealed the vow with a kiss.

* * * * *

Don't miss the next title in the Meet Me at the Altar miniseries from acclaimed author Tara Randel, coming soon!

And for more charming, feel-good romances visit Harlequin Heartwarming at www.Harlequin.com today!